W9-BYG-507

SPARKERS

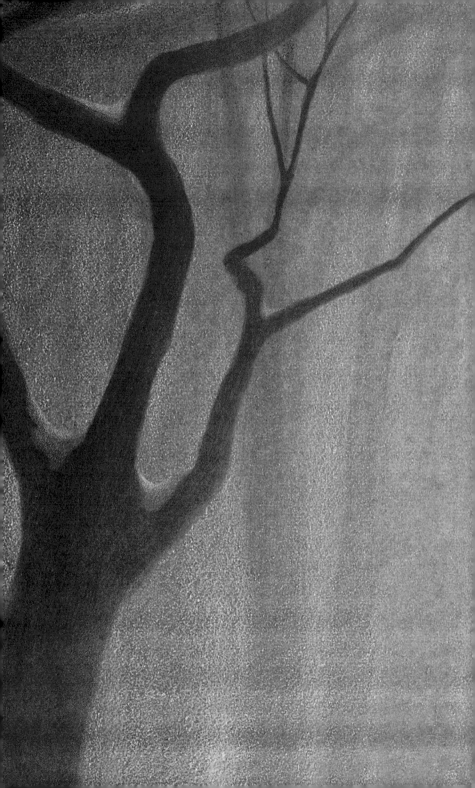

SPARKERS

ELEANOR GLEWWE

VIKING

An Imprint of Penguin Group (USA)

VIKING
Published by the Penguin Group
Penguin Group (USA) LLC
375 Hudson Street
New York, New York 10014

USA / Canada / UK / Ireland / Australia / New Zealand / India / South Africa / China

penguin.com
A Penguin Random House Company

First published in the United States of America by Viking, an imprint of Penguin Young
Readers Group, 2014

LIBRARY OF CONGRESS CATALOGING-IN-PUBLICATION DATA
Glewwe, Eleanor.
Sparkers / Eleanor Glewwe.
pages cm
Summary: "Marah, an underclass 'sparker' in a society ruled by magicians, works with
her friend Azariah to find a cure for a mysterious disease that turns its victims' eyes
black"—Provided by publisher.
ISBN 978-0-451-46876-5 (hardcover)
[1. Fantasy. 2. Social classes—Fiction. 3. Magic—Fiction. 4. Diseases—Fiction.] I. Title.
PZ7.G48837Sp 2014
[Fic]—dc23
2013038475

Printed in the U.S.A.

10 9 8 7 6 5 4 3 2 1

Designed by Eileen Savage
Set in Minion Pro

To my parents, Mary Yee and Paul Glewwe

SPARKERS

Prologue

THE FIRST TIME I WENT TO THE IKHAD BY MYSELF, I WAS eight years old, and my father had just died.

The Ikhad, the biggest marketplace in Ashara, hummed with activity. Around the edge of the vast, cobbled square, shopkeepers arranged their wares on rickety tables outside their stores. Young men trundled in and out of side streets, pushing carts piled high with sacks of flour or coal. Children dashed past me cradling paper cones brimming with spiced nuts.

The jangling of the coins Mother had given me made me nervous. I was afraid they would fall out of my pocket. But this was my first solo errand, and I was determined to carry it out.

The thatched roof of the Ikhad floated above me on spindly wooden posts. A river of shoppers swirled between the stalls. I slipped into the current and had soon purchased a cabbage, a bunch of carrots, and some chard. Feeling proud, I was on my way out of the Ikhad when I noticed a pair of kasiri stalking through the crowd, silver police badges gleaming on their black uniforms.

I froze, terrified they might shoot sparks of magic my way. Innocent or not, all halani knew better than to catch the attention of the police. Once they had passed, I ran in the opposite direction until I found myself in an unfamiliar corner of the Ikhad. I stopped to catch my breath.

On the stall before me rose a mountain of books. I felt a pang; Father had been a lover of books. He had taught me to read when I was small, and on the weekends, he would take me exploring in bookstores in halan neighborhoods. We could rarely afford to buy anything, even though by halan standards he'd had a good job. He'd been the foreman in charge of the blast furnaces at one of Ashara's steelworks.

Now, at the Ikhad, I hugged the cabbage to my chest, grief squeezing my heart. Three weeks earlier, there had been an explosion.

As I stood in front of the teetering piles of books, an old woman peered around one of the stacks. She was small and bony, dressed in layer upon layer of faded clothing. Wisps of white hair drifted out from under her knit cap. Her eyes were light in a wrinkled face browned by the sun.

"Who might you be, little one?" she said.

"My name's Marah," I whispered.

"I'm called Tsipporah," she said. "What sort of books do you like, Marah?"

I was too shy to answer.

From the jumbled stacks, the bookseller picked out a

volume bound in dove-gray cloth. It was filled with stories. Turning the pages, I discovered woodcut illustrations of a sparkling pool, a mountain valley, and a caravan snaking across sand dunes. Cabbage, carrots, and chard were forgotten, along with Mother and Caleb, my little brother, waiting for me at home.

The old woman handed me another book, and I skimmed the table of contents. To my delight, it was sprinkled with the names of faraway lands like Xana and Aevlia. Tsipporah selected still more books for me, somehow knowing which ones I would like.

Glancing down at a thick tome on which I had set the cabbage, I noticed an unfamiliar script on the spine. I touched the flaking gold letters. "What's this?"

"Ah," said Tsipporah, pleased. "That's Old Monarchic, the language of scholars in the days of Erezai. You know about the kingdom of Erezai?"

I had heard the name once or twice, but we hadn't yet learned about Erezai at school, so I shook my head.

"Shall I tell you a story?" the old bookseller asked.

I smiled. "Yes, please."

"Well," she said, "five hundred years ago, before the city of Ashara was a sovereign state, all the north lands were one country: the kingdom of Erezai. It was a land thick with magic, known for its great magicians."

"Magicians?" I said uneasily. I could tell Tsipporah was a halan like me, and as a rule, halani distrusted magicians.

"Not like the kasiri of today," she said. "The magicians of

Erezai were powerful and wise. They had learned the secrets of magic from texts left behind by still older kingdoms. Like our kasiri, they molded the magic with their hands and coaxed it with ancient incantations. But they also harnessed it by painting symbols on stone with pigments ground from cinnabar and azurite. They played music that the magic responded to like a snake to a charmer's flute."

I frowned. "I didn't know you could do magic with music."

"Do you like music?" Tsipporah asked.

"I play the violin," I said. "I just started. But it's my favorite thing to do."

"After reading books, you mean?" She winked before continuing. "Erezai flourished for over two centuries, but then the cold times came. The summers grew shorter and the winters longer until the crops failed each year. In wintertime, snowstorms swallowed the royal roads and choked off whole cities. The kingdom could not withstand it, so Erezai fractured into city-states: Ashara, Tekova, Atsan . . . what we call the north lands now."

The chaos of the Ikhad seethed around us, but all I could hear was the old bookseller's voice. She told me how, after the fall of the monarchy, the city-states had relied on their magicians for survival. In Ashara, the kasiri had cast spells to break up the ice on the Davgir River so boats with grain from the south could get through. Those were the days, she said, when the kasiri first set themselves over us halani, who had no magic.

She described how the cities slowly mastered the cold times, breeding hardier livestock and growing new crops adapted to the shorter growing season. In time, the cities reached out and established ties with one another again. And all across the north lands, it was the magicians who governed.

"And so it has been ever since," Tsipporah said, her gaze inscrutable. "To this day, the kasiri rule Ashara."

Walking home from the Ikhad with Mother's vegetables in my arms, I felt the lightest I had since Father's death. I floated blindly past the newspaper sellers on the street corners and the smoking grills crowded with ears of roasting corn. In my mind's eye, I saw a barge heaped with golden grain nosing through jagged ice floes while, on the banks of the Davgir, kasiri in black stretched out their hands and sent sparks cracking through the brilliant surface of the frozen river.

1

ON A BRISK MORNING IN LATE AUTUMN, I FINISH A SHIFT at Tsipporah's book stall and start across the bustling Ikhad. The produce aisles are packed with halan servants out shopping for their kasir employers, baskets hooked on their arms. When they're not haggling with vendors, they chat with their friends, pulling their coarse woolen cloaks tight against the cold. A kasir family in black tailor-made coats cuts a path through the crowd, their ivory buttons winking in the sunlight. I give them a wide berth.

While navigating the crush, I keep tight hold of the book Tsipporah let me borrow today. It's a volume on music history. Soon after I first met Tsipporah six years ago, I started helping out at her stall in exchange for the privilege of treating her stock like a free library. Occasionally, I even earn a book to keep for my own.

There's more room to breathe past the bakers and butchers and fishmongers. I linger in the artisans' aisle, enjoying the cheerful chaos of market day. I can't resist stopping at the luthier's stall and gazing at the glossy violins and the bows with mother-of-pearl accents. The luthier sits at a work-table dusted with wood shavings, carving the scroll of a viola. My own fiddle at home can't compare with these expensive instruments. I'm grateful for the violin Mother could afford to buy me, but I still wonder what it would be like to play one of these masterpieces.

As I ease around the corner of a soap maker's stand, a young man runs into me. A halan, judging by his patched sleeves. He mumbles an apology and hurries on.

A tingle of foreboding dances up my arms. As I watch the young man slip past a paper merchant's stall, I know some-thing bad is going to happen, something to do with him.

I turn and press forward, suddenly anxious to escape the market. The last time I had a feeling like this was almost a year ago. My brother and I had walked to the Davgir to see the ice skaters. As we watched from a bridge, a terrible certainty of danger seized me, and I made us go home early. By the time Caleb and I reached our doorstep, the deadliest snowstorm of the winter had begun. A dozen people lost their way in the whiteout around the river and froze to death. I still go cold imagining what might have happened to us.

I shove my way out from under the Ikhad roof, and that's when I see them: two black-clad kasiri on the street corner. The sunlight flashes on their metallic insignia. Even from here, the diamond shape of their badges is distinguishable. These are officers of the First Councilor's Corps, the most feared of all the police who serve the Assembly, the supreme political institution of Ashara.

I stumble back and lean against a roof post, my heart pounding. It feels like some kind of attack, but I know it's the halan intuition, our unpredictable ability to know things we shouldn't logically be able to know. It's unique to halani; the kasiri don't have it.

Whatever the young man who bumped into me has done or is supposed to have done, these officers of the First Councilor's Corps are after him. And Yiftach David, the First Councilor of the Assembly, only deploys his personal corps for subversives.

The diamond-badged officers used to be a rare sight, but lately the seven councilors who make up the Assembly have been adopting more and more policies that hurt halani, like encouraging factory owners to cut their laborers' wages and hire only kasiri for management positions. Now all manner of underground groups have sprung up to agitate for change, provoking a wave of raids and arrests. We halani already outnumber the kasiri two to one. The more resistance grows, the harder the kasir government tries to stamp it out.

I look over my shoulder into the market, searching for the young man. I need to do something before it's too late. Not like when Father died.

But before I can act, the officers charge into the Ikhad. One of them clips my shoulder as he tears by, and I fall down, twisting my knee.

As I struggle to my feet, two more Corps officers dash

into the market. Shoppers scream, jostling one another in their haste to get out of the way. Amid the confusion, stalls topple over, sending bottles and bolts of cloth tumbling. Not far from me, a little girl trips over a pumpkin and clings to a roof post, trying to pull herself out from underfoot. She's in danger of being trampled by the mob.

I fight my way over, seize the girl's arm, and lift her to safety.

"Are you all right?"

She nods, her lips trembling.

Dragging her behind me, I pull us out of the thick of the panic only to fall headlong over a sack of potatoes. My palms scrape the cobblestones as the book from Tsipporah skitters away. I swear.

When I stand up, the little girl has retrieved my book and is offering it to me. I finally take a good look at her. She can't be more than eight years old. Her black curls are tied back with a ribbon, and her satin dress is foamy and pink, trimmed with lace like delicate white feathers.

Only a kasir girl would be wearing such a gaudy dress.

Though surprised by her considerate act, I just grab the book and take her hand again. "Come on."

We take shelter in a recessed doorway as people stream from the square. Within minutes, most of the crowd has cleared out. In the middle of the Ikhad, however, a knot of halani is clumped around the young man with the patched sleeves.

The officers of the First Councilor's Corps close in on

the group, raising hideously contorted hands. I can't hear the incantations, but I see colored sparks flash between their fingers. The kasir girl clings to me. I can feel her shaking. The square fills with the bitter scent of magic.

A snake of silver light slithers free from one officer's folded hands and darts toward a woman defending the young man. She collapses, and I stagger as if the spell had struck me.

"Don't look!" I gasp too late, pressing the little girl's face into my cloak.

The halani protecting the fugitive scatter, doubled over from the painful effects of the kasiri's spells. In the aisle of the Ikhad, the young man lies slumped on the ground.

Two officers haul him up and carry him between them. His head hangs down over his chest and his shoes drag along the ground as the police pick their way through crushed vegetables and broken crockery.

Once the police leave the square, someone lets out a wail and rushes to the halan woman lying on the pavement where the kasiri felled her. Others hasten over to help. Vendors begin righting their stalls. Then an old lady breaks free from the cluster of well-meaning shoppers gathered around the unfortunate woman. "She's dead!" she cries, her face stained with anguish.

My head buzzes. For a second, I can't feel my legs under me.

The kasir girl stares up at me with huge, dusky eyes. "Is she really dead?"

I don't know what to tell her.

"Sarah!" A slender woman strides toward us, her face drawn. She's too young to be the girl's mother, and her dark clothes aren't as fancy as the girl's, though they're much smarter than mine. I don't have an immediate impression of whether she's a kasir or a halan, which makes me uneasy.

"What did I tell you about staying by me in the market?" she shouts at the girl.

Sarah hangs her head.

The woman's piercing gaze shifts to me. "Who are you?"

"She saved me," Sarah blurts out, clutching my arm. "When I fell."

Her chaperone looks me up and down. "My thanks," she says stiffly.

Sensing her disdain, I'm about to stalk off when Sarah says, "She's hurt, Channah!" She shows her my grazed palms. "We should drive her home."

"Sarah, I cannot allow—"

"If you don't, I'll tell Father you lost me at the Ikhad," she says pertly.

Channah's lips tighten. I expect her to reprimand her charge, but instead she throws me a furious look. "Very well, Gadin Sarah."

Sarah grins. I glance about the square, but no one is paying any attention to us. I feel a certain fondness for the girl, even though she's the spoiled daughter of a kasir. So while I'm not sure it's a good idea, I find myself following the kasir child and her chaperone.

A few blocks away, we stop in front of a sleek black automobile. Sunlight spills across the silver plating framing the radiator grill and ringing the bug-eyed headlamps. Channah opens the back door, and Sarah climbs into the auto.

"You may sit in the back too," Channah tells me.

I've never ridden in an automobile before. I'm afraid to touch the door lest I leave fingerprints on its polished surface. Inside the vehicle, the seats are lined with black leather. Sarah sits near one of the six rectangular windows, an elegant coat of fine black wool laid beside her.

"What's your name?" she asks as Channah gets into the driver's seat.

"Marah," I say, placing Tsipporah's music history book on my lap.

"Do your hands hurt?"

I check my palms. They've stopped bleeding. "Not much."

"Channah and I—Channah's my tutor—we were going to go to the menagerie today," Sarah says. "At least, before . . ." She goes quiet, looking out the window in the direction of the covered market.

I don't know what to say. I'm remembering the deadly silver light, the old woman's grief.

"Where to?" Channah asks from the driver's seat.

"Five, Street of Winter Gusts, please," I say. "It's in Horiel District. South of—"

"Oh, of course. I have cousins in Horiel. Not a bad sparker district."

I jump when she says "sparker." It's slang for halan, an ironic name coined by kasiri precisely because we *can't* produce sparks from our fingers. Over time, halani embraced the term. It's all right for us to refer to ourselves that way, but coming from a kasir, it's an insult.

"You said a bad word!" Sarah pipes up.

"You're right," her tutor says. "I'm sorry."

Glancing over her shoulder, Channah gives me a knowing look, and I understand at last that she is a halan. Tutor to a kasir child is one of the rare positions that could be filled by either a kasir with few prospects or a very well-educated halan. Using the word "sparker" isn't exactly the way for halani to demonstrate good breeding, but I don't mind. Maybe Channah isn't as snobbish as I first assumed.

The auto lurches forward, and the street starts to slide under the hood. I grab the seat with my hands. I can hardly bear to watch as we barrel around the first corner.

"What's your book about?" Sarah asks eagerly. "Does it have stories?"

"This?" I say, tapping its stained clothbound cover. "No. It's about music history. I'm not sure you'd like it."

"Tell me a story, then," Sarah demands.

The auto careens around another corner. The sight of the buildings swinging past the windshield makes my stomach pitch.

"All right," I say. Anything to forget about the horror of the Ikhad. I draw a deep breath. "Here's a story about Frost. Have you heard of her?"

Sarah shakes her head, her face bright with anticipation.

"Frost was a girl who lived at the beginning of the cold

times. She was small, but very quick and strong, and she could walk through snowstorms that lasted for days without getting cold. She tramped all over the north lands wearing snowshoes and animal furs, and everywhere she went a white fox followed her. His name was Silver.

"One day she met a group of traders in the forest. They were traveling the long road from Atsan to Ashara, but their sleds were stuck in the snow, and their horses couldn't pull them free."

"Why didn't they use magic to melt the snow?" Sarah asks.

I frown. "They were halani, I guess. There aren't any kasiri in this story."

"No kasiri?"

Channah gives a pointed cough from the front seat.

"At the beginning of the cold times, the difference didn't matter so much," I say quickly.

Sarah accepts this. "So what did Frost do?"

"She called her friends the wolves and harnessed them to the sleds in place of the horses. The wolves carried the traders' cargo through the forest while the horses trotted behind, led by Silver the fox. When they came out of the woods, though, the wolf pack would go no further. They refused to journey beyond their territory."

I pause. The little girl beside me is listening raptly.

"So Frost called her friends the ravens. They took up the harnesses in their beaks and talons and flew, so that the sleds skimmed over the snowy fields. There were so many ravens their wings darkened the sky.

"Before long, the traders glimpsed the city of Ashara on the horizon. They were overjoyed to have almost reached their destination, but then they noticed the ravens flying away. As soon as the city came into sight, they would go no further because they would not go near where humans lived. And so the sleds were left in the snow once again."

At that moment, the auto squeals to a halt on the Street of Winter Gusts. "We're here," says Channah.

"But I want to know the end of the story!" Sarah says.

I start to go on, but when I catch sight of Channah's irritated expression in the rearview mirror, I falter. "Maybe I can tell you another time."

I thank Sarah and her tutor and jump out, eager to escape the vehicle and its rumbling engine. Two retired men walking up the block stop and stare at the shiny auto, so out of place against the dull brick of the apartment buildings. I give Sarah a little wave, and she watches me mournfully through the window as Channah drives away.

2

AFTER MY WEEKEND SHIFTS AT TSIPPORAH'S STALL, I always stop by my best friend's, so once the auto is out of sight, I head for her place. The streets of Horiel District are lined with apartment buildings, all built of a yellowish brick that has darkened over the years. The paint on most doors and shutters is chipped or faded, and here and there a broken window is boarded up because its owner can't afford to replace the glass.

When I reach the Avrams' building on Old Spinners' Street, I climb the stairs to the second story. My friend Leah greets me at her door with little Ari in her arms. She has four younger siblings and spends most of her spare time helping to take care of them.

"I was wondering when you'd come," she says, prying her long black braid from her brother's grip and tossing it over her shoulder. "Did something keep you?"

"Yes," I say, my stomach twisting.

I follow her into the apartment. The empty kitchen smells

of mint tea and cinnamon, and someone has left a pair of mittens on the floor. Leah offers me a chair at the cluttered kitchen table and then plops down with her brother in her lap.

The table is strewn with my friend's school papers. A notebook opened to a lesson on literary figures of the last century partially covers a loose page of geometric proofs. Next to that is a list of the kasir inventors who developed, among other things, the automobile and the electric light. The vast majority of her notes, however, feature scrawled evolutionary trees, diagrams of plant cells, and sketches of beaks and fangs. The mundane sight makes me feel better.

"Cramming?" I say.

"As much as Ari will let me," Leah says wryly.

"There's more to the SSE than biology," I observe.

She grins. "Might as well play to my strengths, right?"

We're both fourteen and in Final, the last year of primary school. After that, Ashari students who want to continue their education sit for the citywide Secondary School Examination. Only the four days of the weekend remain between now and the test on Firstday. The exam is the same for kasiri and halani, though kasir students have the extra subject of magic. Virtually all kasiri take the SSE, while in the poorest halan districts, almost nobody goes on to secondary school. Horiel falls somewhere in between; about half our Final classmates registered for the exam.

There was never any question at home of whether or not I'd take the SSE. I don't want to settle for a primary education, and I know Mother expects more.

"You're awfully quiet," Leah says. "Are you anxious? It's not like you need to worry about the SSE."

I smile feebly. "It's not that."

I tell her about the arrest at the Ikhad. She listens, twirling the end of her braid around her fingers. When I reach the death of the woman who was protecting the young man, Leah makes a small noise in her throat and rests her chin on Ari's head. I close my eyes briefly, trying to block out the image of the woman crumpling under the kasir's spell. I finish with my extraordinary encounter with Sarah.

When I stop talking, Leah scoots her chair closer to mine and takes my hand. I squeeze hers in silent thanks.

"I wonder what they thought that man had done," she murmurs.

"Who knows?" The last time I heard about the Corps arresting someone, it was for distributing dissident writings: pamphlets condemning the segregated education system, leaflets counting up factory workers' grievances, and the like. But the young man at the Ikhad could've been suspected of any number of things.

"It's getting bad, isn't it?" Leah says. "Things are so tense."

I nod. Earlier this fall, the workers at an auto factory staged a demonstration to protest the replacement of a supervisor with a kasir rather than a halan promoted from their ranks. The police broke up the gathering with spells, then smashed up a nearby halan bookshop, claiming its owner carried banned books on foreign revolutions that had given the workers ideas. With jobs getting scarcer for halani and the Assembly so quick to use magic against anyone who kicks up a fuss, there's only going to be more trouble.

But something more immediate is bothering me. "Leah," I say, "I had one of those feelings when I saw the young man."

"You mean the intuition?" she says, suddenly sounding reluctant. "Marah, you need to stop obsessing—"

"It came too late!" I burst out, rising from my chair. "By the time I knew something bad was going to happen, I couldn't stop it. It was like when—"

"This has nothing to do with your father," Leah cuts in. "It's no use thinking that way."

The very first time the intuition stirred in me was the day my father died, and this morning is beginning to feel like an ugly echo of that day.

"Then what's the point?" I ask. Unlike the kasiri, who can cast spells at will, we halani have no control over when we get these premonitions.

"I don't know," Leah says. "Please, Marah, sit."

"'Heed the intuition,' the saying goes, right? People say it can guide you, help you make the right choice or do what's wise. But what about when you can't?"

"But you *did* do what was wise," my friend says, grabbing Ari's hand before he knocks her history notebook off the table. "You got out of the Ikhad in time. Without the intuition, you might've been hurt."

I sink back into my chair, deflated. "Maybe you're right."

"The important thing," Leah says firmly, "is that you're safe."

AT HOME, I find Caleb in our bedroom, poring over the yellowed pages of a book. Our room is small, much of it taken up by the bed against one wall and the pine dresser against the other. If we didn't store the extra mattress under the bed, we'd hardly have any floor space at all. There's a cast-iron radiator under the window, which looks out on the street. Next to the radiator are my violin case and the bookshelf Father nailed together for us out of cast-off boards when we were little.

My ten-year-old brother lies sprawled on top of the blue-and-white quilt that was Mother's when she was a girl. He's reading the folktale collection, the first book Tsipporah gave me. He holds it in both hands, his bony wrists poking out of the sleeves of his cotton shirt. His gray wool sweater, handed down from me, lies in a heap on the floor.

I scoop up the sweater and sink onto the quilt beside him. He looks up at me hopefully, his silky dark brown hair falling over his eyebrows. I hand him the new book from Tsipporah's stall, and he begins to leaf through it.

Caleb doesn't speak. When he was three years old, he came down with meningitis and almost died. I remember hovering in our bedroom doorway, my throat tight, watching my brother twist and whimper while Mother tried to cool his fever with a wet cloth. Caleb survived, but as he recovered, Mother and Father and I noticed he no longer turned his head when we called his name. He also all but stopped talking. The illness had left him deaf.

We didn't know any other deaf people, and the only school for deaf children was for kasiri. Forced to figure things out on our own, we devised a system of signs to communicate. Before Caleb's illness, we had been teaching him to read. He had even started to sound out words. But after he lost his hearing, he would only stare silently at the letters on the page. I kept reading him picture books anyway, signing the stories as best I could. Caleb's favorite was about a boy who outwitted a bear in the forest. We always imagined the forest in the story to be the same one that loomed to the west of the city.

One day, I caught my brother examining one of my schoolbooks, a literature text with no illustrations. Somehow, he was reading. From then on, he devoured every book he could get his hands on.

I slide back on the bed and lean against the wall. Caleb curls up against me, propping the folktale collection on his knees.

I tap his shoulder. *Is Mother home?* I sign.

He nods. *She's working.*

I wince. It's going to be one of those weekends when she hardly leaves her study. This is the third time this fall.

Mother works at the Horiel District Hall, one of the neighborhood outposts of the Assembly's bureaucracy. The seven councilors oversee a labyrinthine administration of government officials, all of whom are kasiri, of course. But each District Hall relies on a staff of halan clerks to handle the most tedious tasks, which must be completed over the weekend if they aren't done by Sixthday evening.

She didn't come out all morning, Caleb signs, *so I made the chicken stock. And I swept the apartment.*

Now that he mentions it, the bedroom floor does look shinier. *My thanks. I'm going to study for a bit.*

I SPEND THE afternoon at the kitchen table trying to memorize mathematical formulas and the names of all the First Councilors of the Assembly in chronological order. Every few minutes, I catch myself staring off into space. I can't stop thinking about the woman the police killed. Did she have children? What made her step between the Corps officers and the young halan?

Could I have prevented her death?

And then it's that fateful day again, six years ago. I try to brush away the memory as I usually do because Leah's right, it's no use dwelling on it, but after what happened today, it's impossible.

It was an ordinary weekday morning. I sat eating breakfast in this very spot while Mother, who didn't work then, cut a fried egg into small pieces for Caleb. Father clomped into the kitchen in his work boots, a merry smile crinkling his eyes. He bent to kiss Mother on the cheek and patted Caleb on the head. Then he gave my braid an affectionate tug and walked out the door, off to the steelworks.

At school later, in the middle of mathematics class, I started to feel anxious. I kept picturing Father leaving through our apartment door. A terrible foreboding crept over me: something bad was going to happen to him. I told myself it was my imagination, but I couldn't shake my dread. At morning recess, Leah asked if I was sick. When I explained, her eyes grew big.

"The intuition!" she whispered.

Certainty flooded through me. I'd never had the intuition before, but I'd been told about it. Suddenly I was terrified. I didn't know where Father's steelworks was, but I had to do something.

"I'm going home," I said. "Mother will know what to do."

I ran home as fast as I could and burst in on Mother and Caleb rolling out piecrust in the kitchen.

"Marah, why aren't you at school?" Mother exclaimed.

"Something's going to happen to Father," I cried. "You have to bring him home!"

"What?" she said.

"Mother, I *know* it."

I saw the fear in her eyes then.

As soon as she had found a neighbor to watch Caleb, she left for the steelworks, and I followed. I had to run to keep up with her, my heart thumping against my lungs. By the time we finally crossed the Davgir into the industrial zone on the other side of the river, I was ready to collapse.

I followed Mother to the end of a wide road. Dozens of workers were gathered there, with more joining them every minute. In the distance stood the steel mill. Smoke was pouring from one of its towers. My breath caught in my throat.

The men stopped Mother as she tried to pass. "There's been an accident, an explosion," one of them said. "It's not safe."

"My husband," she said. "Avshalom Levi. He's the blast furnace foreman . . ." She craned her neck, searching the growing crowd for Father.

Some of the workers exchanged glances. A man with an eye patch said halfheartedly, "He's not with us, but we're not all out yet . . ."

The men waited. Mother waited with them. I held Mother's hand.

Finally, the supervisor arrived, shaking his head. His hollow cheeks were dark with stubble, his clothes streaked black. They'd lost three men in the accident. When he said the name Levi, everything went blurry, as though I was seeing the world through rippled glass.

I was home again, and Mother was rocking me in her arms. I felt numb. Night fell. In the dark I started screaming that I'd known, that I'd felt the danger. Mother held me all night and kept repeating to me, fiercely, "It's not your fault, Marah. There was nothing you could have done."

But neither of us knew that for sure. That night, I took my grief and guilt and rage and began to wrestle with the intuition and its cruelty. And since then I've never stopped.

At nightfall, I rummage through the kitchen drawer for matches and light the gas ceiling lamp over the table. Then I light the stove to reheat the chicken stock Caleb made and chop carrots and leeks for a soup. Drawn by the smells, my brother wanders into the kitchen and sticks his face into the steam swirling from the pot.

I raise my eyebrows in a silent question as I bring the knife and cutting board to the sink.

Needs more seasoning, he signs, opening the pantry to survey the jars of dried herbs.

I shrug. On culinary matters, I defer to Caleb's judgment.

Just then, Mother walks into the kitchen. She's wearing an old skirt, and her long braid is down, not coiled up as it would be to go to work. Her tired eyes soften with tenderness as she watches us cooking together, but her fingers pick at a tear near the cuff of her cream-colored shirt.

When the soup is ready, I close the gas valve and ladle up a bowl for each of us. We slurp our meal in silence, content simply to be together. When Mother finishes her soup, she riffles through my notes piled at the empty place.

"It is possible to study too hard," she says.

"I'm not," I say. "I worked at Tsipporah's stall all morning, and then I went to Leah's. And I only have three days left."

"Still. I don't want you working all night."

"I won't, Mother." Watching her brush a loose strand of hair away from her face, I recall when she had the energy to bake a cake with Caleb on the weekend and laugh over my stories of eccentric customers at Tsipporah's stand. Now I just wish she would follow her own advice and rest.

3

Early on Tenthday morning, I set out for the Ikhad again. It's the biggest market day of the week, and everyone is out savoring the end of the weekend before returning to work and school. Today is the last day before the secondary school entrance exam. I'm as ready as I'll ever be.

The crowd thickens on the boulevard that leads to the river. The smell of roasted chestnuts floats in the air. Halan women on their way to the market laugh with each other, their colorful scarves flapping in the wind. At the clop of hooves, they make way for a kasir's gleaming black carriage. The halan driver on the box seat touches the brim of his cap in thanks. Carriages are an unusual sight these days. Like Sarah's family, most kasiri now own automobiles.

The boulevard runs straight into the imposing façade of the most prestigious kasir school in Ashara: Firem. I wish there were a halan equivalent I could try to get into, but there isn't. Firem's great carved doors announce a legacy of wealth, privilege, and magic. The wide stone steps are dotted with university students and secondary school boarders dressed in black. One girl has shoes with heels, and another's hands are hidden in a fur muff. The older boys wear the stiff felt hats kasir men favor.

Past Firem, I fall in with the throngs along the banks of the Davgir. People stream around wagons laden with squash and potatoes from the countryside. Eventually, we all spill into the Ikhad square. The usual crowds eddy between the aisles as shoppers avoid tripping over crates of bruised vegetables. Nothing suggests that the previous market day ended with the First Councilor's Corps killing a halan woman under this very roof.

I hurry to the northeast corner of the Ikhad. Stationed at his steaming griddle, Old Gideon pours batter in a thin stream onto the hot metal. Behind the neighboring stand, Tsipporah is perched on her stool, knitting a sock with gnarled fingers.

"Good morning, Marah!" she calls.

I smile as I approach her stall. "Hello, Tsipporah."

"You made it home safely Seventhday?" she says with concern.

I give a subdued nod. "I saw the arrest though."

Tsipporah shakes her head bitterly. "No regard for anyone . . ."

She sets aside her needles and picks up a leather-bound volume. "Something new," she says, handing it to me across the table of books. Her green eyes sparkle. "Thought you might like to take a look before some stuffy Firem professor snaps it up."

Curious, I open the book. The elegant letters of Old Monarchic flow across the water-stained pages in neat rows. I gasp in wonder. "My thanks!"

Six years after Tsipporah and I first met, I still can't read Old Monarchic. If Tsipporah lent me a primer on the language, I'm sure I could learn. I've taught myself the rudiments of several other languages that way, but hard-up university students always snag Tsipporah's Old Monarchic textbooks before I can get to them. Still, even books written in languages I can't fathom are worth looking at. There's something about the foreign words and the beautiful scripts that I can't get enough of. They're like secret codes begging to be broken.

As Tsipporah takes up her knitting again, I squeeze between her and Gideon's stalls and sit on the ground behind her display. Taking care not to damage the rippled pages, I leaf through the Old Monarchic text, admiring the crisp typesetting. The sweet aroma of Gideon's pancakes wafts through our corner of the market.

At the sound of approaching customers, I jump up. Tsipporah takes care of the first one while I greet the second. For the next hour or so, we keep busy selling books. I steal a moment here and there to pore over the Old Monarchic text. During a lull, Gideon offers us each a thin, delicate pancake spread with jelly and rolled up tight. I eat mine quickly, licking the grease from my fingers. Then I make myself useful sorting out stacks of books haphazardly rearranged by browsing customers.

When I next look up, Tsipporah is standing in the aisle with a woman wearing a gray cloak. I can't see her face, only the long, silver hair escaping from the hood pulled over her head. When she speaks, her voice is hushed. This is not the first mysterious stranger who's come drifting through the Ikhad to talk to Tsipporah without ever touching a book. I've tried asking Tsipporah about her odd friends, but she always deflects my questions.

She notices me watching now and gestures for me to approach. "Have you heard of anyone falling mysteriously ill?" she asks me. The other woman stands perfectly motionless, her hood still up.

"No," I say, perplexed.

"It seems there've been rumors," she says, tilting her head toward the cloaked newcomer. "Strange talk of sickness."

The way she says it, combined with her friend's mute presence, makes the back of my neck prickle. "Winter's coming. There's always illness."

"This is different," Tsipporah says, strands of white hair fluttering against her temples. "A new illness. The eyes of the stricken darken."

"They darken?" I say blankly.

Tsipporah's gaze flicks toward the silent, silver-haired woman. "It may be nothing." She hesitates. "You've done good work this morning, Marah. Isn't that big exam of yours tomorrow?"

I nod, my insides twisting at the reminder.

"You ought to rest up, then," she says. "I think you should go home early."

IN THE MORNING, Mother leaves for the District Hall before Caleb and I have finished breakfast. She wishes me luck on her way out the door. I gulp down my oatmeal, anxious to get to school early for the SSE. First, I need to take Caleb to Leah's apartment. Horiel Primary refuses to accommodate a deaf boy, so he spends school days with Leah's mother and the youngest Avram children.

While I'm clearing the dishes, someone knocks at the door. I cross the kitchen to answer it, wondering who it could be.

The caller is a youngish man, tall and clean-shaven. His black coat, with its silk-covered buttons, betrays him at once.

"Who are you?" he says, frowning.

"I'm Marah Levi," I say, alarmed.

"I'm from the District Hall," he says, holding up an identity card. He steps forward, and I move aside, powerless to stop him from crossing our threshold.

"Does Caleb Levi reside here?" he asks.

"Yes, sir. My brother." I glance toward the table where he's still sitting.

The visitor looks him over. "I've come to summon Caleb Levi to the District Hall. He's missed the deadline for completing his magic examination by several months."

My heartbeat quickens. I thought Mother had taken him.

All Ashari children must be examined for magic before turning ten. The test is usually a formality, since the children of kasiri almost always have magic and the children of halani almost always don't. Nowadays, intermarriage between kasiri and halani is prohibited, which simplifies things. Still, there are exceptional cases in which children's magical abilities don't match their parents', so the examination is required for everyone.

On the rare occasions when a halan-born child is discovered to have magic or a kasir-born child is found not to, the law dictates that they be removed from their home and placed in an adoptive family of the appropriate magical status. There was a boy in my year at Horiel Primary who turned out to be a magician. He disappeared from school, and apart from a terse announcement of his departure, our teachers refused to talk about him. Gradually, we too began to act as if he'd never existed.

Caleb has never shown the least sign of having magic. The ability emerges around the age of eight or nine, so we would know by now if he had it. But the government doesn't know. It has to be official.

They want to test you for magic at the District Hall, I sign to Caleb.

His eyes get big, as though he's just remembered making a terrible mistake.

"Can my mother bring him tomorrow?" I ask the kasir.

The official's gaze slides back to me. "Your brother must

come to the District Hall immediately. It's only a few blocks away."

"But sir, I'm in Final, and the SSE's today. It starts in less than an hour. I promise my mother will—"

"I have orders," the kasir says, a note of regret in his voice. "If you want, I could take him over myself."

I would never leave my brother in the hands of some kasir official, but all I say is, "He's deaf, sir. Someone needs to interpret for him."

Cursing to myself, I sign to Caleb. *He says we have to go now.*

He raises his eyebrows. *What about the SSE?*

Don't worry, I sign. *We'll find Mother. She can stay with you, and I'll go to school.*

Once I've gathered our identity papers and my school-bag, we leave the apartment and proceed downstairs.

At the District Hall, a balding official directs us to a room containing a row of chairs and an unoccupied desk. According to the clock on the wall, it's five past eight. The SSE begins in less than half an hour.

"Wait," I say to the official before he withdraws. "Where can I find Chavah Levi?"

The balding kasir frowns in puzzlement, but he says, "Chavah Levi works upstairs."

Leaving Caleb in the waiting room, I find the staircase and climb to the upper floor. It's a labyrinth. The hallways zigzag, there are too many corners, and nothing distinguishes one stretch of corridor from another except the words stenciled on the doors' frosted panes: Registry of Vital Records, Health and Sanitation, Courtroom . . . Many rooms are empty, and the people I do find send me farther on with confusing directions.

Ready to give in to blind panic, I poke my head into the next office. A man in a plain black suit is standing near the window, his arms loaded with papers.

"Excuse me, sir, where's Chavah Levi?"

He gives me a startled look. "Levi? Oh, they sent her across the city to deliver some documents. She'll be back this afternoon."

This afternoon? There's no hope. My expression must betray me, because he says, "Is it urgent?"

I shake my head and dart out.

Caleb looks alarmed when I rush into the waiting room. The kasir who summoned us from the apartment is here, chatting with another official who has returned to his post at the desk.

"Sir," I gasp, addressing our escort. "Our mother's not here. Would it be possible for the examiner to come at once?"

He purses his lips. "I'll see what I can do."

He leaves the waiting room, and I sink into the chair next to Caleb's.

You should go, my brother signs. *I can stay by myself.*

I shake my head. I'm not abandoning him in this nest of kasiri to fend for himself.

The examiner doesn't come. The SSE will have started by now. Will they let me in late? I feel like the breakfast in my stomach is curdling.

Finally, a pudgy, black-clad kasir enters the waiting room and calls Caleb's name. He ushers us into a cramped side office and motions for us to sit.

"This is the boy?" he says.

"Yes, sir." I hand him Caleb's papers. He glances at them, then flings them onto a chair.

"Stand up. How old are you?" He gestures impatiently, and Caleb leaps to his feet. I sign to him discreetly, and he raises all ten fingers.

"Why don't you speak, boy?"

"He's deaf, sir," I say.

The official becomes, if possible, even more bored. My stomach tightens as he begins a sequence of hand motions and spoken syllables. Pinpricks of light—gold, green, purple —blossom and die at his fingertips. I want to cover my nose against the magic's sharp smell.

The examiner's hands still. He keeps one held out, palm up, and utters a last incantation. A bead of light appears in the hollow of his hand. Its color is indeterminate, an unripe silver. I know from my own test that green means kasir and blue halan. I hold my breath.

The drop of light turns blue.

I let out an audible sigh. The kasir makes me sign a document in Mother's place. After I convince the examiner my brother can write his own name, Caleb signs too.

* * *

Outside the District Hall, Caleb assures me I don't need to walk him to the Avrams', so I let him go on his way. As I sprint toward school, I picture myself ending up on the docks of the Davgir unloading barges of Xanite cotton and Laishidi silk, or working on a factory assembly line.

My calves are burning by the time I reach Horiel Primary. The foyer is empty but for the caretaker sweeping the floor. The door of the headmaster's office looms at the end of the hallway. Steeling myself, I knock.

"Enter," comes a muffled voice.

I let myself into the office and approach Aradi Terach's desk until the fumes from his pipe become too much. His eyes are small and sharp in his broad face, and his thick fingers drum on his armrest. School headmaster is one of the plusher jobs available to halani, a fact which makes Aradi Terach rather smug.

"Good morning, sir. My name is Marah Levi." I haven't been in enough trouble to have wound up in his office for years, so he won't remember my name. "I'm in Final, and I'm supposed to be taking the SSE, but I wasn't able to get to school until now."

He lowers his pipe and squints at me. I already have a feeling I'll never see the pages of this year's test.

"The exam was set for this morning, Levi. Every Final student in Ashara has known this for weeks. What possible excuse might you have for arriving so catastrophically late?"

"My brother was summoned to the District Hall, sir."

"As far as I am aware, it was not your brother who was registered for the SSE," says Aradi Terach.

"Yes, but I had to go with him. He's deaf."

"Surely your mother could have taken him?"

"My mother works, sir." Anxious to head off further questions, I ask, "Since the exam's not over yet, do you think I could start it now?"

"The proctors cannot make irregular accommodations. The rules state—"

"Please, Aradi, there was nothing I could do."

"Did you just interrupt me?" says the headmaster.

The blood reverses in my veins.

"You are dismissed, Levi. The SSE will be offered again next year."

4

"WHERE WERE YOU YESTERDAY?" LEAH DEMANDS when I burst out of the apartment building in the morning, my violin case banging against my leg and Caleb on my heels. My friend is waiting on our doorstep with her own fiddle case.

"You're here already?" I usually meet her at her place when I bring Caleb over.

"Of course I'm here!" Leah signs hello to Caleb before continuing. "I could barely concentrate yesterday, wondering what had happened. I came by after school to find out, but you weren't home. It was the SSE, Marah!"

"I know." I turn to Caleb. *Can you walk to Leah's by yourself?*

He just grins and disappears around the corner. As Leah and I start toward school, I tell her about my morning at the District Hall and the headmaster's total lack of sympathy.

Leah strides faster in her agitation. "What will you *do*?"

"Wait till next year, I guess." That's what I told Mother

last night. After leaving the headmaster's office, I went on a long, dazed walk through the city and didn't return home until the sun was sinking. Mother was waiting for me, distressed and overflowing with apologies even though I didn't blame her. We all knew when Caleb's birthday was.

At school, Leah and I climb to the music room on the top floor for our first class. We play in the medsha, a classical ensemble consisting of twelve musicians: three violinists, two violists, two cellists, two flutists, a lyrist, a horn player, and a percussionist. Each of the six upper years at Horiel Primary has a separate medsha, and Aradi Imael, our music teacher, conducts all of them.

A knot of Final musicians reaches the classroom just ahead of Leah and me. Our friend Devorah, her cello case slung over her shoulder, holds the door for us.

"Where were you yesterday?" she asks me.

"Yes, what happened?" asks Miriam, one of the flute players.

"I missed the exam," I say shortly, following Leah into the room.

"Good morning," says Aradi Imael from her desk.

"You missed the SSE, Marah?" cries Reuven, the third violinist, as he plucks at his instrument.

I wish they would all shut up. Aradi Imael looks at me with concern but says nothing. I take my seat and unpack my violin.

Once everyone is tuned, Aradi Imael takes her baton from the conductor's stand and steps onto her podium. She's not very tall, but her confident bearing commands respect. I think she's younger than Mother, though her black hair, worn in a short, thick braid, is more streaked with gray.

She asks us to pull out "Where Wind Blows Not," an old north-lands folk song arranged for medsha by the Ashari composer Toviah Adam. It's my favorite of the pieces we're performing at our winter concert next week.

Amid the rustle of sheet music, my violist friend Shaul leans across Leah and Reuven and asks, "How'd you miss the SSE?"

"Long story," I murmur. While Aradi Imael scribbles a marking in her score, I tell him and Reuven about the District Hall.

"They could've been more flexible," Reuven says indignantly.

"Bastards," says Shaul. I flinch.

"That's enough," Aradi Imael says sharply. She doesn't tolerate abuse of kasiri in her classroom.

"Sorry. It won't happen again, Aradi." Shaul flashes a lopsided smile, but there's a defiant edge to his gaze. His father was once imprisoned for organizing a factory protest, and one of his cousins was killed in a government crackdown on restless workers.

Aradi Imael raises her baton, and the violins begin "Where Wind Blows Not." I breathe with the music as the sound grows. I love the texture of the strings, the hollow sweetness of the flutes, the depth of the horn. Contentment wells up in me and flows into the warm vibrato of my fingers.

After we've played the piece once straight through, Aradi Imael drills us on some finer points of phrasing. When the period ends, my classmates pack up and flock to the stairs. I'm about to follow when Aradi Imael beckons me.

"So you missed the SSE," she says when we're alone. "How did you manage that?"

I can't meet her eyes as I explain about Caleb and the test.

"Oh, Marah . . ." Aradi Imael sighs and then thinks for a moment. "I might have an idea, but I need to do some investigating first. Visit me at home at the end of the week, all right? Sixthday evening. It's 19 Fayil Street, in Mir District. Now run along."

Surprised but encouraged by her invitation, I join my class downstairs outside Aradi Nabot's room. Three immigrant boys from Xana are joking by the door in their native tongue. A moment later, our teacher pushes through the throng of students, a stack of papers pinned under his elbow.

"Why aren't you lined up properly? Out of my way."

We shrink back, and Aradi Nabot turns his key in the lock. Hardly have we filed in and found our seats than he slaps the papers onto his desk and begins to pace in front of the blackboard.

"I've graded your essays," he says, "and I'll warn you, the class average was abysmal. Some of your classmates' compositions were so dreadful I despair of teaching them anything about the study of literature."

While the teacher's back is turned, Shaul stretches his face into a caricature of Aradi Nabot's and silently mimics his ranting. His impression elicits a few muffled giggles, but I only sigh. The day always goes downhill after medsha.

AFTER SCHOOL, LEAH and I roam the neighborhood. The air is crisp, but we're in no hurry to get home. We pass two women carrying home bags of damp clothes from the laundry. Younger children returning from school leave their books on cracked concrete doorsteps and play in the street, passing around leather balls or breaking apart discarded crates to make wooden swords. On the corner, the coal delivery man's horse and cart are waiting under the street sign, half of which is broken off.

Leah and I reach the neighborhood park and settle onto a bench.

"What did Aradi Imael want after medsha?" my friend asks. "Was it about the SSE?"

I nod. "She said she might be able to help me."

"How?"

"I don't know. Maybe she can find me some work to tide me over till next year's exam."

"What if it was giving violin lessons to children?" Leah says, excited. "You could do it, Marah. You're the best player in the medsha."

I shrug, gazing into the juniper. I appreciate the compliment, but I'm too discouraged about losing a year for it to cheer me.

"What do you want to do later on?" Leah asks as a squirrel scampers across the gravel path at our feet. "Devorah's planning on being a bookkeeper. Miriam wants to study nursing. And Shaul wants to go to the halan engineering school by the river and play with electric wires."

We laugh.

"This might sound strange," Leah says, growing serious, "but I've thought about working in an orphanage."

"That'd be perfect for you," I say, thinking of all her younger siblings. It would make Leah happy to do something so difficult, and so good. I couldn't bear caring for all those children only to send them to the textile factories when they were old enough, so they could repay the government's charity.

"What about you?" Leah asks.

"I don't know," I say quietly. Maybe I could work at a library. Or become a teacher. Everything depends on the SSE, though, and there's nothing I can do about that now except wait.

We rise from the bench and wend our way toward the gate. A flash of red catches my eye. At the foot of a naked shrub, a small bird with a crimson cap and throat huddles on the ground.

"A house finch," Leah exclaims, approaching the bird but stopping at a respectful distance as if to avoid frightening it. "It's injured!"

I sigh. "Maybe it's just stunned. It'll fly away soon."

"No, he won't. Look how his wing is hanging."

She's right. I wince. "It might've been kids. I've seen them throw stones at birds before."

Leah clicks her tongue in disgust, still watching the finch.

"Come on," I say, swinging the gate open. "I don't think we can help it."

She follows me into the street, hesitates, and walks back into the park.

"Leah, the last bird you brought home died," I say, exasperated.

"I can't just leave him," she protests. "A cat will come along and rip him apart."

Fishing a handkerchief from her skirt pocket, she advances toward the limp bird, almost cat-like herself. She drapes her handkerchief over the finch's back and scoops it up, her palms over its wings.

"You're crazy," I tell her. "Are you sure about the orphanage? Wouldn't you rather be an animal doctor?"

Cradling the bird, Leah shakes her head. "Children are more important."

AT THE END of the week, I set off for Aradi Imael's. The most direct route from Horiel to Mir lies through the nicest kasir district outside the city center. Halani usually stay out of such neighborhoods, but skirting this one would add so much time to my walk that I decide to chance it.

Horiel's dinginess first gives way to a different halan neighborhood where the paint on the buildings isn't chipping and useless junk isn't collecting in the street. Some apartments even have window boxes, though nothing is blooming this time of year. Clots of workers saunter down the street, swinging their lunch pails and joking with each other.

I pause at an intersection as people stream out the doors of a fane, a Maitafi house of worship. It's a halan congregation, of course, and most of the faithful coming down the fane's front steps are women. They drape shawls over their shoulders and wind bright, knitted scarves around their necks. Clasped in their hands are copies of the Maitaf, their sacred book. A few of them smile at me, and I try to smile back, feeling awkward because I'm not religious.

When I cross into the kasir quarter, the transition is marked. Here, the limestone apartment buildings are much grander, five or six stories tall with rows of enormous windows on every floor. Elaborate stonework frames the front doors, and wrought-iron balconies extend from the buildings high above the street. I've heard a single kasir family will occupy an entire floor of one of these apartment buildings. This is the sort of neighborhood where Sarah, the girl I saved at the Ikhad, probably lives. I wonder if she still remembers me and the story I told her.

The sun is setting, so I hasten down the neat sidewalks. As I walk along the fence of a large public park, a woman stops in my path and says, "What are you doing in this part of the city?"

She wears a black felt hat trimmed with a striped feather and a fur scarf that looks like it was once a fox. Her outfit makes me very aware of my simple braid, my old-fashioned cloak, and my darned stockings.

"I'm on my way to Mir," I say, edging along the iron fence.

She sniffs. "Well, hurry then."

I walk faster, scowling at the sidewalk. Finally, I arrive in Mir District. I find Fayil Street and number 19 in the fading light. It's a narrow townhouse. When I knock, Aradi Imael answers almost instantly.

"Marah!" A smile lights her face. "Come in."

I follow her into the living room, where a fire is blazing in the grate. Above the mantelpiece hangs a plate with a Laishidi-style brush painting in its center.

Aradi Imael offers me a threadbare armchair, and I sit down. She passes through a curtain into the kitchen and reappears bearing a tray with two tea glasses, a teapot, and a plate of almond biscuits.

"This must have been a distressing week for you," she says, pouring the tea. "I'm sorry about the SSE, but I might have a solution."

She hands me a glass of hot tea, and I take a sip. It's black and smooth and calming.

"I spoke to a friend of mine about you," Aradi Imael continues. "He's the headmaster of a secondary school for musicians called Qirakh."

I glance at my teacher in surprise. In the firelight, her golden skin takes on a reddish cast.

"You're a talented violinist, Marah," she says. "Any music school would be lucky to have you."

I flush. "My thanks."

"I explained your problem to my friend. He said they'd be willing to consider an application from you based on your primary school record alone, without the SSE. And while Qirakh's focus is music, you'd receive a more than adequate secondary education." Aradi Imael raises one eyebrow at me. "What do you think? Are you interested?"

Does she even need to ask?

"Yes," I say at once. "Music school sounds wonderful. And if there's any way for me to go to secondary school next year, I want to try."

"Good!" Aradi Imael beams. "I should mention, Qirakh was founded by Xanite immigrants, and the student body is still predominantly Xanite. There are those who don't think well of it."

I nod my understanding. Many Ashari look down on Xanites, who have immigrated to the north lands in droves to flee a decades-long civil war in their homeland. Nevertheless, Xana is the country with which Ashara and the other city-states have the closest economic ties and the most in common culturally. In fact, the people of the north lands descended from Xanite migrants who crossed the sea and established the kingdom of Erezai centuries ago.

"That doesn't bother me," I assure my teacher. Tensions between Ashari and Xanite students have never been high at Horiel Primary.

"You'll have to audition, of course," says Aradi Imael.

"Oh." The only auditions I've ever played have been for seating in medsha, and I've never faced any real contest for first violin.

"I'll be frank," she says. "Most students who audition

for Qirakh take private lessons. You'll have to work hard in order to compete with them."

My apprehension grows. As if sensing this, Aradi Imael gives me a reassuring smile. "I think you could do beautifully, Marah. Auditions are in five and a half weeks. We'll find you a solo to play. Why don't you stop by my classroom after school next Thirdday? That will give me a couple of days after our concert to think about repertoire."

I get to my feet, thanking Aradi Imael profusely. Then I step out into the wintry night, filled with excitement and hope.

5

I SLEEP LATE THE NEXT MORNING SINCE IT'S SEVENTHDAY, the start of the weekend. At breakfast, I explain Aradi Imael's proposal to Mother and Caleb.

A cloud seems to lift from around Mother. "What an opportunity! I'm so glad, I've been worrying all week about your education. . . . I must thank your teacher."

After we polish off Caleb's spiced oatmeal, she disappears into her study. Caleb remains at the table, reading. It's a market day at the Ikhad, so I take my cloak from its peg, eager to leave for Tsipporah's stall.

Want to come? I sign to Caleb.

He shakes his head. *I'm learning about fungi,* he signs earnestly. There's a strange air about him, like he's trying too hard to look innocent. I almost have the impression he's waiting for me to leave. I watch him for a moment, but soon he's absorbed in his book again, and I decide I'm imagining things.

Outside, I tighten my cloak against the biting cold and set off at a quick pace. At the Ikhad, the Seventhday market is in full swing. Merchants' voices rise above the creak of cart wheels and the melancholy neighs of horses as they vie for customers. At one stall, women in furs and plumed hats examine a stack of hand-knotted carpets only kasiri could afford. I brush past them and weave through the vegetable stands. Two farm boys standing guard over several bushel baskets of turnips watch the swelling throng with their mouths hanging open. The way they're gawping, they must be from some remote village in the northern reaches of the city-state. Granted, the aisles *are* especially crowded today, and the shoppers' conversations seem unusually agitated.

When I reach Tsipporah's stall, Gideon the pancake vendor is missing. A tarpaulin is spread over his griddle.

"Tsipporah, where's Gideon?"

"Good day, Marah," she says, her wizened face carefully blank. "All well at home?"

"Why wouldn't it be? What's wrong?"

Tsipporah draws her eyebrows together. "Marah . . . Gideon has died."

I stare at the empty stall. For as long as I've been visiting Tsipporah, Gideon has been a fixture of the Ikhad, always ready with a free treat for his fellow vendors. How can he be gone?

"What happened?" I ask.

"He took ill," Tsipporah says, tugging her knit cap lower over her white hair. "Do you remember the dark eyes sickness we heard about last weekend? That's what it was. It was very sudden, his daughter said. And it's not just him." She gestures at an open newspaper spread over the poetry section. "Three other such deaths were reported in the *Journal* today too."

That must be why today's shoppers are so worked up. Still, if it turns into a real outbreak, I'm sure Ashara's physicians will find a way to treat it.

Business is brisk this morning, leaving me little time to dwell on Gideon's empty stall. I leave the Ikhad toward noon, hoping to meet Leah for lunch. A few solitary snowflakes drift down from the blank gray sky as I walk back to Horiel District. When I knock on the Avrams' door, it swings inward, and a three-year-old boy peers out.

"Hello, Ilan. Can I come in?"

"Who is it?" It's Leah's mother's voice.

"Gadi Yakov?" I call. "It's Marah."

She comes to the landing, shooing her son out of the way. Gadi Yakov is tall and sturdy and wears her braids pinned up in a crown. Today her face is drawn.

"Is Leah around?" I ask.

Gadi Yakov sighs. "Come in, Marah."

Puzzled, I follow her into the familiar apartment. In the kitchen, Ilan has returned to building a tower of blocks with the help of his sister Yael. Ruth, the eldest after Leah, greets me from near the window, holding Ari on her hip.

"Leah's sick," Gadi Yakov tells me, removing her apron and winding the strings around her chapped hands.

"Oh, I'll come back another time then," I say, turning to go. Then I hesitate. "What does she have?"

"I'm not sure," her mother says. Something in her expression sends a shiver up my spine. She motions me into the hallway and continues in a low voice, "She's running a high fever, but . . . it's no ordinary illness. Her eyes have turned black."

My heart stops. "Can I see her?"

"It could be contagious," Gadi Yakov begins, but I'm already halfway down the hall.

"Marah, wait!"

I turn the loose knob of the girls' bedroom door. "Leah?"

She's lying in bed, awake. I hasten to her side and kneel on the floor, drawn to her eyes in spite of the dread sloshing around inside me. Normally a lively brown, her irises are now so dark I can barely distinguish her pupils. The sight is paralyzing.

"Marah," she says. Her lips are puffy and dry.

"Leah . . ." I slide into a moment of panic, thinking of Gideon the pancake vendor. What if Leah . . . ?

I don't let myself even think it. "How do you feel?" I ask.

"Cold," she says, shaking beneath the heavy quilt. "Tired. I have an awful headache. Everything aches." She offers a wan smile. "But I'm glad you're here."

"I have some exciting news." I tell her about Aradi Imael's friend, the headmaster of Qirakh, and my decision to audition for the Xanite music school.

"Oh, Marah!" Leah's cracked lips break into a real smile. "I'm so happy for you." With some effort, she sits up and scoots to the far side of the bed, peering down at something on the floor. "Want to see Raspberry?"

"Raspberry? Don't tell me you named the bird." I walk around the bed. At the foot of the nightstand is a battered hatbox pierced with air holes. The lid is off, and Leah is gazing fondly into it.

"Yael named him," she says.

I peek into the box. Though Leah has mentioned the injured finch every day at school, I haven't seen it since that afternoon in the park. The red-throated bird is nestled in a soft dishcloth, its left wing bound to its body with a strip of rag. A saucer of water and another of seeds lie within pecking distance.

"I can't believe it's still alive," I say.

Leah beams, falling back against her pillow. "He's a tough little one. Mother tried to take him out of my room last night, but I wouldn't let her. If I can't see my siblings, I'm at least going to keep Raspberry."

I snort.

"That's the advantage of being sick, you know," Leah adds dryly. "People have to cater to your every whim."

"Do you think it'll fly again?" I ask, anxious to steer the conversation away from her illness.

"I hope so." She kneads her forehead. "Yesterday after school I asked Aradi Lamech if he had any advice for taking care of a bird with a broken wing."

"Aradi Lamech?" I say, making a face at the mention of our science teacher.

Leah shrugs. "He likes me all right. And he does know a lot about animals. The first thing he said was most rescued birds die of shock pretty fast and mine probably would too. So I told him I'd already had Raspberry for five days. That shut him up."

I giggle.

"Anyway, then he talked about what to feed him, how to keep him calm . . ." Leah yawns, and I realize my visit is tiring her.

"I'm going to let you sleep," I say, getting up.

"Wait." My friend is silent a moment. "I've seen my eyes, Marah. Mother told me I'm not the only one. I'm scared."

"Don't be scared," I say even as my stomach drops. "You'll get well."

Back in the kitchen, Gadi Yakov is ladling up bean soup for Leah's siblings. Ilan and Yael wait at the table while Ruth feeds Ari spoonfuls of purée.

"Would you like some, Marah?" Gadi Yakov asks, setting two bowls on the table.

"No, my thanks."

"Is Leah asleep?" she says.

"Not yet, I don't think. We were looking at . . . Raspberry."

Gadi Yakov makes a sound of irritation. "That filthy bird. Leah pitched a fit when I suggested moving it out of her bedroom. Her *sickroom*."

I struggle to hide a smile, but my amusement is fleeting. I can't forget Leah's night-black eyes.

"Can I visit her again?" I have no intention of staying

away, but I should at least pretend to ask permission.

She sighs. "Talk to your mother first. And tell her I don't think Caleb should come back until Leah's better."

At dinner that night, I pick at Caleb's latest concoction—mashed potatoes with salted fish—until Mother asks me if I'm all right. Everything comes spilling out of me, from Tsipporah's tidings to Leah's black eyes.

By the time I finish, Mother and Caleb have both gone still. I stand and drift from the table, abandoning my supper. In our room, I sink onto the edge of the bed. A few minutes later, Mother comes in and sits next to me. I don't protest when she drapes her arm around my shoulders and pulls me close.

After going to bed, I lie awake on the mattress on the floor listening to Caleb breathing softly on the bed. We read three folktales together before turning out the light, comforting stories about loyal friends and homeward journeys, but still he wouldn't stop clinging to me, his fingers clutching my shirt, his breath on my cheek.

I turn restlessly under the covers. It feels like hours have passed when the door creaks open. I lie still. Even with my eyes closed, I can feel Mother standing over us.

It snows during the night. In the morning, glittering icicles hang like daggers from the eaves. I begin my homework after breakfast, but my thoughts keep wandering to Leah. At last, I give in.

On my way to the Avrams' apartment, I pass people

gathered in knots on the street corners, clutching newspapers and talking of the illness. Everyone already seems to know of someone, kasir or halan, who's died.

I stay with Leah and her invalid house finch for most of the morning. When Gadi Yakov brings her a hot infusion of horehound leaves, I help her drink it. Between sips, she gives me a smile, half embarrassed, half grateful, but I'm only doing what she would do for me if I were in her place. I wish I could do more.

I return home around lunchtime. When I reach the Street of Winter Gusts, there's a boxy black auto rattling in the cold in front of our building. I stop dead. What's a kasir doing on our street?

The auto's back door swings open, and the little girl from the Ikhad hops out. Her dress snags on the running board where it rises to swoop over the back wheel. Above the gleaming hood, the girl's halan tutor looks out through the windshield. Then she steps out of the auto too, her heart-shaped face pinched with annoyance.

"You're here!" says Sarah, running up to me and seizing my icy hand. "Can we go inside?"

"Inside?" I say, uncomprehending.

"Gadin Sarah wished to call," Channah says. "We were just leaving, as nobody appeared to be home."

I can tell by her uneasy expression that Channah feels the impropriety, or at least the profound oddness, of a kasir girl visiting a Horiel apartment. But she makes no move to steer her charge back into the auto, and Sarah looks so eager I suppose I must let her in. She's a kasir, after all. And she is kind of sweet.

Luckily, there is no sign of our nosy neighbor, Gadi Yared, in the entrance hall. Channah and I hurry after Sarah as she skips up the steps.

When we reach the fourth floor, my guests follow me into our apartment. The kitchen is empty. Mother is putting in extra hours at the District Hall this weekend to finish a pressing project, but Caleb should be here. He must be in our bedroom.

"Please sit down," I say, embarrassed. The wooden floor has never looked so scuffed, the gas range so battered.

Channah pulls out a chair for Sarah, who plops onto it, her legs dangling. Channah and I also sit, but then I jump back up.

"Would you like tea? May I take your coats?"

Channah wraps hers more tightly about her narrow shoulders. So much for halan solidarity.

Sarah, on the other hand, offers me her coat, revealing a delicate orange frock. "I only drink our cook's spiced tea, but Channah will take some of yours," she says.

She's awfully presumptuous. I glance at her tutor, who nods, so I fetch the tea tin from the pantry and brew a pot. After pouring glasses for Channah and me, I sit down at the table.

"May I ask why you're visiting?"

"To hear the rest of the story!" Sarah says.

Channah sniffs. "Gadin Sarah gets fixations," she says under her breath.

"I do not," says Sarah, sticking out her chin. "I like Marah. And I want to find out what happens to Frost."

I hide my smile. Channah's view of the matter is probably right. It occurs to me that Channah might not like me because I remind Sarah of their ill-fated visit to the Ikhad. That wasn't exactly Channah's best moment as a chaperone.

Sarah stands up. "Where's your room, Marah?"

Channah breathes in sharply, but Sarah is already in the hallway. I catch up to her and nudge open our bedroom door. To my surprise, Caleb isn't there. Where could he be?

Sarah spots the bookshelf and rushes to it. "I knew you'd have books. Look, Channah, I have a book of tales like this one!"

"Don't touch without Marah's permission," her tutor says from the doorway.

"It's all right," I say distractedly. "Could you hold on a moment?"

I dart back into the kitchen, but no one's there. I check Mother's bedroom, even the study, but Caleb's gone. I've never discovered him missing before. Mother doesn't let Caleb leave home alone, lest he be run over by a cart or an automobile he can't hear.

I'm tempted to go out searching for him at once, but I have no idea where to look. Besides that, I have my hands full with Sarah and Channah in the apartment. Anxious, I return to my room to discover Sarah sorting through our books. She tosses most of them aside, pronouncing them boring, but then she happens upon my foreign grammars.

"You have books in other languages."

"I know," I say, joining her on the floor next to the shelf.

"Can you speak them?" asks Sarah.

"I've learned to read a couple."

I watch her inspect my prized books. The first sketches out the grammar of a language written with a huge syllabary. I gave up on it, though I like to leaf through the book now and then to appreciate the mystery of those symbols. The second book is an Aevlian grammar. Since Aevlian uses the same script as Ashari, I learned the basics without too much trouble. The third grammar is for a language called Hagramet, which has its own alphabet. It's more exotic than Aevlian, but not impossible. Tsipporah told me books in Hagramet are incredibly rare, which made the endeavor doubly exciting. Of all the languages I've dabbled in, it's the one I've studied most.

"You should meet my brother," Sarah says. "He's trying to translate some old books right now, and he's angry because he can't figure them out."

"There's no need to talk about Azariah like that," Channah says. Just then, Caleb comes into the bedroom. He freezes at the sight of me and my visitors.

Where have you been? I sign, my fingers flying as I rise from the floor.

He ignores this. *Who are they?*

Sarah scrambles to her feet. "Are you Marah's brother?" she asks Caleb.

The question is predictable enough that he can read her lips. He nods.

Our signing hasn't escaped Channah's notice. "He's deaf, Sarah," she says.

"So?"

With that one word, Sarah wins me over. My heart swells with a rush of warmth.

Sarah spots a stack of loose-leaf paper on the bedside table. "Can I use a piece of that?"

"Sarah . . ." Channah begins. She falls silent when I hand Sarah a pencil stub.

Sarah bends over the nightstand and painstakingly writes something in the corner of a sheet of paper. Then she holds it out to Caleb, and I make out the question: *What is your name?*

My brother looks at me as if to say, *Who are these people, and why are they in our bedroom?* I just nod toward the piece of paper. Resigned, Caleb takes the pencil and prints his name.

Sarah sounds it out. "Caleb?" She beams at him. "I'm Sarah." She writes her name next to his. Caleb looks at me again. If I weren't furious with him, I would have to laugh. Instead, I glare back at him. He drops his gaze and slips out of the bedroom.

"Will you finish the story now, Marah?" Sarah asks.

"Where did I leave off?"

"Frost and the traders were almost to Ashara, but the ravens that were helping them flew away," Sarah prompts. She settles onto the floor, sitting cross-legged, and starts drawing on her piece of loose-leaf.

"Right. Well, the traders were near despair, but then Frost called her friends the mice."

"The *mice*?" Sarah drops her pencil and wrinkles her nose.

I laugh. "Yes. Thousands of mice came scurrying to the travelers' aid. At first, they were disgusted, but when they saw the mice grip the harnesses in their teeth and begin to drag the sleds, they were grateful.

"The mice brought the sleds all the way to Ashara. When they reached the city, the traders gave a great cheer, frightening the mice, who went scampering back to their burrows. The traders began to unload their goods. Suddenly, they remembered Frost. They looked for her to thank her, but she and Silver had already disappeared into the frozen landscape."

Sarah looks up and seems to contemplate the end of the tale. Then she rewards me with a glowing smile. Scooting toward me, she lays her piece of paper in my lap. "Look what I made for you."

Underneath her written exchange with Caleb, she's drawn three people and a tabby cat in descending order of height. The humans are labeled, from tallest to shortest, Marah, Caleb, and Sarah.

"My thanks," I say. "But where did the cat come from?"

"I just want a cat," Sarah says, standing up and dusting off her dress. She hesitates and glances up at me. "He doesn't have to eat mice."

I laugh.

"We must be going, Gadin Sarah," Channah says.

I usher them out through the kitchen. Sarah pauses on the threshold to give me a hug and then waves good-bye again from the landing. Once she and Channah are gone, I return to my room. On the bed is Sarah's slightly creased drawing. I smooth it out and pin it up on the inside of our door.

6

WHEN I WALK BACK INTO THE KITCHEN, CALEB is ferreting in the pantry. I march up to him, snatch a jar from his hand, and slam it down on the shelf.

Where were you earlier? I sign.

He draws back from the pantry, guilt flitting across his face. *Out,* he gestures. *I like to go walking.*

You like to go walking? I could shake him. *You do this often?*

He avoids my gaze. *I thought you'd be gone longer.*

It's not a straight reply, which tells me everything. But before I can react, he counters, *What about you? Those were kasiri.*

Only the girl, I sign. *The woman is the girl's tutor. She's a halan.*

Caleb looks at me in disbelief. *You just had a kasir girl to tea?*

Don't change the subject, I sign. *You can't go off by yourself like that! What if something happened? You couldn't . . . You're not . . .*

He jerks away from me, his cheeks coloring. *I can write, can't I? I'm not a baby!* He turns his back on me and drops into one of the chairs at the table, refusing to face me.

Regretting my harshness, I find a stale spice roll in the pantry, slice it up, and grill it. Then I spread jam on each wedge and offer it to Caleb as a peace offering.

My thanks, he signs when I set the plate in front of him. He takes an uncertain bite, his eyes fixed on me. *Honey is better than jam on these.*

I laugh in spite of myself. Then, unwilling to let him off so easily, I sign, *How long have you been lying about what you do all day?*

He bristles. *I've never lied to you.*

Shevem says truth and lies aren't only a matter of words, I reply. Shevem was a great philosopher, as well as an artist and composer. Tsipporah gave me his famous book of essays when I was eleven, and Caleb and I both pored over them. His writings are like poetry, lovelier than the lines of the Maitaf.

Caleb frowns. *Shevem also says truth isn't always right and lies aren't always wrong.*

I lift my hands to dispute that and then give up. I'll never win this debate, not when he's spent hours at the Avrams' reading Shevem while I've been in school.

My gaze strays to the cloak hanging from the back of his chair. Something white peeks out from the folds of gray wool:

a rolled-up *Journal* folded in half and stuffed into the pocket.

I toss the newspaper onto the table. *Where did you get this?* I sign. Neither of us has pocket money to spend on newspapers.

It was blowing down the street, Caleb signs. At my skeptical look, he adds, *I swear!*

Flattening the front page, I scan the headlines, afraid of what I might find. There it is: "More Deaths from Inexplicable Illness Confirmed." In the first paragraph, the words "black irises" leap out at me. The article reports four new cases: a kasir banker, a halan autoworker, a kasir cloth merchant, and a halan mother of three. Nothing appears to connect their deaths.

I slide the newspaper in front of Caleb and jab my finger at the article. *This is why you shouldn't be walking around the city by yourself.*

He barely glances at the page. *If you can, why can't I?*

I don't want you to get sick! I sign.

Caleb glares at me. *I can take care of myself.*

Stung, I cast about for a cutting retort. Before I can think of one, he adds, *You were younger than me when you started going to the Ikhad to see Tsipporah.*

That stops me short. I want to argue, but I can't deny the unfairness of it. *Where do you go?* I sign helplessly.

Caleb doesn't answer for a while. Finally he signs, *Just here and there. I like to walk around the city without anyone knowing who I am or that I'm . . .* After a brief hesitation, he taps his ear, then his mouth.

For a long moment, I don't know what to say. The stillness between us stretches on.

Here, I sign at last, *let's make omelets for lunch. And from now on, just tell me when you're leaving the apartment.*

On Firstday, I trudge to school alone. Leah is still sick, so Caleb isn't going to the Avrams, though I can't trust he'll actually stay home. Our medsha concert is this morning, and it occurs to me this will be my first time performing without Leah beside me.

At school, instead of climbing the stairs to the music room, I head to the decrepit auditorium for our dress rehearsal. The stage is set up for the medsha, and everyone is tuning. I unpack my violin, trying not to look at the empty chair next to me. My throat feels tight, and my fingers slip on the strings as I warm up.

The sounds die away when Aradi Imael walks out from the wings with her stack of scores.

"Where's Leah?" she asks.

"She's ill," I say. "The dark eyes."

For a fleeting moment, Aradi Imael looks shocked, but then her expression eases to one of gentle concern. "I'm sorry to hear that. We'll miss her today. Perhaps you could play her solo in the dance suite, Marah? I have extra parts."

"I can try to do more than that," I offer. "I know the places where her part is more important than mine."

Our conductor blinks at me and then hands me a folder of extra music. I pull out all the second violin parts. Putting two stands together in front of me, I arrange my music on the left and Leah's on the right, already thinking through the passages where I'll change to her part. I can't be two musicians at once, but I'll attempt to preserve as much of the melody as possible.

We turn first to "Where Wind Blows Not." Aradi Imael lifts her baton, and I tuck my violin under my chin. We breathe as one, and the music begins.

Despite the weekend's grim news hanging over me, my arms tingle. Reuven and I shift from note to note, creating the peaceful opening chords. The cellos enter with the plaintive melody. I play the first violin descant and, as it draws to a close, switch seamlessly to Leah's soaring line. The opening is exquisite, until Miriam falters on her flute entrance. Soon after, Tamar's horn comes in at an unexpected place, and we fall apart.

Aradi Imael raps her music stand with her baton. "Start seven bars before the horn entrance."

Halfway through the piece, we flounder again. We lower our instruments, contemplating the musical wreckage. The concert starts in two hours.

"Does anyone know the words to this song?" Aradi Imael asks.

"I've heard it sung before," says Devorah. "It starts with 'Where wind blows not,' and you sing that over and over for a bit. Then it's 'Where shadows darken not.' I can't remember the lines after that, but in the end it circles back to the beginning."

"There's no place without wind and shadows," Tamar says.

"I think that's the idea," says Shaul.

"Those aren't even sentences," says Zeina. "The lines are incomplete, unfinished."

I see what she means. The song invokes an impossible land without naming a true wish. The yearning is buried in the words that aren't there.

"Think about those words, what they express," Aradi Imael says. "And then listen to one another. I know you have other things on your minds, but you must play together."

She raises her baton once more. We start again with new purpose, inspired to create the atmosphere of that imaginary country. This time, the music is something we're all shaping together, and no one makes any noticeable mistakes.

The rehearsal passes quickly. I thought it would be trickier to juggle Leah's part and mine, to judge where to splice first and second violin parts, but the more I open my ears to the whole medsha's sound, the more the music comes alive within me and nudges me in the right direction. I only get lost twice, and I find my place before anyone notices. Aradi Imael looks startled each time I change over to Leah's line, but after a few measures she always nods in approval.

At eleven o'clock, students begin filing into the auditorium, from the littlest children in Preparatory to our classmates in Final. As Horiel's top medsha, we perform for the entire school. The hall, so still during our rehearsal, echoes with coughs and murmurs. Glancing at the pale faces floating in the sea of darkness, I wipe my palms on my skirt.

Aradi Imael bows to subdued applause. As she turns back to us, a hush falls over the audience.

"Energy!" she mouths.

We raise our instruments and look up. Aradi Imael holds her baton poised above the score. In the second our eyes meet, I sense a perfect trust between us. She gives the upbeat, and raw joy sweeps through me as I spring into the theme.

The three pieces flash by, and my spirits soar. It's oddly exhilarating weaving between Leah's part and my own, and I almost forget how much I wish she were here.

At the end of our performance, the school bursts into applause. Glowing with pride, Aradi Imael waves us to our feet. I stand up with the whole medsha and smile as I face the crowd. My heart is warm. The audience claps for a long time.

At the end of the school day, Miriam, Devorah, Zeina, and I leave Horiel together along with Reuven and Shaul. We walk down the street in a cluster, exulting in the success of our concert and trading compliments.

"I can't believe you went back and forth between the first and second violin parts without getting lost," Devorah tells me. "I've never seen anything like that."

Shaul begins to describe his efforts to repair a discarded music box to give his little sister for her birthday. He's telling us how he plans to fix the clockwork mechanism when Reuven raises his hand. "Quiet!"

After a moment, I make out an eerie melody on the wind.

"Mourning music," Zeina says, her voice hushed. "It must be a funeral procession."

Soon, we encounter the crowd. The street is clogged with silent mourners holding black books with silver lettering on the spine. The Maitaf.

"Do you suppose whoever it is died of the dark—?" Shaul begins, but we shush him.

The sight of the body, draped in blue linen and borne on a litter by four men, steals my breath away. I shudder, disturbed by the Maitafi custom of burying the dead without coffins. Not that coffins make me feel much better. I glance at my friends' drawn faces and wonder if we're all thinking of Leah.

Lately it seems I haven't been able to get away from death. First the woman killed at the Ikhad, then Gideon the pancake vendor. Now, death is actually before me, close enough to touch. Somewhere, the flutes play their hypnotic lament.

7

TWO DAYS AFTER THE MEDSHA CONCERT, ARADI LAMECH brings us starfish to dissect. Leah will be so envious; much as she loves animals, she has no qualms about slicing open a specimen to study it. Since she's sick, I partner with Miriam. We claim a spot at one of the long counters at the back of the classroom and cover our work surface with old newspapers from the stack by the sink. Aradi Lamech passes out the starfish on metal trays.

"This dark eyes illness . . ." Miriam begins after our teacher has moved off.

"What about it?" I say brusquely.

"My father says it's caused fifty deaths since last Seventh-day. Kasiri and halani."

"So many!" Each day another school desk is empty, and our mathematics teacher is ill too.

"There's talk of plague," Miriam says.

Her words frighten me. I stare at the flabby starfish, wishing it didn't look so lifeless.

"I'm surprised kasiri are dying too," I say. "Their doctors use healing magic on top of medicines." I wonder if Sarah's family has been affected by the illness. Every time I look at her drawing on my bedroom door, I marvel again that she dragged her tutor all the way back to Horiel to see me.

"My father says healing spells aren't effective against the dark eyes. They relieve symptoms but don't cure the disease."

I glance up from our specimen. "How does he know that?"

"He works for the post, remember? He delivered a package to a kasir pharmacy near Firem and overhead a doctor talking to the pharmacist. Apparently the doctor and his colleagues don't know what to make of the dark eyes, and the Assembly's just telling everyone to keep calm while they investigate."

"Of course," I say bitterly.

"The strange thing," Miriam pursues, "is that the grown-ups who've gotten sick have died within days of their eyes turning black, but—"

"Miriam, could we please not—"

"—not a single child has died."

I pause. If she's right, there's hope for Leah.

"My father . . ." Miriam hesitates. "He's been talking about leaving Ashara."

I look at her in astonishment. "Where would you go?"

"One of the other city-states, I guess." Miriam takes up a knife and prods the starfish's shortest arm. "Atsan, maybe. I don't know."

"It's not easy," I say. "Remember when Shaul's family tried to emigrate? Their passport petition never got approved." Leaving Ashara requires obtaining the proper documents, and it's rare for the government to issue them to halani.

"I know," Miriam says. "You have to know someone, and we don't."

"Quiet in the back!" shouts Aradi Lamech. "Are you following your charts?"

We peer down at ours. The first step is splattered with ink.

The day trickles by. At half past three, we troop into the history classroom for our last period. To our surprise, Aradi Mattan is hovering near the back row of desks, and a stranger stands on the teacher's dais. When I take my seat, I realize with a start that it's the District Hall official who knocked on our apartment door just over a week ago.

"Good afternoon," the kasir official says once the class has fallen into a wary silence. "I've come today from the District Hall to talk about what lies ahead for you as Final students, insofar as it concerns the district.

"As I am sure you are aware, you will become adults in the eyes of the district when you graduate. I understand approximately half of you sat for the SSE. Whether you go on to secondary school or whether you seek employment right away, you must complete the appropriate procedures at the District Hall. We maintain education and employment records for all Horiel residents . . ."

Listening with only one ear, I gaze out the window at the grimy snow lining the street. This is even more excruciating than one of Aradi Mattan's history lessons. Somehow, the kasir manages to stretch his explanations over half an hour, but finally he runs out of forms to describe. "Do you have any questions?" he asks.

When Shaul's hand shoots up, half the class tenses while the other half perks up. The official calls on him, and Shaul stands.

"Is the Assembly going to find a cure for the dark eyes?" he asks.

The question takes the District Hall representative off guard. "That is not strictly relevant," he says nervously. "I cannot speak in any official capacity, but yes, I am sure the Assembly will find a cure, most likely in the form of new healing spells."

"These healing spells," Shaul says. "How do they work, exactly?"

"Excuse me?" says the kasir, nonplussed.

"I want to know how magic works."

"Sit down, Shaul!" says Aradi Mattan.

"No, no," the kasir official says, "it's a harmless question. That is, if you really do not know . . ."

He looks out across the classroom as though beginning to suspect we're all playing a practical joke on him. Doesn't he know the Assembly prohibits sparker schools from teaching about magic?

"Well," the kasir says cautiously, "magic works through spells. Each spell comprises two essential components: the hand shape and the incantation."

Some of my classmates nod. It's not like we've never seen a magician cast a spell. At the back of the room, Aradi Mattan looks alarmed. Halan students are not supposed to receive this kind of instruction. On the other hand, he doesn't dare contradict the District Hall official.

Heartened by our interest, the kasir continues. "Spells are useless when magic isn't plentiful in the environment, however. Ashara was founded on the banks of the Davgir, between the Sohadir and the Shatarai Rivers, precisely because magic is dense here.

"Magic has certain effects when it flows along a certain course. Each hand shape corresponds to a desired effect. Uttering the right syllables causes the magic to move along the contours of the hands."

Aradi Imael once explained magic in a way I understood better. We were laughing because Reuven's music stand kept buzzing when he played his open D string. Aradi Imael said it was because the frequency of that note matched the music stand's natural frequency, producing sympathetic vibrations.

She told us magic worked in a similar way. Instead of finding the right note to make the music stand vibrate, magicians form the music stand with their hands in order to capture the right note among all those already present. To Aradi Imael, magic is one great unending chord, an inaudible symphony all around us.

"When magic is drawn into a spell, it produces secondary substances which are magical derivatives, by-products," the kasir is saying. "Some of these are useful, strengthening the spell. Others are of no use and merely dissipate. While most spells deal with the elements, some can influence men: making them invisible, putting them to sleep . . ."

Now we're all alert, waiting for him to take this point to its inevitable end. But he doesn't. Shaul does.

"Or killing them?" he says, eyes narrowed.

"Shaul!" Aradi Mattan explodes.

The kasir looks ill at ease. "The healing spells you originally asked about can do things like purify the blood, suppress or stimulate various physiological—"

"But sir," Shaul interrupts, "even if the Assembly discovers new spells to cure the dark eyes, how will that help halani? We can't afford healing spells."

Some of my classmates gasp. The District Hall representative stands frozen on the dais with his mouth open.

"Class dismissed!" shouts Aradi Mattan. Everyone starts talking at once, and I make my exit, glad to escape. Deep down, though, I admire Shaul's boldness. New healing spells *won't* be of any use to Leah if her family can't pay for them.

It's Thirdday, so while some of my classmates stream down the hall, I go upstairs to meet Aradi Imael as planned. As soon as I walk through the door, she hands me a Qirakh application and an audition pamphlet. On the front of the pamphlet is a Xanite flag. Inside, fragments of text jump out at me: dates, procedures, the required number of octaves for different scales. Solos and sight-reading. I fold it back up, feeling queasy.

"We should choose a solo today," says Aradi Imael. "Why don't you take out your instrument?"

While I tune, she fetches her own violin and plunks a pile of scores onto the conductor's stand. The possibilities seem infinite: countless sonatas by the great Atsani masters, works by more obscure composers like Toviah Adam, and even some modern compositions.

In the end, I select a piece by the philosopher Shevem.

"It's an unusual choice," Aradi Imael says. "Shevem's music tends to get forgotten, what with everything else he did. It's sure to surprise your judges."

She probably hopes that will work in my favor, since the other students will doubtless be performing famous concertos beyond my ability.

Before I leave, she has me attempt a few tricky sections under tempo. She listens and watches, sometimes playing along with me until the notes begin to feel familiar. At the end of the lesson, in addition to the music for the Shevem, she hands me another book, *Medsha Excerpts for Violin: Volume I.*

"Practice sight-reading out of that, but focus on your solo," she says with an encouraging smile. "See if you can learn the notes this week. Let's meet again after school next Fourthday. In the meantime, mail in your application to reserve an audition time."

"I will," I say, clutching my new music. I'm determined not to mess up my one chance of getting into secondary school this year. "My thanks, Aradi. For everything."

8

EARLY THE NEXT MORNING, CALEB IS STEWING SQUASH and I'm dashing off the conclusion to an essay that's due today when a thumping at the apartment door makes us both jump. Answering it, I come face to face with Sarah's willowy tutor. She is bareheaded, her brown hair parted severely and smoothed back into a knot at the nape of her neck.

"Channah?" I say, astonished. "I mean, Gadi . . ."

"Hadar," she finishes. "Good morning."

I invite her in, but she doesn't want to leave the landing.

"I'm in this part of the city on personal business this morning, so Sarah asked me to deliver this," she says, passing me an envelope.

I unseal it and unfold a note written in an elegant hand.

Dear Marah,

Sarah has asked me to invite you to our home for dinner this evening. I apologize for her fancies and urge you not to feel

*obligated to accept her invitation. We
would, however, be delighted to have you.*

Nasim Faysal (Sarah's mother)

Nasim Faysal. A Xanite name. So Sarah's Xanite? I
wouldn't have guessed, but it's not easy to distinguish
Xanites from Ashari.

"If you accept the invitation," Channah says, "I'll come
back at five o'clock to take you to dinner."

She knows as well as I do that kasiri and halani hardly
ever socialize. The rare friendships that do spring up tend to
be between well-off halani and kasiri of modest means, gen-
erally in the same profession. Before he died, Gadi Yared's
husband was a draper who occasionally took tea with the
kasir owner of a small cloth shop. But even that was unusual.

"The Rashids are liberal-minded," Channah says, guess-
ing my thoughts. Her expression is unreadable.

Despite my misgivings, I soften when I think of Sarah.
And I am curious to see the inside of a kasir home. This is
probably the only chance I'll ever have.

"I'll come," I tell Channah.

"Very good," she says. "I'll see you this evening." She
turns on her heel.

Caleb gapes at me from the stove. Grinning, I sign him a
brief explanation and then head for the study. Mother is gathering papers at her desk, about to leave for the District Hall.

"Mother? Can I go somewhere for dinner?" I explain how
I know Sarah.

"Well, I can't see any reason why you shouldn't go," Mother says. "It might even be impolite to turn down such an invitation. I'm surprised, though, that you're so attached to an eight-year-old kasir girl you've hardly known two weeks."

I hesitate. "It was the way she treated Caleb. You know how everyone acts like he doesn't exist once they realize he's deaf? Sarah wasn't like that."

Mother smiles tiredly. "Don't stay out too late, Marah."

A FEW MINUTES before five o'clock, a sleek automobile turns onto our street, and I run downstairs. Snow dusts the auto's flat roof and gathers in the wheels' metal spokes. Channah motions for me to sit in front. Just before I climb in, I notice one of our neighbors standing on the doorstep of the apartment building opposite ours. He stares openmouthed at me and the automobile. Wincing inwardly, I duck inside, and Channah speeds down the street.

We rumble westward, leaving the city's crowded districts behind. We pass courtyards full of dormant potted plants wrapped in burlap and twine. Curlicued wrought-iron gates guard the homes. Another auto rolls past us, headed into the city, and a little later, we overtake a carriage. Still farther down the road, the fashionable suburbs give way to open country dotted with austere mansions.

Channah eases the auto around a curve. Birch trees, their white bark standing out starkly in the bluish evening, line the gravel road and part to reveal a huge house on a rise. The driveway's open gates glint in the headlamps' light.

We glide through, fresh snow crunching under our wheels. After Channah parks the automobile in an outbuilding, I follow her across the driveway to the mansion's least imposing entrance. We stamp the snow from our shoes and go inside.

"This way, through the kitchen," Channah says, unwinding her scarf. I take off my cloak as we step into a room filled with clanging and sizzling. I smell roasting meat, herbs, butter, mushrooms. The cook, stirring something on the stove, looks me over curiously.

Apprehensive, I follow Channah down a corridor. In a mansion like this, I'd expect electric lights, but we're too far out for that. Only kasir buildings in the center of Ashara have electricity. Here, two gasoliers with gold branches hang from the ceiling, their flames throwing shadows onto the wallpaper. A door swings open, and Sarah races down the hall to grab my hand.

"Marah, you're here!" she cries. "Come meet Azariah."

I can't help smiling at her clear voice and bright face. She drags me into the room she burst from. It's a study, its walls lined with floor-to-ceiling bookcases. A carved wooden music stand and a chair occupy one corner of the room. Opposite the door, a tall window framed by velvet curtains looks out onto the snow-blanketed lawn. I can distinguish the dark edge of the forest on the western horizon. Facing this view is a glossy wooden desk with lion's feet and pewter drawer knobs.

A lanky boy rises from the desk to greet me. I'd guess he's

in Final too. He has short black hair that curls a bit, deep-set dark eyes, and a sharp chin. He doesn't seem to realize his crisp white shirt has come partly untucked from his trousers.

"Azariah, this is my new friend I told you about," Sarah says.

The boy nods. "Hello."

"I'm Marah Levi," I say.

"It's nice to meet you," he replies.

An awkward silence stretches between us. I've never spoken to a kasir my own age before, and it occurs to me Azariah may never have spoken with a halan his age either.

"Is Cha—I mean, Gadi Hadar, your tutor too?" I venture at last.

Azariah looks taken aback. I must've asked a stupid question.

"No, I go to Firem," he says, gesturing toward his desk chair. A black jacket lies draped over the back. Sewn onto the lapel is the badge of the elite kasir school. "Sarah had a bit of a bad time of it in Preparatory, so Mother and Father pulled her out of school and hired a tutor for her."

Sarah tugs on her brother's sleeve. "I wanted Marah to help you with your books."

"My thanks, Sarah," he says with a little smile, his eyes resting doubtfully on me. I return his gaze coolly.

"She's eating with us first," Sarah says, clapping her hands. "With Melchior home from boarding school, it's almost like a party!"

Azariah grimaces as the door creaks open behind us. An

older boy, maybe seventeen, sticks his head in and peers at me. He resembles Azariah but for his stocky build.

Sarah flits up to him and slides her hand in his. "This is Marah, Melchior."

"So *you're* Marah." Melchior smoothes Sarah's hair and walks into the room. His faintly suspicious gaze makes me self-conscious, so I don't meet his eyes, staring instead at the Firem Secondary pin fastened to his jacket.

"Why do you always barge into my study without knocking?" Azariah complains.

"Try a lock spell next time," Melchior says, already on his way out. Azariah rolls his eyes.

Sarah, Azariah, and I soon join the rest of the family for supper. The Rashids' dining room is twice the size of our kitchen, with a soaring ceiling that makes me feel small. Ornate gas light fixtures are evenly spaced along the walls, and the furniture is all made of dark wood.

When we come in, Melchior is speaking to a man with a graying beard at the head of the table. "Yes, I realize Azariah's grades are astronomically better than mine, but I—"

He breaks off at the sight of us. The man, whom I take to be Sarah's father, welcomes me and introduces himself as Jalal Rashid. Then he presents his wife, Nasim, a dazzling woman with sleek black hair. I learn that they both work for the government, he in the Foreign Commerce Department and she at the Education Bureau.

"Sit by me, Marah!" Sarah says, bouncing in her seat. Gadi Faysal flashes a reproving look at her daughter. Then she reaches out her hand, murmuring a word, and flames dance on a silver candelabrum on the table.

I sit down beside Sarah and wait, now wishing I'd stayed home to eat squash with Mother and Caleb. Sarah may be endearing, but the Rashids are kasiri, and I feel totally out of place.

A maid appears bearing a silver tray of crystal glasses into which drinks have already been poured: wine for Sarah's parents, water for her brothers and me, and juice for Sarah.

"My thanks," I tell her when she sets down my glass.

Without replying, the maid glides out of the dining room and returns with porcelain bowls of some kind of herb-infused broth.

"I hope you like it, Marah," Gadi Faysal says warmly. "Tell us, how old are you?"

"Fourteen," I say. I taste the broth; it's bitter and soothing at the same time.

"The same age as Azariah, then. Where do you go to school?"

"Horiel Primary."

Gadi Faysal's cordiality only throws me more off-balance. When she asks me to tell them a little more about myself, I don't know what to say. I rack my brains while the maid serves mushroom soup and roast duck. At last I remember medsha.

"Music? Splendid," Sarah's father says. "Azariah plays the violin too."

"Marah also tells stories," Sarah pipes up. "She told me one in the auto about—"

There's a blinding burst of light, like a photographer's flash, and the sound of breaking glass. I blink away the black spots floating in my vision to see the shards of Sarah's tumbler glinting on the table and the deep red juice, cherry or pomegranate, soaking into the cream tablecloth.

Sarah gives a cry of surprise and turns red. A smoky smell permeates the dining room, as intense as if a wood fire were burning under the table.

"It's all right," Gadi Faysal says at once, extending her hand, palm down, toward the spreading stain. Across from me, Azariah curls his fingers around empty air and looks intently at the jagged pieces of glass. For a second, I can't understand how Sarah's grip could have shattered crystal, and then I remember she wasn't even holding her glass.

Gadi Faysal and Azariah utter incantations. The crimson stain shrinks with breathtaking speed, leaving unblemished cloth in its wake until all evidence of the spill is gone. At the same time, the crystal fragments leap together as though by a magnetic force, and the glass stands whole on the table once more.

"Show-off," Melchior says to Azariah.

"You weren't about to do it," Azariah retorts, examining the repaired tumbler for cracks.

"I'm sorry!" Sarah squeaks, ducking down in her chair.

"It's all right," her mother repeats. "You couldn't help it."

"That was nothing," Melchior reassures her. He leans across the table as if to share a secret. "When Azariah was your age, he exploded a stuffed pheasant."

Azariah glares at him, but Sarah giggles, and without thinking, I say, "The taxidermy kind or the edible kind?"

Melchior looks at me as though seeing me for the first time and bursts out laughing.

Azariah finally grins. "The edible kind," he says ruefully. "Don't think I don't remember when you were growing into your power, Melchior."

"Did you see, Marah?" Sarah turns to me, her cheeks still pink. "It means I have magic."

Now that she's certain no one is angry with her, Sarah's proud of having shattered a glass with her nascent powers. I feel a small pang, knowing she's not just a little girl but a little magician.

The Rashids settle into the rest of their meal, and I feel awkward again. Banar Rashid and Gadi Faysal launch into a discussion of Xanite politics. The maid serves buttery vegetables and date confections, and I eat mechanically. The next thing I know, Sarah is towing me back to Azariah's study.

The room is frigid, and snow is falling outside. After following us into the study, Azariah pauses, his expression thoughtful. Then he turns toward the door, holds out his hand in a strange shape, and pronounces a word. A purple spark floats between his fingers. I catch a whiff of something acrid and wrinkle my nose. It's not as strong as the wood smoke smell at dinner, but it's less pleasant.

Sarah says something in Xanite, but Azariah nods at me. "Speak Ashari, Sarah. And no, I doubt Melchior could break that." He smiles fleetingly. "Even I don't know the theory behind lock spells, and I'm sorry, but Melchior's practically flunking out."

I stand uncomfortably on the luxuriant carpet until Sarah drags up a chair for me.

"Will you help Azariah now?" she says.

I shift uneasily in my seat. "What exactly do you need?" I ask her brother. "It's getting late."

"Sarah said something about you and languages. It was her idea. Now that you're here, I might as well see if . . ." He trails off, looking embarrassed.

"Show her the books," Sarah says.

He crosses to the shelves covering the wall. The sight of so many books fills me with excitement and envy. Azariah chooses four or five volumes and hands them to me one by one.

"The university was cleaning out its library," he explains, "and I fished these out of the discard boxes. They're all in languages I don't recognize. That's probably why they were thrown out, actually: they're in languages too obscure to matter to the librarians, or else nobody can read them."

"Firem's librarians are *throwing away* books just because they're not interested in them?" I say, aghast.

"I know." Azariah looks pained. "That's why I rescued these. I haven't gotten around to asking my teachers about them. They don't have much patience for this sort of thing. If it's not in Ashari or Old Monarchic . . . We're lucky the university library even has a Xanite collection. Anyway, I haven't gotten anywhere with these books yet, but Sarah's convinced you might know something."

He throws me a doubtful glance. I pretend not to mind in case I can't identify any of his mystery languages.

The first book is written in a twisting script I've never seen before. Even though I don't recognize it, its symbols are so marvelous in their strangeness I can't help lingering over the pages. I admire a graceful letter that stands alone, a word in itself, perhaps. It appears again a few lines down, and once more at the bottom of the page. This is what fascinates me about a new language: the tantalizing glimpse of a pattern in an otherwise incomprehensible text. Of course, the real excitement comes when I can decode enough to begin unlocking the contents of a book.

"I don't know what this is," I say at last, setting the thick tome aside. Sarah looks disappointed.

In the next volume, I recognize a vertical script I've glimpsed at the Ikhad book stand, but Tsipporah never had a book that taught how to read it. Then I open a third book, which has a faded cover.

. . . Bezhir, the eighth king of the House of Agrav . . .

I look up at Azariah. "This is Hagramet."

"It's what?" he says, startled.

"Hagramet. You know, the language of Hagram."

According to Tsipporah, Hagram was a civilization that

flourished in ancient times in what are now the north lands. Its people possessed unparalleled knowledge of medicine, mathematics, astronomy, and magic. But by the time our ancestors, the migrants from Xana, arrived from across the sea over seven hundred years ago, Hagram had collapsed. During the Erezai monarchy, scholars studied Hagramet texts preserved by the descendants of the fallen kingdom, but the ruins of Hagram have never been discovered.

"I know what Hagramet is," Azariah says. "It's just . . . Hagramet books are banned."

"Banned?" I say, frowning. "Why?"

"I don't know," he says with a shrug. "I was talking once to Firem's rare book librarian, and he mentioned the law, and the fact that there are hardly any Hagramet texts left anyway. He said even he wouldn't recognize Hagramet if he saw it. How on earth did you learn it?"

"From a grammar," I say, my heart hammering. I've broken a law. Unintentionally, but still.

"Where did you get it?"

I start to answer and then stop. Does Tsipporah know she wasn't supposed to sell me that book? Icy fear slithers in my stomach. I shouldn't be telling a kasir all this. Won't Azariah follow the law now that he knows?

He doesn't press me. "It'd be exciting to try some translation. Will you bring me your grammar some time?"

"Are you going to confiscate it?" I say warily.

"Of course not!" he says, appalled. "No one will know. The Assembly's probably forgotten about Hagramet anyway."

I look down at the book lying open on his desk. For most Ashari, the name Hagram is synonymous with a lost civilization. Our teachers at Horiel spent almost no time on the history of the north lands before the Xanite migrations and the founding of the Erezai monarchy. But maybe it's different at kasir schools.

"What do you know about Hagram?" I ask Azariah.

He looks surprised. "Just what they've taught us. Nowadays historians can only study Hagram secondhand through texts dating from the Erezai era. Those scholars admired Hagram, especially its magicians, because Erezai magic—and thus our magic—was originally the magic of Hagram."

He brushes the page of the Hagramet book with his fingertips. "This is incredible."

"Well," I say after a pause, "I should be going home."

Azariah nods and looks at Sarah. "Find Channah, will you?"

"What does that say?" she asks, peering at the book and tapping a heading on the page.

"Later, Sarah," Azariah says.

"It says 'Day of the Rose.'" I point. "This is *zhikin*, 'rose's,' and this is *enga*, 'day.'"

Sarah's eyes light up, and she smiles at me before skipping out of the study.

My brief demonstration has made Azariah even more delighted. "I can't wait to find out what's in this book. The next time you come—"

"What do you mean 'next time'?" I say.

He flushes. "I'm sorry, I shouldn't have assumed . . . I just thought, if you'd bothered to learn Hagramet, you might like to . . ."

I've never spoken to a humble kasir, let alone a mortified one. Azariah's curiosity is compelling, and the prospect of deciphering this rare volume is tempting. Still, I'm hesitant to embark on an illegal project, even one as harmless as translating a book. I don't like this kasir knowing something he could use against me. His willingness to break the law amazes me.

"I guess if you just want help translating, it's all right," I say.

"My thanks, Marah," Azariah says. "We'll keep it a secret between us, I promise. It'll be just for the sake of knowledge."

9

B Y THE TIME CHANNAH DROPS ME OFF, IT'S ALMOST TEN
o'clock, and I'm afraid Mother will be upset with me for
staying out so late on a school night. But when I climb up
to the apartment, only Caleb is there, looking worried and
forlorn at the kitchen table.

Isn't Mother home yet? I sign, astonished.

He shakes his head. There is a plate of cold stewed squash
at her place.

I join my brother at the table, and for a nerve-wracking
half hour, we wait for Mother to return from work. When
she finally arrives, her bun is coming undone, and there are
two deep lines carved between her eyebrows.

"I'm sorry I'm so late," she says, sinking into her chair
across from Caleb and me. "You've been to Sarah's and back,
Marah?"

I nod. "What kept you?"

She reaches into her cloak pocket and slaps a bundle

of twelve- and sixty-stone banknotes onto the table. "The District Halls fired all the halani."

I stare at the money and then back at her. "How can they do that?"

"The orders came down from the Assembly," Mother says, her voice taut with anger. "They can do whatever they want. God knows how the government expects to get anything done without us. They'll probably hand our jobs off to young kasiri fresh out of secondary school. As if the halan unemployment crisis weren't bad enough."

I feel frozen inside. I haven't seen Mother this furious in ages.

"We heard the Gishal District employees tried to protest," she continues. "Refused to leave. The First Councilor's Corps was called in."

"God of the Maitaf," I say. "Was anyone hurt?"

"Do you think they want us to know?" Mother says.

In a daze, I cross to the stove to warm the leftover squash for her. Caleb offers Mother a slice of bread with her favorite raspberry preserves from the icebox. She smiles wearily at him.

Only after she has eaten a little do I dare ask, "What will we do about money now?"

She sighs, pushing a chunk of squash around her plate without bringing it to her mouth. "Let me worry about that, Marah."

* * *

As if the District Hall firings weren't shocking enough, the Second Councilor of the Assembly succumbs to the dark eyes later the same night. On Fifthday morning, the news spreads like wildfire through Horiel Primary. Copies of the *Journal* pass from hand to hand in the corridors between class periods, and teachers keep the newspaper on their desks, compulsively checking the headline in case their eyes have deceived them.

At morning recess, the schoolyard is abuzz. Though the Second Councilor's death is no calamity from our point of view, the fact that the dark eyes can take someone as powerful as him comes as a shock. It's been several days since I've visited Leah, and now I desperately want to see her. I'm sure she's holding up—children are safe, after all—but the councilor's death rattles me.

I overhear a few students suggesting the Assembly got what it deserved for ordering the firings. I'm not the only one with a parent or relative who worked at one of the halls.

Miriam and I join our friends at the back of the schoolyard by the spruce trees, whose boughs are frosted with new flurries.

"The councilors can't even protect themselves," Devorah is saying. "The best drugs and healing spells counted for nothing."

"Who cares about the Second Councilor?" Shaul says cheerfully. "Good riddance."

"It's wrong to rejoice in someone's death," Zeina admonishes him. "Even a councilor's."

He rolls his eyes. "Anyway, it's no wonder they can't protect themselves. The kasiri have fallen into decadence."

Everyone stares at him. Not only is his remark absurd, but there's also no way he came up with it himself.

"Where did you pick that up?" I ask.

Shaul scowls. "My brother has some friends who meet and talk in the back room of a pharmacy near the Ikhad. They look out for each other, loan each other money, get around the bureaucracy when they can to help each other out. Lately my brother's been letting me come. They're all secondary students except me, but they think I'm—"

"Shaul!" Devorah cuts in. "Do your parents know? I can't believe you're hanging around with a pack of subversives."

"They're not subversives," he scoffs. "It's not illegal to air your grievances in private."

"What if you get hauled in for questioning?" Miriam says. "If you get arrested, you'll never get into engineering school."

"Get arrested! They're not plotting the kasiri's downfall," Shaul says, with a note of bitterness. "It's not like they'll ever do anything."

"So why even meet?" I ask. It's these kinds of gatherings that land halani in prison. If his brother's friends are going to risk that, they might as well make a real effort to undermine the councilors.

Shaul glares at me. "We discuss important things."

"Oh, it's *we* now," Devorah says, but Shaul talks right over her.

"Like our right to halan representatives in the government. Think, if there were halan councilors, we wouldn't be shut out of the best secondary schools."

A hint of longing stirs in Zeina's eyes, but Reuven snorts. "Halan councilors? Good luck."

"Things can change," Shaul insists. His tone has become a bit self-important, and I can tell he's just repeating ideas he's heard from his older brother's friends. "The kasiri aren't what they were. Three hundred years ago, when the cold times began and the monarchy fell, that's when they were truly great."

"Because they saved us from starvation, you mean?" Reuven says with a crooked smile, offering a familiar refrain from history class. Nobody laughs.

"Nowadays, the kasiri rely more on technology than on magic," continues Shaul. "They sit around watching sparker laborers lay bricks and build autos. But we're the ones who actually understand how all the factory machinery works because we operate it."

"You can't say the kasiri do nothing with their magic," Zeina objects. "They disperse and convert much of the smoke and ash the factories spew out, for one. And magic is useful in medicine—"

"Worked well for the Second Councilor, didn't it?" Shaul says, sneering. "The point is, magic used to make a bigger difference than it does today. Yoel—my brother's friend—he says we don't have to depend on the kasiri's magic the way we used to. Everybody has gas now, and he thinks we'll all have electricity soon too. Yoel told me halani are inventing and improving things all the time even if kasiri take all the credit."

"That's just it, though, isn't it?" Zeina says, her expression sharpening. "The kasiri have the money. They own the factories. They control the gas supply and what little electricity there is. I know you want to be an engineer, Shaul, but what if it's not enough? Maybe it doesn't matter how smart we are if the kasiri have all the power."

It's depressing to hear the brightest student in our year say it doesn't matter how smart we are.

Shaul gapes at Zeina. "Halan workers just need to *organize*," he says. "And there's another thing we talk about at the pharmacy. The sparker intuition."

I tense.

"What about it?" Miriam asks.

"The intuition is our power," he says. "Like the kasiri's magic."

"No, it's not," I snap. "The kasiri wield their magic. The intuition is just something that happens to us."

My friends look taken aback. I never told them about my intuition of Father's death; it was too painful.

Shaul looks mutinously at me. "It's more valuable than we think. One of the students I've met knows a woman who ran an underground press that printed banned materials. The police raided it a few months ago, but thanks to the intuition, she and her workers escaped beforehand. They even saved their stock."

I hate stories like that. They fill me with a mixture of rage and envy that's hard to stomach. Since I don't want to lash out at Shaul again, I keep my mouth shut. I'm grateful when Reuven speaks up.

"For every time like that, there are ten times the intuition doesn't come when it'd be really useful," he says. "It may be a gift, but Marah's right, it can't be harnessed."

"You shouldn't involve yourself with these people anyway," Devorah says. "Have you forgotten the steelworkers' massacre?"

Shaul clenches his jaw, and I stare at the ground. Devorah is referring to what happened three years ago when the government abruptly ended pensions for injured steelworkers and their families. Mother's widow's pension had long since run out, so the decision didn't affect us, but we were as outraged as everyone else. Hundreds of workers marched on the Assembly Hall and stormed the building. In response, the First Councilor's elite corps slaughtered dozens of steelworkers, some of them fathers and uncles and cousins of Horiel students. I sometimes wonder if Father would have marched that day if he'd been alive.

"And what about what happened last night in Gishal after the District Hall firings?" Devorah continues. "Three people were injured in the confrontation with the Corps."

"How did you hear?" Miriam says, shaken.

"My uncle told me," says Devorah. "He was a Gishal employee." She turns back to Shaul. "Listen to me. You can't count on the intuition. Don't go back to that pharmacy."

He smirks. "I didn't know you cared so much, Devorah."

If it weren't for Zeina stepping between them, I think Devorah would punch him. Instead, she stalks off. Zeina follows, looking reproachfully over her shoulder.

"Well done, Shaul," says Reuven.

I risk a sideways glance at Shaul. Once he was content to make mischief in the classroom and play handball in the street after school. Now he's beginning to move in dissident circles. Maybe this is what it means to grow up, but it frightens me.

10

THE WEEKEND ARRIVES, THE FIRST SINCE THE HALAN firings at the District Halls. On Seventhday, when I pick my way through the Ikhad, my only reward is Tsipporah speaking darkly of plague. Under the thatched roof, a number of stalls stand empty, not only because people have fallen ill, Tsipporah says, but because vendors and craftsmen from the outlying hamlets are avoiding the city and its contagion. I don't stay at the market very long.

On my way out of the square, I notice a peculiar current in the streets. It seems to be carrying both kasiri and halani in the direction of the Assembly Hall, where the seven councilors meet and the city government offices are located. I follow the herd, catching snippets of my fellow citizens' conversations.

"—don't know why we bother, nothing the First Councilor can say is—"

"—proper medical report, or some concrete numbers about—"

"—pray there's good news."

My heart beats faster. The First Councilor hardly ever makes public appearances. This is a rare opportunity to hear words directly from Yiftach David's mouth, and I might learn something I could bring back to Leah.

The crowd bears me into a plaza teeming with people. The Assembly Hall looms on our left. Unlike most of Ashara's venerable edifices, it's made of brick, not stone. After the original Assembly Hall burned down seventy years ago, it was rebuilt in a newer style.

Today, a wooden platform has been set up in front of the hall. Around it is a cordoned-off section, complete with folding chairs, which the arriving kasiri are filling. Police officers are stationed along the rope barriers to keep the mob of halani from pressing in too closely.

A diminutive man with gray hair approaches the lectern at the front of the platform. Having seen him once on a school trip, I know this is Yiftach David, First Councilor of the Assembly.

David begins to speak, but we can't hear his voice. On the platform, another kasir joins him. He removes his gloves and curls his hands at chest level. A spray of tiny white-hot lights, bright as a welder's sparks, bursts from his fingers, and abruptly David's amplified voice booms through the square.

"—confirm to you that one hundred and thirty-four Ashari have died of a new and as yet unidentified illness within the past month."

The First Councilor pauses to let the death toll sink in.

"By now," he continues, "you are all familiar with the disease, whose symptoms include chills, fever, aches, and respiratory difficulties. In many ways, it resembles influenza or pneumonia, but the illness can be diagnosed with certainty due to the darkening of the patient's irises.

"I understand the anxiety this epidemic is causing the people of Ashara. I regret to say that we do not yet know what the origin of the disease is, but on behalf of the entire Assembly, I pledge to determine the nature of the illness and develop a treatment for it as speedily as possible. The untimely death of Second Councilor Yitzchak has deeply saddened us all, and we are reminded that, kasir or halan, councilor or ordinary citizen, we are all at risk until a cure is found. We seek to honor his memory in working to treat the illness."

The halani around me shift restlessly while David lowers his head in a moment of reflection. So far this speech isn't proving very helpful.

When David next speaks, his tone is brisker. "My colleagues and I have appointed a committee of physicians to study the new disease. Its members are accountable to me, and I will personally oversee their work." This statement garners a smattering of applause from the kasir section, but the woman digging her elbow into my ribs snorts.

"I urge the public to resist panic," the First Councilor says, his magnified voice steady and reassuring. "I am confident the people of Ashara will weather these difficult days as we weathered the beginning of the cold times so long ago. I ask only for your patience."

But how long can we wait for a cure?

I visit Leah every day after school. I wash my hands when I arrive at the Avrams' apartment and again before I leave. Gadi Yakov constantly warns me not to sit too close to Leah. I think she'd prefer I stay away entirely, like the rest of her children, but I'm already careful not to touch my friend. Besides, if I haven't caught the dark eyes from her by now, I'm probably not going to.

Leah's fever has subsided for now, but she complains of achiness, and a nasty cough has set in. She can't shake her exhaustion; a walk to the kitchen leaves her spent. The only task for which she can summon much energy is caring for Raspberry the house finch. Gadi Yakov brings her supplies so she can clean out his hatbox and replenish his food and water. I watch her rebind his wing, marveling at how gentle and nimble her fingers are and how he seems to trust her. I look forward to these moments because they make it easier not to think about how sick she is.

Once, though, I suggest taking care of the bird is tiring her out. Leah rolls her eyes.

"If it weren't for Raspberry, I'd have died of boredom by now."

Often she's not awake when I arrive, so I do my homework on the bedroom floor. When she does wake up, she's too weak to talk much, so I tell her about Sarah the kasir girl, describing in detail the dinner at the Rashids' house. I also try to amuse her with stories from school.

"Aradi Mattan called me Leah this afternoon," I say one day. "He's so absentminded. It reminded me of when we were younger. Remember how people would always ask us if we were sisters?"

Leah nods. We loved being mistaken for siblings.

"There was that old woman who sold mugs of pea soup at the Horiel market," I recall. "We never corrected her. Then one day your mother overheard her telling us how she'd never seen two sisters get along so well . . ."

"Yes, and Mother scolded us for lying!" Leah says, lifting her head.

We both giggle. Then Leah lets her head fall back onto the pillow and shuts her eyes.

When I'm not at school or at the Avrams', I'm busy preparing for my audition. I send my application off to Qirakh as Aradi Imael instructed me and throw myself into learning the Shevem solo.

On Fourthday morning, seven days after the First Councilor's speech, I arrive at school to find dozens of students clustered around the front steps, talking noisily in the snow. Miriam elbows her way through the crowd to me.

"What's going on?" I ask.

"Nobody knows. The doors are locked."

Miriam and I hold our instruments close and search the throng for our friends. Then the school doors open. The headmaster appears at the top of the steps, flanked by several teachers. He begins to speak, but we can't hear him.

A hand falls on my shoulder, and I jump. It's Aradi Imael, and her face is grave.

"Girls, the school is closed."

"What?" says Miriam.

"The Assembly has closed all the schools in the city to prevent the spread of the dark eyes," our teacher says.

Miriam and I exchange stunned looks.

"Marah, I know we were going to practice after school today," Aradi Imael says, "but now I'm going to be busy with staff meetings. Maybe you could come to my house this weekend instead. Would Seventhday afternoon work?"

I nod.

"My thanks," she says before rushing away.

ASIDE FROM MEDSHA, I never thought I'd miss school, but without it the hours are interminable. Visiting Leah helps, but it's hard to watch her suffer: from the cough that makes her ribs sore, from the aches in her limbs, from the fever that keeps returning. I find myself feeling glad that Raspberry's wing was broken because the little finch is the only thing that seems to cheer her.

To distract her from her misery, I bring my violin every day and play. While she listens, I practice my three-octave scales, sight-read passages from *Medsha Excerpts: Volume I*, and work on the Shevem solo. I receive a letter from Qirakh setting my audition for a date a little less than four weeks away.

On Seventhday morning, while Mother is out shopping, Channah Hadar calls again.

"I'm only staying a minute," she says when I greet her. "You're invited to the Rashids' again tomorrow evening. For supper. Also, Azariah asked me to tell you he'd like your help again. I didn't realize you two had gotten on so well."

"I'll come," I say, excited at the prospect of discovering what Azariah's Hagramet book contains.

"I'll pick you up at the same time, then," Channah says.

After lunch, I leave for Aradi Imael's house with my violin, cutting through the kasir neighborhood and its grandiose apartment buildings again. I've almost reached Mir District when I turn a corner and slam into someone coming the other way.

"Excuse me," I gasp. I look up into the face of Melchior Rashid.

He steps back on the sidewalk, his eyes wide. "What are you doing here?" he says in an undertone.

Before I can reply, two kasir boys his age, both wearing Firem Secondary pins, come up behind him. Melchior turns to go back the way they came, but one of his companions catches him by the shoulder. "Wait. It's a sparker."

My heart starts thudding. It's the middle of the day, and there's no one on this block but me and the three boys.

"Let's go, Shimon," Melchior says.

Ignoring him, Shimon seizes my arm. "Your kind doesn't belong around here."

I glance at Melchior, but Sarah's brother looks at me as though he's never met me.

"Let go of me," I croak, trying to wrench away from Shimon.

He shoves me so violently I stumble, and the third boy takes this opportunity to grab my violin.

"Give it back!" I lunge for my instrument, but Shimon holds me fast as his friend opens my case on the sidewalk.

"Leave it, Ayal," Melchior says.

Ayal lifts my fiddle from its case and wrenches out the wooden tuning pegs. I watch in a stupor as they bounce on the cobblestones. Then, while the strings swing pathetically from the tailpiece, Ayal presses his thumbs into the belly of my violin.

The sound of breaking wood shatters my daze.

"No!" I throw myself at him, but Shimon pushes me into the snow piled along the edge of the street. I scrape my knee on the pavement and taste grit. Snow trickles down my neck. Hiding my face, I lie there and wait for them to go away.

I hear more cracks, then laughter.

"Come on, we'll be late."

"Shemuel's waiting for us."

Their voices fade. I stand up and see my pegs lying amid the unwound strings on the ground. Numbly, I gather them and stuff them into the abandoned case. Then I spot my snapped bow hanging over the park gate down the street. My violin lies nearby atop a dense hedge.

I burst into the park and seize my instrument. Ayal smashed the bridge into the front, splintering the polished wood down the middle. No luthier could repair it, and I can't afford a new instrument. Holding my ruined fiddle, I feel as though something inside me has broken. I slump onto a park bench, my throat aching with the effort of not crying.

Then a terrible thought dawns on me. How will I audition for Qirakh now? My violin, my key to secondary school, is destroyed. It's too much to bear. Huddled on the bench, I weep into my folded arms.

Eventually I remember that Aradi Imael is expecting me. I get up, wincing, and attempt to wash my face with a handful of snow. A few minutes later, I arrive at my teacher's.

"Hello, Marah," Aradi Imael says when she opens the door. "I was afraid you'd forgotten your lesson."

"I'm sorry I'm late," I murmur. I wobble a little crossing the threshold. My knee stings, and I can't help grimacing.

"Are you all right?" she asks. "Come into the living room and sit down."

"My violin . . ." I sink into an armchair. The story comes out in fragments. When I unclasp my violin case to show Aradi Imael the damage, her expression confirms what I already knew.

"You're hurt," she says. "Wait here a moment, I have gauze and tape."

While I self-consciously clean my scraped knee and press a bandage over it, Aradi Imael strokes the threadbare arm of her chair, looking troubled.

Finally, she says, "We'll find a violin for you to borrow. For today, you can play mine."

BEARING MY BROKEN violin, I take the long way home from Mir, avoiding the kasir district and sticking to halan neighborhoods. When I get back to the apartment, Caleb is occupied with my school books, and Mother is sitting in her study. I don't have the heart to tell them about my fiddle yet, so I drop off my case and go over to Leah's.

Yesterday, she felt well enough to sit by the window in a chair dragged in from the kitchen. She even spent half an hour fastening large squares of cheesecloth to the sides of a huge crate her sisters found in the street to make a bigger cage for Raspberry. I watched her ease the bird out of the hatbox, untie the strip of fabric securing his wing to his body, and set him in the crate.

When I arrive today, the finch is chirping in his new cage near the window, but Leah's back in bed, holding a mug of poplar bud tea for fever.

"Are you all right?" I ask.

"I'm fine," she says impatiently. "Look at Raspberry!"

Through the cheesecloth, I can make out the bird's silhouette as he hops around. Suddenly he flaps his wings and flies in an arc from one end of the crate to the other.

"Oh," I say.

"His wing is healed!" Leah seems disappointed by my lack of enthusiasm. Then she notices something. "You didn't bring your violin."

Unable to speak, I shake my head.

"I was hoping to hear some music," she says. "Would you play mine? It's there in the corner."

I don't hesitate. I unpack my friend's fiddle, tighten her bow, and tune. Once I begin to play, it's a long time before I stop. For a moment, I think Leah's fallen asleep, but then, at the thwack of Raspberry's wings, she stirs.

"You play so politely," she says with a sleepy smile. "You should be bold at your audition."

I cradle her violin in my arms. "Leah," I say, "can I borrow your fiddle?"

The memory of my encounter with the kasir boys is searing as I explain.

"How could they be so cruel?" she breathes. "Who were they?"

"Sarah's brother was with them," I say. "The older one, Melchior."

"I'm so sorry, Marah. I wish I'd been there with you." She draws herself upright and looks intently at me with her black eyes. "Keep my violin for as long as you need it."

"It won't be for long," I promise. "I only need it to practice and to audition. If I get into Qirakh, I'll get a new violin."

I just have no idea how.

11

THE FOLLOWING MORNING, I SECURE MOTHER'S PERmission to visit the Rashids before she goes out. She's been looking for work, but even her mathematical prowess and bureaucratic experience don't seem to be enough. I'm afraid of what will happen if she can't find a new job.

I shut myself in my room for most of the day and practice the Shevem on Leah's violin, trying to learn her instrument. I imagine our elderly neighbors downstairs listening to me through their ceiling and strive to impress them.

At dusk, I wait for Channah, torn between my eagerness to decipher Hagramet and my fear of confronting Melchior. I try to forget him by paging through the Hagramet grammar I'm bringing to show Azariah. The glow of headlamps alerts me to Channah's arrival.

As we drive through the falling snow, I can't help watching Sarah's tutor. She's acted less standoffish since Sarah first invited me to dinner. Her haughty glances have all but stopped, and she speaks to me with more familiarity. Even so, I'm never quite sure what to expect.

When I next glance through the windshield, I stiffen. We're crawling behind a gigantic funeral procession headed for the City Cemetery. It's a secular funeral, not a Maitafi one; the mourners are clad in white instead of blue and are following an ornate hearse instead of a litter. Points of colored light float above the crowd like huge fireflies.

"Is that the Second Councilor?" I ask.

Channah nods.

"Isn't it late for the burial?" The Second Councilor died fourteen days ago.

She shrugs. "Yiftach David invited a horde of dignitaries from all over the north lands to attend. The Assembly had to wait for them to arrive from Atsan and Tekova and Kiriz . . ."

"Oh." I wonder how she knows. I think if I were an official from Tekova or Kiriz, I'd be leery of traveling to a plague-ridden city.

"In any case, *we* don't have much reason to mourn his loss," Channah adds under her breath. She glances expectantly my way, and I shake my head nervously.

At the Rashid mansion, Channah sends me to the front entrance. Sarah opens the door and throws her arms around my waist, almost hitting her head against the huge book in my hands.

"Good evening, Marah." Azariah, coming up behind his sister, notices the grammar right away. "Is that the . . . Is that it?"

"Yes."

"We can leave it in my study till after dinner," he says.

"Is Melchior here?" I ask, a little too nonchalantly, as the three of us walk down the corridor.

"No, he's at his friend's house," Sarah says. I breathe a silent sigh of relief.

In the dining room, the Rashids and I exchange polite remarks over chicken and saffron rice until talk turns to the illness. I can't stop picturing Leah's gaunt face and dark eyes. At last I must inadvertently make some sound because Sarah's father invites me to speak.

I flush, momentarily tongue-tied. "I just wondered . . . Has anyone figured out what's causing it?"

Banar Rashid wipes his mouth with his napkin. "I'm afraid not, Marah. You know of the Assembly's special committee of physicians, of course. From what my colleagues in the Health and Sanitation Department tell me, their efforts have not yet met with much success."

Abruptly, Banar Rashid turns his head toward the doorway, as if he's heard something. I think I see a shadow in the corridor, but it's gone too quickly to be sure.

"Just this morning, however," Banar Rashid continues, "the physicians announced that they are now confident the illness is not transmitted from person to person."

Across from me, Azariah murmurs in surprise. This news is a comfort, however small. Now there's no reason for anyone to worry about me visiting Leah.

"So will they reopen the schools?" I ask.

Gadi Faysal shakes her head. "Too many students and teachers are ill right now. Classes won't recommence until the disease is brought under control."

"Has anyone actually recovered from the dark eyes?" Azariah asks.

"Not that I've heard," says his father. "The reason the physicians are having such trouble identifying the cause of the illness is that it exhibits few patterns in choosing its victims. At first, it was believed that the young, though just as likely to get sick as adults, did not succumb to the dark eyes. There are apparently dozens of children who fell ill ten or even twenty days ago still fighting the disease. However—" He breaks off and glances at Sarah, the corners of his mouth tightening. She is absorbed in tracing her fork through the pool of currant sauce on her slice of almond cake.

"Sadly, the first children have died this weekend," Banar Rashid finishes in a low voice.

I sit up straight in my chair. If the dark eyes has begun to claim children, there's no safety in youth anymore. Leah is as vulnerable as anyone.

After dinner, Azariah and I return to his study. Sarah tags along with a drawing pad and pencil. Her brother has already laid out the Hagramet text, a new blank book, and several steel-nibbed pens on his desk. As we sit down, I notice a Maitaf next to his desk lamp. The gilding is wearing off the edges of its well-thumbed pages. I throw Azariah a curious glance. I didn't know he was Maitafi.

"So this is your grammar," he says, looking at the heavy book on the desk, his face bright with eagerness.

"Yes." I place one hand protectively on its dark, cloth-bound cover.

"My thanks for bringing it." He reaches for his own Hagramet text. "This week I drew up an inventory of all the signs in this book. It's an alphabet, isn't it?"

I nod, opening my grammar. While Sarah draws in the corner, I guide Azariah through the alphabet chart, pointing out the Ashari transliterations of each Hagramet letter. His eyes drink in the page as I sketch out the bare bones of Hagramet grammar.

"This took me years to learn," I say eventually. "Should we start on your text?"

"Yes, let's," he says.

I glimpse some of Sarah's childlike enthusiasm in him as he opens his Hagramet book to the title page and sets the new notebook in front of me. With a shiver of anticipation, I dip one of his pens in the inkwell and begin.

As it turns out, I can't even get through the title without consulting the dictionary in the back of my book. Not the most impressive beginning, but Azariah watches attentively as I look up a word.

"There," I say. "'Histories.' And the rest of this . . ." I trace the remainder of the title with my finger as I sound it out for him. "'Of the Agrav Dynasty.' Underneath there are some dates, probably a span of time, but I'm never going to work them out. Hagramet dates are absurdly complicated."

"Well, the original text had to have been written at least a thousand years ago," Azariah says. "What do we need to know beyond that?"

I shrug.

"Speaking of which," he says, "I went to the library and looked up the ban on Hagramet texts."

"And?"

"It was passed a hundred and sixty years ago, and as far as I can tell, it hasn't been repealed. Probably because everyone's forgotten it's there."

I move on to the inscription at the bottom of the page, recharging my pen and writing my translation in the notebook. What with Azariah wanting to look up words in the dictionary himself, deciphering the brief line of text takes us almost ten minutes.

Compiled by the court magicians, servants of the kingdom

"Court magicians," Azariah muses.

"Maybe they're like the seven councilors of the Assembly," I say.

"Six, now. Councilor Yitzchak's dead, which isn't entirely unfortunate," Azariah says quietly.

I stare at him, thunderstruck. The Second Councilor's death isn't entirely unfortunate? I think of Shaul and his pack of subversives. But Azariah's a kasir, not some resentful sparker student in a pharmacy back room.

"Shall we go on?" Azariah says hastily, trying to cover up his imprudent remark. "We've got an idea what we're dealing with now."

I persuade him to let me work independently, pointing out that the translation will go much faster if I don't have to deconstruct every sentence for him. While Azariah leafs through my grammar, I dive into the first page, borrowing the dictionary whenever I encounter an unknown word I can't just skip over.

> In the first year of the Agrav Dynasty, the Year of the Persimmon Tree, the new capital of the kingdom of Hagram was built ? between two rivers and ?? two regions ? a third. The Suhodri River, on the western border ?? cliffs ? mines of ? rock. The towns along the Dobigri River, ??? peasants grew corn and ?. On the eastern border, the mightiest of the three, the Chotrae, which flows down from ? mountains.

I pause to take stock. "Azariah, read this. It's about the location of Hagram's capital."

He leans over the notebook for a long time. All I can hear is the scratching of Sarah's pencil. Azariah begins to mutter the names of the rivers. "Suhodri, Dobigri, Chotrae . . ." Then he jumps to his feet. "Don't you see?"

"See what?"

"The rivers!" Azariah says. "Suhodri, Dobigri, Chotrae.

And, let me see, the western border is the Suhodri—"

"There are no such rivers in the north lands," I say. Sarah is watching us now, enthralled.

"What river flows through Ashara?"

"The Davgir."

"Dobigri."

I shrug, unimpressed.

"What about the one to the west?"

"Sohadir."

"Suhodri. And to the east?"

"Shatarai," I breathe. "Chotrae. The capital of Hagram must've been where Ashara is today!" None of our history books could tell us exactly where Hagram was located. Discovering its capital once stood where we live today makes the almost mythical kingdom feel like it actually existed.

"Yes!" Azariah breaks into a huge grin. Then he grows thoughtful. "Maybe I shouldn't ask, but . . . You wouldn't be willing to leave your book with me for a few days, would you?"

Stony silence should be a sufficient answer, but he doesn't deserve that. "I'm the one who knows Hagramet," I say instead. "Would you be willing to let me take your book home?"

He looks down at his text, considering, and then meets my gaze again. We both know neither of us is prepared to relinquish our rare book.

Azariah sighs. "I suppose it'd be best if we kept working together. Do you mind if I copy a few words out of the dictionary, though, so I have something to look for in the meantime?"

I consent, and we spend a few minutes writing Hagramet words with their Ashari transliterations and meanings in a different notebook. Azariah is interested in the magic of Hagram, so he asks for terms like "spell" (*dhak*) and "magician" (*naethul*).

When we finish, Sarah jumps up from her corner, waving her pad of paper. "Marah, come look at the pictures I drew!"

She has penciled a whole world of triangle-eared cats and girls with twig-like hair.

"This one's you," she says.

I look at the figure she's pointing at, a taller girl set apart from the others. Somehow, with her wobbly lines, Sarah has given the girl a distinctly sorrowful air. I wonder how she captured it, and if that's really me.

12

ON TENTHDAY, I RISE TO MEET TSIPPORAH AS SOON AS the Ikhad opens. There are questions I need to ask her. The sun has hardly risen, but men in shabby coats and women in shawls are already crowding the streets, making way for wagoners and the odd auto. The snow is dusted with coal ash the kasiri's spells haven't scattered.

The Ikhad is bursting with people, but no one seems to be buying. Tsipporah, her hands in fingerless gloves, is knitting on her roost.

"I'm glad to see you, Marah. Business has been glacial this week."

"Tsipporah," I ask, "do you remember the Hagramet grammar?"

The yarn darts around her knitting needles in a hypnotizing dance. "I remember."

"Have you ever had another book in Hagramet?"

"No," she says. "They're very rare."

"Where did mine come from?"

She hesitates. "I'd rather not say, Marah."

"Because Hagramet books are banned?"

Tsipporah stares at me, baffled. "Why on earth would they be banned? I hardly think the Assembly is worried about the subversive nature of grammars."

Reassured that she's unaware of the law Azariah mentioned, I join her behind the book stand. Tsipporah fishes a ragged blanket out of the pile by her stool and throws it at me. Gratefully, I wrap myself in it and huddle on the ground. But I'm not done yet.

"If there's nothing wrong with Hagramet books, why can't you tell me where you got that grammar?"

"Marah, there are some things you don't need to know," she says.

Hurt by her unwillingness to answer my question, I keep silent. I don't understand why she's being so secretive. After an hour passes without any customers, I decide to leave.

I WALK TO the Avrams' apartment. In the bedroom, Leah's eyes are half closed, the blanket pulled up to her chin, her face partly buried in the pillow. This is the frailest she's looked yet. Raspberry's crate is by the window, but someone has taken him out of the bedroom, no doubt to keep his chirps from disturbing Leah.

"Marah." Her eyes open as she croaks my name.

I rush to her side, my knees buckling. "Leah, you need a doctor."

"We can't spare the money," she says, struggling to sit up.

She coughs so hard I'm afraid she'll break a rib. "Besides," she adds when she catches her breath, "there's nothing a doctor could do that Mother isn't already doing."

"Herbal infusions aren't enough."

"Do you think the kasiri who've died didn't have the best medicine there is?"

I have no answer. Leah fixes her black eyes on the distant window, her cheeks hollow.

After a little while, she says, "You know those feelings, when you're sure of something and you can't explain why? I . . . I can't see any future for me, Marah."

"What are you talking about?" I say, clutching her hand. "We're graduating Final at the end of the winter. We're going to secondary school."

Her fingers press back. "I don't know anymore. I don't see a springtime for me. It's this feeling, like I'm not going to . . ."

I feel a stab of terror. "Leah, no!"

"Marah—"

"I hate the intuition," I say savagely. "I hate it."

"Just listen."

"Shaul called it our power," I add bitterly. "More like our curse."

"I'm going to die," Leah says, her voice quivering.

"We all are."

"Stop it. You're making this harder. I'm going to die before spring." She laughs, her laughter edged with hysteria.

It turns into a coughing fit. "I don't really believe it, though, do I? How can I say I'm going to die?"

I slide onto the bed and put my arm around her shoulders. "Leah, you're not going to die. Hardly any children have died of the dark eyes. And anyway, they'll find a cure soon."

Leah ignores me. "Did Shaul mention the intuition's never wrong? You of all people should know that, Marah."

Her words hit me hard. She knows ever since Father died I've trusted absolutely in the intuition. Now I would give anything to believe it could be fallible. My mind scrambles for a way around it, and at last I hit upon it.

"It's not the intuition," I say with all the certainty I can muster. "You've mixed up what you know and what you're afraid of." I study her sunken dark eyes, her newly sharp cheekbones. "Have you told anyone else?"

She shakes her head.

"You have to try to get better, Leah," I say fiercely. "Don't give up because you think it's no use. Promise me."

"I promise," she says, but I fear she's only saying it for me.

AT HOME, I take out Leah's violin and play until the music leads me into a trance. The piney scent of rosin from her bow resurrects an old memory.

We were nine years old, and I had brought one of Tsipporah's storybooks to school to show Leah. We were admiring its magnificent color plates at recess when an older boy snatched it and ran off laughing. Leah and I skulked about the edge of the schoolyard, watching the thief from afar until he stuffed the book into his bag and left it against the wall of the school. We raced over and rummaged through his things. While I retrieved the book, Leah chanced upon a spice roll wrapped in sticky paper.

"Take it," I said.

We split the spice roll behind the spruce trees at the back of the schoolyard. No pastry had ever tasted so sweet. But at the end of the day, the boy was waiting for us outside with two of his friends.

"We'll have to run for it," Leah said.

"I can't run as fast as you," I said.

Leah grabbed my hand and pulled me down the school's front steps. We made it halfway down the block before we heard footfalls pounding behind us. Leah yanked me into a narrow alley, and we clambered over a barricade of trash and empty crates, rotten slats giving way beneath our feet. The alley spat us out by the park, where I stopped, gasping for breath. Up the street, the boy and his friends came running around the corner.

"This way!" Leah cried, dashing through the park gate. While I lagged behind, she ran up to a pine tree and started climbing. "Hurry, Marah!"

I got to the tree and wrapped my arms around the lowest limb as Leah had done, but I couldn't pull my legs over it.

"Come on!" she said.

"I can't!" I said, dropping down to the ground.

She jumped down a branch and stuck her hand out. I grabbed it and finally scrabbled up into the tree. We climbed out of the bigger children's reach, the bark rough and sticky under our hands, the resin sharp and fragrant. My heart beat wildly in my chest, but I was safe with Leah.

Now, as my bow saws across the strings and sends up puffs of rosin dust, it occurs to me how small my terror was then compared to what I feel now.

13

IT'S BEEN A WEEK SINCE LEAH CONFIDED IN ME, AND thankfully she's said nothing more about her intuition. Some days, as I play at her sickbed, I even think she looks stronger, her gestures quicker and her cheeks less flushed.

I visit Aradi Imael twice more to work on my solo. She has a way of coaxing miracles from my fingers by describing the feel of a phrase: this one is like the flight of a swallow, that one has the cadence of a halting question. I discover myself capable of a velvety tone in one place, of icy, slashing bow strokes in another. Still, my scales are too slow and my sight-reading of challenging excerpts spotty at best. I feel anxious whenever I think of my audition, now only three weeks away.

When I'm not at Leah's, I stay home to keep Caleb company and help him cook meals. With Mother unemployed, we have to make sure not a scrap goes to waste.

On Tenthday afternoon, after fruitlessly trying to bring

my minor scales up to the required tempo, I drift into the kitchen just as Caleb comes in from one of his walks. He tosses a newspaper onto the table.

I scan the front page. In a box at the bottom, I notice DEATH COUNT in block letters, and underneath, the number 237. A chill like ice water washes over my skin.

Caleb taps my arm and hands me an envelope. *It's for you. It was in our mailbox downstairs.*

The envelope is made of fine white paper and bears my name and address in blue ink. I break the seal and unfold a sheet of yellow stationery.

Dear Marah,

Would it be convenient for you to come to our house every Thirdday to continue our work? I have spoken to my parents of our common interest in studying languages, and they have no objection to such an arrangement. If you agree, there is no need to reply. Channah will pick you up at five o'clock every Thirdday, starting next week.

Azariah Rashid

I read it again, indignant at his kasir arrogance. *No need to reply* indeed.

Caleb peers at my letter, and I don't hide it from him.

It's from that kasir? he signs.

I nod. Azariah's lucky I'm so curious what else is in his book.

On Thirdday, the Rashids' gleaming auto rolls up at nightfall. A few men returning from work glower at me as I come out of our building. I pretend to ignore them. If I were them, I'd disapprove too.

During the drive, Channah is unusually cheerful.

"You're visiting Azariah more than Sarah now, aren't you?" she says.

"I guess." I wonder how she feels about having to chauffeur me, a fellow halan, to and from the city so I can spend the evening with her kasir employers' children.

Channah keeps asking questions. What sort of dinner conversations do I have with the Rashids? What do Azariah and I talk about in his study? Bewildered by her inquisitiveness, I give short, vague replies.

When we drive up to the Rashids' outbuilding, I notice another auto parked near the house. Channah breathes in sharply and swears.

"What is it?" I ask.

She shakes her head.

I stumble out of the auto, my shoes crunching on the snow. At the front door, Azariah lets me in, a wide-eyed Sarah at his side.

"Follow me," he whispers. The three of us hurry to his study, and he shuts the door behind us.

"What's going on?" I demand.

"We have dinner guests," Azariah says darkly.

"The Seventh Councilor of the Assembly," Sarah says, her voice hushed with awe.

"And her personal secretary," says Azariah.

"What?" I say, aghast. "I can't have dinner with the Seventh Councilor." I take a step toward the door. "I should go."

"No." He makes as if to hold me back. "My parents want you to stay. You were invited. The Seventh Councilor wasn't."

"She wasn't *invited*?"

"No." Azariah stuffs his hands into his trouser pockets. "I'm sure she's snooping for Yiftach David. Mother's furious."

I can't think straight. Shouldn't the Rashids be honored by this visit? Azariah's parents must work high up in the government hierarchy if they can afford a mansion like this one. Then I recall what Azariah let slip last time about the Second Councilor.

My confusion must show on my face because Azariah says, "The Assembly doesn't trust us."

"Why not?"

"Well, for one thing, we're Xanite, but mostly it's because of Mother and Father's radical views. They believe in halan representation in the government. And Mother's argued for integrated schools for years."

I stare at him. I didn't think there were any kasiri who supported halan representation or integrated schools. I wonder what Shaul and his pharmacy friends would make of this.

"It means the councilors always pass them over for promotions," Azariah adds, "but Mother and Father came from rich families in Xana and don't need to rely on the Assembly's good favor." He pauses. "At least they don't think they do."

I glance at Sarah, who looks sad and scared perched on Azariah's desk chair. "Isn't this all the more reason for me to leave? A halan guest will make it look like—"

"That's why the Seventh Councilor can't find out you're not a kasir," Azariah says.

I gape at him. "What, you want me to pretend?"

"Yes." Azariah turns to Sarah. "Hear that? For tonight, Marah's a kasir."

She nods gravely.

"You can't be serious," I say. "Look at my clothes. It'll never work."

Azariah's gaze moves reluctantly over my plain skirt and scratchy wool sweater. I should've known a boy wouldn't notice that kind of thing.

"It's true," Sarah says. "She doesn't look like a kasir."

"We'll have to find you something else," he says.

"This is insane," I begin, but then Sarah leaps up.

"Let's look in Mother's wardrobe!"

"Your mother's taller than me," I say.

"Yes, but Hala and Isra's things are in there," Sarah says with a gleeful smile.

"Whose things?"

"Our cousins from Atsan," Azariah explains. "They visited a while ago, and some of their clothes are still around. Come on, let's see what we can find."

Azariah cracks open the study door, and Sarah slips through and darts down the hall. Her brother and I follow her into a vast bedroom. Azariah lights the gas lamp overhead with a spell.

Sarah walks around her parents' massive bed, throws open the doors of a rosewood armoire, and starts rooting through the richly colored wools and silks of her mother's dresses. I'm still wondering how many clothes their Atsani cousins must own in order to think nothing of leaving some in Ashara when Sarah pulls out a dress.

"You should wear this!" she says, running her fingers through the folds of dark blue velvet.

"I'm not sure—"

"At least try it on," Azariah pleads.

Sarah shows me into an adjoining dressing room and leaves me with the dress. I change into it and study my reflection in the oval mirror above the dressing-table. The gown fits all right, though I'm not as filled out as the girl it was made for. The sleeves end in snug cuffs at my elbows. I'm unaccustomed to the way the skirt reaches my ankles and the neckline exposes my collarbones, but it's the kasir style. I almost don't recognize myself.

Sarah peeks into the dressing room, then grins and bounds up to me. Before I know what's happening, she has climbed onto the dressing-table stool and untied the cord securing my braid.

"Sarah, what—?" Then I understand. A kasir girl wouldn't be caught dead wearing a single braid down her back. Sarah combs her fingers through my hair, smoothing out the kinks, and arranges it around my shoulders as elegantly as she can.

"There," she says, beaming at our reflection. "You look so pretty!"

When I emerge from Gadi Faysal's dressing room, Azariah's eyes widen.

"I feel like an impostor," I say. "I *am* an impostor."

"Don't think like that," he says. "You look perfect."

I highly doubt that.

The three of us are the last to enter the dining room. Seven porcelain plates are laid out on a shimmering tablecloth. Gadi Faysal and Banar Rashid sit at the head and foot of the table, and when they see me walk in wearing a velvet dress that clearly isn't mine, they both stare. Luckily, their astonishment goes unnoticed by the two strangers present. The first, a woman in a dark red dress, must be Ketsiah Betsalel, the Seventh Councilor. She's young, even for the most junior member of the Assembly. Her olive skin is smooth, her black hair cut short in a daring new style. Her gawky secretary, dressed in a white shirt and a black jacket with silk lapels, sits beside her.

Azariah nudges me forward, and I move to the spot next to Sarah, keeping my back as straight as possible. To my dismay, I find myself directly opposite the Seventh Councilor.

"Good evening, children," she says with a condescending smile.

"Good evening, Gadi Betsalel," Azariah says.

"What are your names?" she asks.

"I'm Azariah," he says. "And this is my friend Marah."

The Seventh Councilor looks at me. My instinct is to shrink in my chair, but instead I pull my shoulders back, lift my chin, and respectfully meet her gaze. "Good evening, Gadi Betsalel."

While Sarah introduces herself, I watch Gadi Faysal whisper to the maid at her end of the table. Then Azariah kicks me in the ankle, and I realize the Seventh Councilor has just asked me where I go to school.

My mind goes blank for a moment. Recovering, I affect an offhand tone and say, "I go to Firem with Azariah."

I catch Banar Rashid's sharp glance, but there's not much he can do now. I'm counting on Azariah to buttress my lies.

"The first course is served," Gadi Faysal announces, smiling with flawless grace as the maid sets bowls of soup in front of us. "A Xanite delicacy, made from a rare desert plant."

I watch Azariah's mother, picking up the same spoon

she does and imitating the way she sips the soup. Garnished with sprigs of a spiny herb, it's almost unbearably bitter.

"Ah, the flavors of your native Xana," Gadi Betsalel says, her face smooth. She smiles at her secretary. "Delicious, isn't it, Lavan?"

"I asked the cook to prepare it the moment I heard you were coming," Gadi Faysal says, feigning modesty. Councilor Betsalel's secretary grimaces as he swallows another spoonful.

Soon after the maid serves barley and roasted hare, the Seventh Councilor brings up the subject of immigrating Xanite kasiri. Lavan, her secretary, brightens and forgets all about his dinner.

"Xanite kasiri tend to arrive unaccustomed to our institutions' traditions," Gadi Betsalel says as I swallow a forkful of meat. "Despite their accomplishments, they are outsiders until they adapt to our practices and our theory of magic."

Banar Rashid clears his throat. "Keep in mind that Xanite immigrants have made significant contributions to the modern craft of Ashari magic."

"But it was Ashari magicians who refined those contributions and extended their applications," Lavan pipes up. "You'll notice none of the Assembly councilors is Xanite."

Gadi Faysal lowers her silverware. "Perhaps if the councilors were elected, it would be different," she says dryly.

"If Xanites don't like Ashara," Lavan says, "they can go back to their country."

"The civil war there has been raging for thirty years, as you well know," Gadi Faysal says, her cheeks bloodless. "And must I remind you that the people who settled the north lands and founded the Erezai monarchy came from Xana?"

"That's ancient history," Lavan retorts.

"That will do, Lavan," says the Seventh Councilor, a smile playing on her lips. "You'll find Gadi Faysal difficult to sway."

"Do taste this fish, Ketsiah," Banar Rashid says as another course arrives. I expect him to steer the conversation into less treacherous waters, but then he says, "What can you tell my family about the outbreak of the dark eyes?"

I don't know if I can handle talk of the illness. But maybe the Seventh Councilor can tell us something no one outside the Assembly knows.

"We are devoting considerable time and funds to the study of the illness, Jalal," she tells Banar Rashid. "Yiftach David himself examines each progress report submitted by the physicians' committee."

"Shouldn't these reports be available to the public?" says Gadi Faysal.

"What do you mean?" the councilor asks.

"The committee's work is shrouded in secrecy, and we've seen no evidence of progress in treating the disease. The Assembly has still not identified the illness, nor can any doctor explain the darkening of the irises."

"You are the first person I've encountered who is not satisfied with our swift response to the outbreak and our energetic pursuit of a cure," the Seventh Councilor says.

Gadi Faysal's eyes flash. "Am I the only person who is paying attention?"

Banar Rashid straightens, alarmed. "Nasim, I believe the children may be excused."

The Seventh Councilor protests, but Banar Rashid is firm. Sarah, Azariah, and I file out.

Sarah slips off by herself, and Azariah and I walk down the carpeted hallway. When we reach the safety of his study, he sinks into his desk chair, his whole body sagging.

"Can I take off this wretched dress?" I ask.

He shakes his head. "Better wait until we're sure Councilor Betsalel's gone."

Resigned, I pull the other chair up beside him. He opens the Hagramet book. "Remember the words I copied out of your dictionary?" he says. "'Spell' and so on? This is a section where they appear a lot close together."

I pull the book toward me, and the page I'm holding starts to rip at the edge. I jerk my hand away, but Azariah simply twirls his fingers over the tear, murmuring, and the fibers of the paper knit themselves back together. Impressed, I reach for a pen.

We begin to translate, consulting my grammar to check constructions or to use the dictionary. Azariah's swift mastery of the Hagramet alphabet amazes me, but he doesn't know many words. He's torn between his impatience, which would have me forge ahead, and his desire to learn the language, which requires me to explain everything I do. It takes us a good ten minutes to translate our first two sentences.

Magic is all around us; it is a single, uniform ?. In some places it is more abundant and in some places scarcer.

Wonderful, a treatise worthy of one of Aradi Mattan's history lectures.

"Single, uniform what, I wonder?" Azariah says, jotting down the unknown word in his own notebook. "This reminds me of a description in a Xanite manual." He rises and crosses to a bookcase, tilting his head to read the titles.

"Shall I go on?" I ask.

"Please."

I tackle the next few sentences, my translation littered with question marks, but the gist seems consistent with my very basic understanding of magic. Then I reach an easier passage.

With each spell, the magic produces secondary ?, both beneficial and harmful. After a spell is cast, the magician performs a special spell to ? the harmful ? to become harmless. Magicians have cast these ? spells for as long as they have cast spells, in order to protect the kingdom. People are

? to the harmful ?, some more than others. The abandonment of the ? spells in the forty-third year of the Agrav Dynasty led to a surfeit of harmful magical ? in the air. After many years, a plague of ? destroyed the House of Agrav. When

"Look at that!" Azariah exclaims.

I start, unaware he was reading over my shoulder. "What?"

"Aren't you reading this?"

I skim my translation. "It's about your secondary residues, your by-products."

"It says they're harmful!"

"So?"

"Well, it's odd, isn't it?" He gestures at the notebook. "All this describes exactly how I cast my spells. It suggests a thousand years ago magicians in Hagram used magic more or less the same way Ashari do today. Except I've never heard of any by-products that are considered harmful, or these special spells that sound like they neutralize them."

I rest my head in my hands. "It's probably not really the same. A lot has happened in the last thousand years." Hagram collapsed, for one thing. Then centuries later, Erezai rose in its place, only to split into independent city-states of which Ashara is only one.

"Everything else fits," Azariah insists. "Remember, Erezai's magicians considered themselves the heirs of Hagram."

I reread my translation. A surfeit of harmful magic in the air. A plague that destroyed a dynasty. I glance back at the original text, and the word *eyes* jumps right off the page.

. . . the eyes become black.

"God of the Maitaf," I say, and someone knocks on the door.

14

AZARIAH AND I SHARE A LOOK OF HORROR. THE NEXT instant, he sweeps books, pens, and notebooks into his desk drawer. We draw ourselves up and stand side by side in front of his desk.

My head pounds. Black eyes. The dark eyes.

"Come in," says Azariah.

Councilor Betsalel sweeps in and pauses at the sight of the two of us standing stiffly apart.

"My," she says, her lips curving upward, "a secluded study is a fortune, isn't it?"

Azariah blushes at once. My stomach boils with panic. As Sarah slips into the room behind the Seventh Councilor, I adopt my perfect medsha posture and stretch my mouth into a smile.

"May I help you?" Azariah asks Gadi Betsalel.

She crosses to his bookshelves. "Your sister is showing me around. Your parents tell me you have an impressive library for one so young."

When she fingers the spines of some of his books, he tenses. Sarah yawns. I pray the councilor will go away so I can return to the Hagramet text. Leah's black eyes smolder like cold embers in my mind's eye.

Gadi Betsalel seems to spend eons inspecting Azariah's collection. She asks him some questions, but she doesn't seem interested in his replies. When she finally leaves, Azariah locks the door, swearing under his breath.

"What an evening," he says, returning to the desk. "I'm sorry."

"Azariah, it's true," I say. Now that the Seventh Councilor is gone, I can't stop shaking.

"What?"

"Just before you closed the book, I read something else. The plague during the Agrav Dynasty. It's the dark eyes."

"What?"

"It says their eyes turned black!" I cry. "The harmful magic. The illness. Black eyes."

His mouth opens silently. Then he swallows. "It's happening again?"

"Yes!"

"But . . . but the . . ." Dread transforms his face. "The magic is the same. Somewhere, somehow, we lost the neutralizing spells. And the harmful by-products have built up in the city."

I speak over my thudding heart. "It's strange, isn't it? The truth about the illness is in some book only you have, written in a language that's not only been outlawed but is so rare most people wouldn't recognize it."

Lost in his own thoughts, Azariah doesn't seem to hear me. "We've all been casting spells for years, never knowing this poison was accumulating around us. And now there's too much for us to tolerate. I almost can't believe it, except . . ."

"Except for the eyes," I say.

"Right." He lights up with sudden understanding. "That's why the illness isn't contagious! It has nothing to do with spreading microbes. It's about the level of tainted magic in the environment reaching a tipping point and—oh! Maybe that explains why children are more resistant, because the magic hasn't been building up in their bodies for as many years as—"

"Azariah," I say, uninterested in his theories, "my best friend, Leah, has the dark eyes."

He catches his breath. "I'm sorry." After a pause, he says, "Marah, we have to tell someone about this. My parents, for a start."

I'm about to agree when a wave of terror rushes through me, accompanied by a sudden, absolute conviction. "No! Azariah, we can't."

"What do you mean? It's killing people right now!"

"No," I choke out. The fear clogs my throat. "We can't tell anyone, Azariah. I know we can't. There's something wrong. The Hagramet . . ." My intuition won't take me any further, but I'm determined to heed it. I won't make a mistake this time. If the feeling tells me we can't reveal this to anyone, we mustn't reveal it.

"What do you mean you know we can't—oh." Azariah

goes still. He looks uneasy, and when he speaks again, his voice is hushed. "It's the sp—your intuition."

I feel strangely exposed. Shaul's defiant words come back to me. *The intuition is our power.*

"Don't be afraid," I tell Azariah. It's not what I expected to say.

"I'm not afraid," he says. "I've just never . . . been around the intuition. Up close."

"I'm used to it," I say, not without sadness.

"It's uncanny."

"As long as you believe me."

He mulls it over while I let the feeling settle inside me.

"Let's keep translating," Azariah says at last. "Maybe we can learn more."

I nod.

We stay like that awhile, bound together by dread. The study is silent, the heavy velvet curtains still. On their dark-stained shelves, Azariah's books stand as mute witnesses to our pledge. Finally, Channah comes to take me home.

ALL NIGHT, I lie stiff under the covers, picturing poisonous magical residue falling onto my skin like ash from a burning building. I listen to Caleb's gentle breathing and wish I could hide him and Mother away somewhere. Perhaps in a sleepy village in the Ashari hinterlands, or deep in the forest that borders the city. When I drift into slumber, the Hagramet alphabet is branded onto my dreams.

I hurry to Leah's apartment in the morning. For the

first time, I feel the weight of history on my shoulders. Here, on the banks of the Davgir, trapped in a crucible of magic formed by the Sohadir and the Shatarai Rivers, a dynasty of Hagram collapsed in a mess of fouled magic. We're drowning in the same brew now, and I can't bear the loneliness of being the only one besides Azariah who knows.

When I arrive, Leah is buried in blankets as usual, her eyes closed, her forehead creased.

"It's me," I say.

Her black eyes fasten on me at once. "I've been waiting for you, Marah." Her voice is as thin as onion skin, her cheeks sunken. I imagine tendrils of magic probing her skin and shiver.

"Waiting for me?"

"To release Raspberry."

I glance at the silhouette of the house finch in his crate.

"I don't want to let him go," Leah says. "He keeps me company. But I've waited too long. He's ready." She pushes off her covers. "Help me get up."

"Get up? You can't do that."

"Yes, I can. Just to the window."

So I help her rise, and she staggers across the room, leaning against me. She's lost a frightening amount of weight.

"Open the window," she says.

"What? No. You'll catch your—" I break off. After a moment's indecision, I do as she says. A chilly blast of wind blows in, rippling Leah's nightgown.

Clutching my arm with one hand, she bends over

Raspberry's crate and rips the cheesecloth away. The finch flits up to one of the slats and warbles. Leah coaxes him out of the cage, and he alights on the windowsill, only to fly to her nightstand. I groan. Trembling in the cold air, my friend wheedles until the bird flutters back to the window. He hops back and forth on the sill, tilting his head. Then, without warning, he spreads his wings and soars into the air above the street.

"He's free," Leah breathes, radiant with joy. "He's the first creature I've ever sent back into the wild. Did you see him fly?"

Unexpectedly moved, I can only nod.

"Leah, I need to talk to you," I say when she is tucked back in bed. I sink to the floor, wondering where to begin. "Remember how Sarah invited me to dinner with her family? Well, I've been twice more."

Leah's astonished expression makes her look more like her old, healthy self. "All this for an eight-year-old?"

"It's not just Sarah," I say. "I'm working on something with her brother."

"What? The one whose friends broke your violin?"

"No, the other one. His name's Azariah. He's our age."

"Is he good-looking?" Leah asks, a trace of mischief discernible even in her darkened eyes.

"Leah."

"Well, is he?"

"Leah, he's a kasir! Besides, that's not the point." I take a deep breath and tell her about the forbidden Hagramet book and the translation project. Then I describe the Seventh Councilor's visit yesterday evening. When I come to the forgotten spells and the origins of the dark eyes, I hesitate. Last night, when Azariah wanted to confide in his parents, I swore him to secrecy, but right now my intuition is quiet.

"Leah," I say, "you can't tell anyone what I'm about to tell you."

When I finish, she sucks in her breath. "God of the Maitaf. Can it be true?"

"We're all going to pay for the magicians' mistake," I say bitterly. "They've always hurt us."

"Stop it," she says. "Aren't kasiri dying too?"

She sighs and gazes toward the window. Then she turns back to me. "Marah, I want you to have my violin."

I feel a chill deep inside me. "This is about your intuition."

Leah says nothing.

"You'll need your violin when you're well," I say.

"You're going to get into Qirakh," she says. "You'll need an instrument, and I want you to play mine."

"No," I whisper, tears welling up in my eyes. I smear them away. Leah reaches for my hand. I don't know which of us is shaking.

THIRDDAY FINALLY COMES again, with the death count approaching three hundred. At the Rashids, Azariah welcomes me in the entryway.

"Melchior's here tonight," he says. "Not at his friend's, for once."

Something heavy settles onto my chest. As we pad down the hall, I hear voices coming from the dining room.

"—grades remain disappointing," Gadi Faysal is saying.

"Why should I bother to raise them, Mother?" I recognize Melchior's voice. "So I can attend Firem University and graduate a puppet of the Assembly? You despise them. Do you want me to follow in their footsteps?"

Azariah mutters something that sounds like *not again*. As we pass the doorway to the living room, Sarah comes dashing out and gives me a hug.

"Will you read me a story tonight, Marah?" she asks.

"Of course," I say, ignoring her brother's aggravated expression.

As soon as the three of us enter the dining room, Melchior stops talking. I avoid looking at him as I sit down.

The meal proceeds calmly enough until dessert, when Sarah lets something slip about the Seventh Councilor's visit. She proceeds blithely into a story about Channah taking her to the archaeology museum, but Melchior interrupts her.

"Ketsiah Betsalel came to dinner last week?"

The dining room falls silent.

"Are you serious?" he says. "God of the Maitaf."

"Maybe if you spent a little more time around here," Azariah says, "you'd know what was going on. Even Marah was here."

"You let her see a sparker at our table?" Melchior says, appalled. I bristle.

"Be civil, Melchior!" says Gadi Faysal, her cheeks blazing.

"If I'd known Betsalel was coming," he says, "I would've made sure I was here to prevent you from doing stupid things like that. You always do, when it's easy to send those vultures away happy."

"It is not your responsibility to navigate politics on behalf of this family," Banar Rashid says sternly.

"It is your responsibility to attend to your studies," says Gadi Faysal.

Azariah throws down his napkin. "Here they go again," he says in my ear. "Let's not stay for this."

Neither Melchior nor his parents take any notice as Azariah, Sarah, and I leave the dining room.

"Why are they fighting?" Sarah says, distressed. When Azariah rolls his eyes, she seizes my hand. "You promised to read to me."

I glance at Azariah, who shrugs. "Come join me after."

Sarah's bedroom has none of the scholarly elegance of Azariah's study. The only sign of any academic pursuits is a desk by the window, where presumably she works on her lessons with Channah during the day. Sarah sinks onto an elongated yellow cushion next to a lacquered cupboard. She yanks it open and pulls out a thick book.

"Sit next to me," she says. She folds her hands mournfully in her lap. "You don't like me anymore."

"What?" I plop down beside her. "What do you mean?"

"All you do is study with Azariah. You never talk to me."

"Yes, I do," I say lamely.

"Not really." After a moment, she asks, "Want to see something?"

I nod.

She sets aside her book and cups her hand in front of her, staring intently into her palm. It reminds me of the examiner at Caleb's magic test at the District Hall, except Sarah's gesture is full of innocence and wonder.

A pearl of golden light appears in the hollow of her hand. She blows on it, as though sending off a butterfly. The light floats up from her palm and soars toward the ceiling before vanishing just below the gasolier.

"Oh! That was beautiful. Well done!" The words take me by surprise. Am I praising a budding magician for honing her skills?

Sarah smiles at me. "It's not a real spell, but I can do it every time now." Reaching for her book, she says, "Now read me a story."

She chooses a fairy tale about a princess who disguises herself to escape an arranged marriage to an evil king. The story is predictable, but I get caught up in it. Just as I reach the end, there's a knock on the door. It's probably Azariah, wondering where I am.

The door swings open. It's Melchior. He can't seem to lift his gaze from the floor. "Sarah, I want to talk to Marah for a moment. Why don't you go see what Azariah's up to?"

Sarah looks from me to her eldest brother in confusion. "All right." She kisses me on the cheek before scurrying out.

I stand up and try to slip around Melchior, but he says, "Marah, wait. Please."

"I don't want to talk to you."

"I—"

"You called me a sparker at dinner like I wasn't even there," I say, my voice shaking.

Melchior reddens. "That was stupid of me. I'm sorry. For that and for everything. Please hear me out."

I wait. It strikes me how absurd it is for us to be having this conversation in Sarah's room, surrounded by pastel cushions and watched by a row of porcelain dolls nestled on the bed.

Melchior looks me in the eye. His hair clings damply to his forehead, and he swallows. "I'm sorry for letting my friends hurt you. For letting them break your violin."

"Why didn't you stop them?" I ask.

"I don't know," he says bleakly. "I guess I didn't want Shimon and Ayal to think . . . It's not easy being Xanite at Firem. If you don't make them like you, they call you an immigrant, a foreigner, sand spawn."

When he utters that name for Xanites out loud, I can't help a small gasp. As insults go, sand spawn is pretty foul.

Melchior seems not to notice my shock. "Then on top of that, being a Rashid . . ."

"Azariah seems to manage," I put in.

Melchior snorts. "Azariah's a genius. And unlike me, he wants to go into government so he can fix things." He shakes his head. "I owe you a new violin—"

"I don't need it," I say. Then I realize with a pang that I'm thinking of Leah's fiddle.

"Are you sure?" Melchior says.

I nod. "You weren't the one who broke it."

He grimaces. "In a way, I was. I'm really sorry."

"I know." After a pause, I add, "My thanks."

I feel strangely relieved, though I still can't wait to escape. "Azariah's waiting for me."

Melchior nods. I edge out of Sarah's bedroom, feeling the slightest twinge at leaving him looking so miserable.

When I enter the study, Sarah is no longer there. Azariah looks up from the Hagramet books. "What on earth did Melchior want?"

"He was apologizing to me," I say.

"Apologizing?" he says incredulously. "For what?"

I hesitate before telling him what happened.

"He did that?" Azariah sounds horrified.

"It's nothing to do with you," I say. "We need to get to work. The dark eyes."

"Oh. Right." He takes a breath. "I think I've determined the spot in the text with the most discussion of spells. With any luck, there'll be a description of the neutralizing spell."

The section Azariah has picked is near the end of the book, about twenty pages past the passage about the Agrav Dynasty's collapse. I sit down and tackle the first sentence while he scribbles notes in his blank book. The words are simple, but their arrangement is complex, and after a moment I realize the paragraph consists of instructions.

"You're right, Azariah. I think this is a spell."

"Really?"

"Here." I translate aloud. "'Written down to preserve . . .' Something about forgetting. Then here, 'a spell,' 'harmful to harmless' . . . I think you've found it!"

He clenches his fists. "God of the Maitaf. We're saved."

"But what if it doesn't work anymore?" I say, glancing down the page. "I can't make much sense of these directions."

"Well, you're not a ka—" He flushes. "Translate the spell, and I'll do it."

Once I've finished, we read the text together. I'm skeptical. The words are plain, but the hand movements they describe are anything but clear. Worse yet, with nothing but my grammar to guide us, we can only approximate the pronunciation of the incantation.

Azariah's face falls as he peruses my translation, but he still says, "I want to try it."

With some apprehension, I ask, "Is it safe? What happens if you cast a spell incorrectly?"

"Nothing, usually." He squints at my handwriting, contorting his hands in front of his chest. "What sound do you think 'ae' is?"

"How should I know? That's how the chart transliterates this Hagramet letter, but Ashari doesn't even use that digraph."

He raises one eyebrow. "What's a digraph?"

"Just try, Azariah."

While he utters syllables in slow succession, I chip away

at the next section of the text. I'm hunting for a word root in the dictionary when Azariah sighs. "It's not working."

"How do you know?"

"I can feel it. The magic's not moving." He glances at the notebook where I've written, *This describes how to . . .* "If I could just ask the advice of a more skilled magi—"

"Azariah, you can't!" My voice catches on a spike of terror as the intuition surges inside me.

"All right, all right," he says, half grudging, half offended.

Just then, I find the dictionary entry I was looking for. Next to the Hagramet verb is its Ashari translation: *treat (as illness), cure, heal.* My heart pounds.

"Look!" I say, scrawling *cure* in the notebook. I seize the original text. Familiar words leap out at me: plants, numbers, simple directions.

"It looks like a recipe for some kind of potion," I say breathlessly.

Azariah looks blank. "I don't—"

"Here," I say, showing him in the book. "Below the neutralizing spell. Azariah, I think it's a cure for the dark eyes!" I jump up from the chair as tears of joy, or relief, sting my eyes.

Azariah's face lights up. "Then we can save Ashara! I'll figure out the neutralizing spell, we all will, but first we'll heal everyone who's ill."

Hope rises in my chest, burning so brightly it almost scares me. The task before us is so daunting.

"We're going to save the city, right?" I say.

Azariah nods. "We have to."

* * *

AFTER CHANNAH DROPS me off, I stand in the street for a moment, motionless in the snow. The world is so quiet. Out here, it is the loneliest of winter nights, but I'm not afraid, not even of the poison in the air.

At home, Mother is in our bedroom leaning over Caleb, who lies curled up in bed, the blankets pulled up to his chin. The peace of the snowy street deserts me.

"Mother?" My voice sounds high-pitched. "Caleb?"

Mother looks at me, her face empty. "He's sick, Marah."

I rush to the bed and place my palm on my brother's forehead. His skin is burning, his body trembling. I stroke his hot face until he opens his eyes.

His irises are black.

15

THE CURE IS ON MY MIND THE MOMENT I WAKE. I CRAWL out from under the covers and check on Caleb. He's still feverish. As I pile my blankets onto him, a powerful wave of longing for Father sweeps through me. I miss him more intensely than I have in years, and with missing him comes fear as deep and black as the sea. We've already lost Father. We can't lose Caleb too.

I can't wait a whole week to start deciphering the cure. I want to go to Azariah's house today, but I would have to walk, and I don't know the way well enough to be sure I wouldn't get lost in the country. So instead I grab a piece of paper from the nightstand and a pen from my schoolbag. I scribble a letter to Azariah asking if we can meet sooner than next Thirdday. If I mail it today, I can hope to hear from him as early as the beginning of this weekend. Even that feels too far off.

When I walk into the kitchen with the letter, I'm surprised to find Leah's sister Ruth sitting with Mother at the table.

"Good morning, Marah," Mother says. "I didn't get a chance to tell you last night, but I've found a new job."

"Really?" I say. This is the last thing I expected to hear. "Where?"

"At the Maitafi Graveyard, in Gishal District."

"You're going to be a *grave digger*?"

Mother laughs. "No. I'll be record keeper."

After the secular City Cemetery, the Maitafi Graveyard is the largest burial ground in the city. Nowadays only halani are interred there. And only the religious ones at that. I'm surprised they hired Mother when we aren't Maitafi.

"Today's my first day," she continues, "and you have your violin lesson this morning, so—"

"Maybe I should stay with Caleb," I interrupt.

Mother shakes her head. "Ruth will watch him while we're gone."

"It's the least I can do," Ruth says.

I grudgingly give in. After a hasty breakfast, Mother and I leave the apartment together. She watches me tuck Azariah's letter into our mailbox without asking who it's for. Before we part ways in the brittle cold, she places her hand on my shoulder and says, "We'll make it through this, Marah."

I take the direct route through the kasir neighborhood again. Even as I keep a nervous eye out for Firem boys, my thoughts circle incessantly around Caleb and the promise of a cure. I walk along the icy sidewalks with reckless haste, wanting to hurry through every moment I'm away from my brother.

When I reach her house, Aradi Imael greets me with a warm smile. "How are you, Marah? Only seven days now."

I nod distractedly. Caleb's illness has overshadowed everything, making my upcoming audition feel much less real. I want to be translating Hagramet right now.

While Aradi Imael brews a pot of tea, I tune and try to coax some limberness back into my fingers. Then she asks to hear the Shevem. I begin to play, my tone thin and colorless.

"Fuller sound," says Aradi Imael, watching me.

I draw my bow more deeply into the strings, but each phrase is more barren than the last.

"Stop, Marah." My teacher's face is calm, her fingers steepled under her chin.

I let my bow arm drop to my side.

She leans forward in her armchair. "You need to give it more."

"I'm trying," I mumble.

"No, you're not," she says. "Start again. Make that crescendo fill the whole room."

My fingers are trembling, and suddenly I'm sure I can't play the Qirakh audition. In my effort to keep myself together, I play like a clockwork creature.

"Marah, is something wrong?"

Yes. Everything. I can't trust my voice.

"Marah," Aradi Imael says gently, "you won't play with your whole self unless you risk vulnerability. You must not be afraid of your fear."

I concentrate on breathing for a few excruciating seconds.

How can she ask this of me? If I don't shove down my terror for Caleb, I'll break down completely. And what does it mean to play with my whole self?

At last, I adjust the fiddle under my chin. Instead of suppressing my fear of losing Caleb, I try to let it wash over me. I lift my bow again, holding it with a looser grip. Then I take the Shevem from the beginning. I'm still holding back, but now my tone is purer, sweeter.

When I stop, Aradi Imael nods. "Better."

THE NEXT DAY, Fifthday, Mother leaves for the Maitafi Graveyard just before sunup. I practice in my bedroom all morning, standing over my brother like some sort of guardian. My audition is on Firstday, only days away. Caleb wakes now and then and watches me sight-read medsha excerpts or polish the Shevem. I almost can't bear the eclipse of his eyes.

From our bedroom window, I spot the mailman leaving our building. I race down to the foyer to check our box, hoping for a postal miracle. It's empty, of course.

Mother returns at dusk, a basket hanging from her arm. She sets a fragrant loaf of bread, a jar of pickles, and something wrapped in butcher's paper on the kitchen table.

"We can afford fresh meat?" I say.

"Yes," she says with a tired smile. "Thanks to my new job."

"How do you bear it?" I find myself asking. I can't imagine being around the endless funeral processions, the murmured prayers, the gaping graves. "Doesn't it make you think of Father?"

She looks sadly at me. "I have never been able to avoid reminders of your father, Marah."

Later, I watch her tending to Caleb. Her sure hands help him get up and lie down, gauge the heat of his fever, and coax broth and herbal tea into him. Her movements stir up dim memories of my own childhood illnesses, of Mother's presence, always near, imparting the confidence through the haze of sickness that all would be well. But all won't be well until I can get back to the Hagramet book.

On Sixthday, Caleb's fever breaks. He begins to cough.

On Seventhday, I finally receive a letter from Azariah. I tear it open in the entrance hall.

> Dear Marah,
>
> I'm sorry to hear about Caleb. I'm afraid I only have more bad news. Sarah fell ill with the dark eyes on Fourthday. I agree we can't wait until next week to continue our work, so I've asked Channah to bring you to our house on Eighthday evening.
>
> Azariah

Sarah too! I picture her on the yellow cushion in her bedroom, paging eagerly through her fairy-tale book. The letter flutters in my hand. Tomorrow night can't come soon enough.

At dinnertime, I tell Mother I'm going to the Rashids' again.

"Tomorrow?" she says. "Weren't you just there on Thirdday?"

I nod, blowing on my soup.

Mother sets down her spoon. "Marah, more than a few neighbors have asked me why you're associating with kasiri. Gadi Yared told me she couldn't imagine what kind of mother would let her daughter ride around in some government official's auto."

I feel angry on both our behalfs. "I'm sorry."

"What the neighbors think doesn't matter if I understand why you're going to the Rashids," Mother says more gently. "Are you really still visiting these kasiri just to humor a little girl?"

Her perceptiveness makes me squirm a little. "Not exactly."

She waits, expecting me to elaborate.

"Sarah has a brother who's also in Final, at Firem. His name is Azariah."

Mother raises her eyebrows. "You've been going to the Rashids to see a boy?"

"It's not like that," I say hastily. "We're both interested in foreign languages and old books. That's what we've been talking about."

This makes Mother laugh. "You and your languages, Marah. But why do you need to see this Azariah tomorrow? Isn't it enough to talk about obscure languages once a week?"

I hesitate. If I reveal the whole truth to Mother now, she'll never stop asking me questions. She'll want to see the evidence with her own eyes. Inevitably it will come out that Azariah and I have been translating a banned book, and I'm still convinced we can't tell anyone about that.

"We've found something," I say at last. "Something I think might help Caleb."

Mother stills. "You mean something that might heal him?"

"Maybe," I say, bracing myself for an onslaught of inquiries. But Mother just shakes her head.

"You can go to the Rashids, Marah," she says, "but try not to chase false hopes."

On Eighthday, Channah picks me up later than usual, after supper. At the Rashids', Azariah doesn't even look up when I enter his study. Books litter the floor, and he kneels among them, his lips moving silently.

"It's me," I say.

He stands up and wipes his dusty fingers on his trousers. "I'm sorry about Caleb."

"I'm sorry about Sarah," I say hollowly.

I pick my way to the desk where the Hagramet text lies open to the instructions for the cure.

"The first ingredient's an herb, something about bears," Azariah says.

I glance at the Hagramet. He's right, the first item on the ingredients list is "the herb called foot of bear cub."

"Cub's foot?" I guess. "Does that sound familiar?"

He shakes his head. "Sorry about the mess. I was looking in my father's herbals."

I reach for a pen and our translation notebook. The next few items are also rather culinary: more herbs, a couple of spices, some kind of nut oil whose name I recognize from the market. The dictionary furnishes us with the Ashari names for these ingredients, but neither of us is certain what they are.

"Perilla?" I say. "Oxalis? I've never heard of these plants."

"Good thing we have these herbals, then," he says.

While he combs the indexes of his father's books, I move on, deeper into the Hagramet. It's calming to wrestle with the text. The focus it demands distracts me from my worries, and at least we're doing something.

At last, I look up from the book and read the list of translated ingredients aloud. Three entries remain undecipherable.

"This doesn't look *too* bad," Azariah says, sounding a little desperate as he examines the page. "I've found all the herbs and spices, and most of them shouldn't be difficult to buy."

"Most of them?"

"A few are uncommon," he admits.

"Still, isn't it odd a magical cure should include such ordinary ingredients?"

"I'm not sure. We don't study apothecary magic till secondary school."

"I can ask about the unusual ingredients at the Ikhad," I

offer. Never mind how we're going to make the cure if I can't translate the last three items, or if Azariah has to dabble in a kind of magic he's never learned.

"I'll do some more research too." He grits his teeth in frustration. "I wish we were making this already!"

For the first time, I decide to leave my grammar with him, but only after I tear a sheet out of the notebook and make myself a copy of the ingredients list.

"When can you come back?" Azariah asks. "There are still the instructions to translate."

"The Ikhad's not open till Tenthday," I say. That's in two days, but it feels an age away. "I'll come that night."

"Eat dinner with us. I'll ask Channah to bring you."

"My thanks." I should be getting home, but something holds me back. "How's Sarah?"

"Not well," he says. "The doctor was here a few days ago, but he couldn't do much except give her medicine and use some healing magic to bring down her fever." He seems embarrassed, as if he wishes he hadn't mentioned healing spells.

"And your brother?" he asks.

"I don't know."

In this fragile moment, we're both afraid to breathe.

"Can I see her?" I ask impulsively.

Azariah nods, and I follow him to Sarah's bedroom. Across from the cushion and the lacquered cupboard where I read to her, Sarah lies on a low bed under a thick pile of blankets.

"Azariah?" she mumbles, squinting at us from her voluminous pillow. It's a shock to see her like this, drained of her vivacity.

"Marah's here," Azariah says. He leads me to Sarah's bedside, and I kneel to return her black and wondering gaze.

"Marah?" she says in disbelief.

"It's me." I try to smile, but my lips crack.

"I don't feel good," Sarah says, butting her head deeper into her pillow.

"I know," I say. "But you'll get better soon."

She bursts into stormy tears. I look at Azariah in alarm, but he just shakes his head.

"Sarah," I whisper, stroking her damp hair as she cries. "It'll be all right." Her sobs are already abating. She's too weak for such noisy despair, and soon she falls asleep.

I stand up and catch sight of Azariah's clenched jaw.

"I'm sorry," I say.

"Don't be silly," he says, wiping the tearstains from Sarah's cheeks with his thumb. "You made her happy."

CHANNAH HAS AN unsettled air about her as she starts the auto's engine to take me home. Once we're rolling along the snow-dusted road, she asks, "What do you keep coming to the Rashids for?"

"I'm working with Azariah," I say evasively.

"Don't you think it's unusual for you to be spending so much time with a kasir family?"

Is she warning me off? Does she think I've betrayed our

kind by fraternizing with her employers? She knows as well as I do the Rashids are different.

"Is your work something to do with languages?" Channah persists.

"What?"

She guides the auto around a bend between the bluish snowbanks. "The reason Sarah wanted you to meet Azariah in the first place was because of your foreign books."

Suddenly, I remember that Sarah was in the study the night Azariah told me it was illegal to own books written in Hagramet. She could've told her tutor everything.

"What's it to you?" I ask, my heart beating fast.

Channah draws herself up, and I regret my rudeness. "Anyone would be curious," she says. But she stops asking questions.

16

AT THE IKHAD ON TENTHDAY, I JOSTLE MY WAY TO THE book stall and greet Tsipporah.

"Marah!" she exclaims, breaking into a smile of relief. "I was beginning to worry." An impish light appears in her green eyes. "Forgot about me, did you? How do you expect to keep a job when you go three weeks without showing yourself?"

"Tsipporah," I say, "Caleb's ill."

At once, her lined face looks much older. "The dark eyes?" she says.

I nod. Before she can say anything else, I draw the translated list from my cloak pocket and hand it to her. "Do you know where I can find these ingredients? Especially the cub's foot, the oxalis tubers, and the perilla oil?"

Tsipporah squints at the page, wisps of her silvery hair rippling in the wind. A look of wary surprise spreads across her face. "Oxalis tubers were cultivated in this region before the cold times, but they can't be grown this far north anymore," she says. "And cub's foot is contraband. It's considered dangerous."

"Does that mean they're impossible to come by in Ashara?" I ask, my heart sinking.

"I didn't say that," Tsipporah says with a hint of a grin. "Does this have something to do with the Hagramet grammar you were asking about last time?"

I hesitate, then nod. "I've met someone who has another Hagramet book," I explain, keeping my voice low.

"Really?" she says. "I'd like to see it."

"There's something in that book I think might help Caleb get well," I say. "That's why I need to find these ingredients."

Her gaze is searching. I can't tell if she thinks this is a futile pursuit.

"You asked me where that grammar came from," she says at last. "Where I found it, you can find what you need. It's a place where many strange goods are sold."

"We also need to translate a few more words of Hagramet."

"Who's we?"

"Me and my friend. The one with the book."

"Well," she says, "it just so happens I know someone who reads Hagramet. He was the one who told me what I had when that grammar of yours fell into my hands."

I feel a surge of hope. "When can you take us, Tsipporah?"

She considers. "Tomorrow night? It must be at night, Marah. It isn't the safest of places."

"It's not?" Wouldn't it be better to go in daylight, then?

Though I suppose if cub's foot is contraband, there must be an element of evading the authorities involved.

"Oh, you'll be fine with me," Tsipporah says, waving her hand as though batting away invisible worries. "But best not tell anyone where you're going. And you'll need money to pay the vendors."

We'll figure out the money somehow. I think for a moment. My Qirakh audition is tomorrow. After that, there will be nothing left to worry about but the cure. "Tomorrow night's perfect."

"Meet me here after dark," Tsipporah says. "And bring a lantern."

"My thanks, Tsipporah." Standing on the cobblestones beneath the Ikhad roof, I feel something stir in my chest. If it weren't for the books between us, I would throw my arms around her.

EVENING COMES, AND headlamp beams scythe through the wooly darkness. Channah's greeting is subdued, and she doesn't meet my eyes as I climb into the auto. She grips the steering wheel with pale, bony fingers, and she looks so gaunt I wonder if she's lost weight. I expect to have to deflect more questions about my increasingly frequent visits to the Rashids, but she makes no attempt at conversation.

When we arrive, Azariah ushers me into the dining room, where his whole family is gathered. Only Sarah is missing. I cast Melchior an uncertain glance. He looks miserable. For the first time, I feel a strange closeness to him because of our shared worry for Sarah.

Everyone picks at the exquisite dinner, and conversation is scant. Azariah excuses us right after dessert. We hurry to his study in silence. In front of the door, he arranges his hand in a curious way and reaches for the knob. He begins to speak, starts, and jerks back.

"What's wrong?" I say.

"Someone's tampered with my lock spell!"

He flings open the door, and I dart after him to stop it from slamming against the wall. Azariah lets out an explosion of Xanite. When I turn to survey the study, he's on the floor snatching up papers. Before I can warn him, he plants his knee into a seeping pool of ink. Someone appears to have knocked an inkwell off his desk along with a stack of books. I rush over and right the bottle before picking up the books and setting them on the desk. There I notice Azariah's Maitaf, opened to a page marked with a silver ribbon.

"It was Melchior!" he spits, slapping a few pieces of sheet music onto a chair.

"Are you sure?" I say. "He's still at the table."

"Who else would it be? It might've been before dinner. Melchior's always barging in here, borrowing books, stealing pens." Azariah spreads his hand over the inky carpet and growls an incantation that makes the stain fade. He stands and repeats the spell on his trousers. "I can't believe he broke my lock spell. I didn't think he could."

"He must've left in a hurry," I say, indicating the mess, but Azariah's not paying attention.

"Why couldn't he have knocked *this* into the ink?" He picks up a folded edition of the *Journal* lying next to his Maitaf and thrusts it at me. I glance down at the article, which is about insulation problems in the District Halls. Then I notice a box squeezed in the corner.

Rashid Rebuked Following Remarks to Assembly

AFTER A MOTION was put forth by First Councilor Yiftach David, the Assembly voted unanimously to issue a formal rebuke censuring Jalal Rashid (Foreign Commerce) following statements he made before the Assembly at its weekly public session. In addition to their slanderous nature, Rashid's remarks were made in violation of Assembly procedural rules.

"What did your father say?" I ask Azariah.

"He said the Assembly hasn't shown it's done enough to address the dark eyes, even as the death toll mounts. He specifically mentioned halani and how most of them can't afford medicine or a doctor's visit. He argued the government should be providing medicine to those who are too poor to buy any."

"Medicine hasn't prevented anyone dying."

"I know," he says with a pained expression, "but it eases their suffering. Anyway, Father went past his allotted time. He said he wouldn't yield as long as the kasiri refused to lift a finger to help those we'd placed beneath us. I'm sure plenty of kasiri agree with Father, at least about the Assembly not doing enough about the dark eyes, but everyone else is too scared to complain."

"Your father did the right thing."

"Yes, well. . . . When I think that we know more about the dark eyes than anyone else in Ashara, that we've found a cure, I wonder why we haven't—"

"We don't know if this cure will work," I interrupt, my heart thumping. "We haven't even translated the instructions for making it. If we manage to heal Caleb and Sarah and my friend Leah, then maybe we can think about going to the Assembly." I have no intention of telling the councilors anything, but I need Azariah to stop harping on this.

He sighs. "Let's start working, then."

He crouches behind his desk and runs his fingers along the back panel. A drawer pops out, revealing the Hagramet texts and the notebooks nestled inside.

"You hid them?" I say.

He nods. "They are illegal, after all, and with things turning sour for my parents . . ."

We sit down at his desk with the books in front of us.

"I've found someone who will take us somewhere to buy the unusual ingredients tomorrow night," I say. "The cub's foot, the tubers, and that oil. She also told me someone there can read Hagramet, so we'll be able to translate the last three ingredients. We're going to leave from the Ikhad after nightfall."

His jaw drops. "You managed all that this morning? Who is this person?"

"Her name's Tsipporah. She's the bookseller who sold me the grammar."

"You said tomorrow?"

"Yes, after my audition."

"Thank God! I didn't think we'd find everything so soon." He frowns. "Wait, what audition?"

"I'm auditioning for Qirakh Secondary School."

"The music school? That's a Xanite school. You're applying there?" He grins. "You at a Xanite school!"

"I have to get in first."

"Oh, I'm sure you're really good," he says blithely. I can't help smiling.

Having deciphered all but the three impossible ingredients two nights ago, we set to work translating the instructions for making the cure. Luckily, the text proves relatively simple. Most of the words have to do with preparing ingredients for cooking, and there's a lot of repetition. Both of us marvel at how straightforward it is until we come to a mysterious direction.

"It's talking about what to do with your hand." I point the

words out to Azariah. "I think it might say 'cupped hand.' And then here, I don't think this is even a real word, it's just a . . . a syllable. God of the Maitaf, they're spells." I look up at Azariah in consternation.

A hint of alarm crosses his face, but he says, "Let's get through to the end."

After another hour, we succeed in translating the entirety of the instructions. I'm confident our translation is accurate, but the result concerns me. It's a recipe for an herbal remedy interspersed with sequences of spells, all meticulously described.

"What are we going to do about these spells?" I ask.

Azariah rereads the instructions. To my surprise, he brightens. "I think I can do them."

"But when you tried to cast the neutralizing spell, it didn't work."

"These spells are different," he says. "I recognize them. They're the simplest kind that exists. Instead of producing a specific effect, they alter magic on a fundamental level, and they can be layered in complex ways. I think that's what's meant to happen in the cure."

I raise my eyebrows.

"Think of it as playing open strings on a violin," he says. "The most basic thing you can do."

"Fine, but this text is ancient. How can we be sure the spells haven't changed?"

"We'll just have to trust they've been passed down properly over the centuries."

"Oh, right. It's not as if magicians failing to pass down their spells properly got us to where we are today or anything."

Azariah looks incredulously at me, and suddenly, despite everything, we're both laughing.

"I should go home," I say, sobering. "It's getting late."

"Of course," he says. "Good luck on your audition, Marah."

"My thanks." I hesitate. "Azariah, when we buy the ingredients tomorrow . . . I don't have any money."

He shakes his head. "I'll take care of that."

Relieved, I say, "Don't forget, then. Tomorrow at the Ikhad. Meet me at the northeast corner, after dark."

"After dark," he echoes. There is a pause. "I'll go find Channah now."

Neither of us moves for a while though. The study is absolutely quiet.

17

AT DAYBREAK, I WAKE TO THE PATTER OF RAIN, A strange sound for the dead of winter. I twist out from under the covers and tiptoe to the window. The snow on the sill has melted, and the cobblestones below shine with moisture. Down the whole street, the eaves are crowned with icicles as long as swords.

The knowledge of what day it is grabs me by the throat. As I dress, my stomach feels hollow one moment and fluttery the next.

The kitchen is empty, but while I'm frying bread for breakfast, Mother appears in the doorway. With the heat of the stove warming my face and the cooking to occupy my hands, I realize now is the time to tell her.

"Mother, I'm going to be gone this evening."

"Must you see the Rashids every day?" she asks wearily.

"No, I'm not . . ." I falter. "Azariah and I are going somewhere. We might be gone late."

"How late?"

"I'm not sure. I'll come home as soon as I can."

Mother purses her lips. "Marah, I don't like the idea of you two going out after dark."

I clench my teeth, checking the undersides of the bread slices. "We won't be alone. Tsipporah's coming with us."

"Tsipporah?" Mother says in disbelief. "I hardly think the company of an elderly bookseller is any reassurance."

"She wouldn't let anything happen to me," I say as persuasively as I can. "She's known me since I was eight."

"She's been kind to you, Marah, but what will an old lady do if you encounter someone dangerous?"

I suspect Tsipporah is more capable than Mother thinks, but I don't say anything.

She comes up behind me as I spread honey on my bread. "Is this about you thinking you've found some way to help Caleb?"

I nod, keeping my eyes downcast.

"What is it, exactly?" she asks gently.

"Some . . . some herbs," I say, "different, rare herbs . . ." It's difficult to lie to her, but she seems to think I'm stammering from emotion.

She rests her hands on my shoulders. "It's all right. Try to calm down. You need to focus on your audition. We can discuss this afterward."

"I have to do this, Mother." I muster the courage to look her in the eye. "If I don't, and Caleb . . . I'll always wonder if I could've done something more for him."

Mother gazes at me for a long moment. "All right, Marah. You can go."

Qirakh Secondary School lies between a modest but respectable commercial district and an impoverished Xanite neighborhood. Built of gray stone, the building hunkers lower than the surrounding roofs, as if ashamed. The ripples of nervousness intensify in the pit of my stomach.

Inside the school, a spiral staircase leads to a landing that wraps all around the foyer. The wooden banister has been polished by many hands, but the hall is empty. I adjust the strap of Leah's violin case on my shoulder, comforted by the instrument's weight.

"Are you here for an audition?" The voice rings under the high ceiling. A stocky, middle-aged man in Xanite tunic and trousers beckons me from the corridor.

I walk with him down the hallway, wondering how I'll play with such cold hands. It's a good thing Aradi Imael told me to arrive early.

"What school do you attend?" my escort asks. His garb may be traditional, but his Ashari is unaccented.

"Horiel Primary," I reply.

"Oh!" He smiles. "You're Elisheva Imael's student."

"Yes."

The corridor ends in a large hall. A handful of students are scattered across the room, warming up. Swallowing hard, I retreat to the farthest corner and unpack. The minutes go by slowly while I play some scales and various passages of the Shevem, trying to wring some blood into my fingers. Yet when a young woman calls my name, it feels like only moments have passed.

I follow her into an adjacent room where she leaves me at the mercy of three women. I start to greet the judges, but my voice fails me. Two of them have copper ornaments in their hair. In Xana, copper is for mourning.

"Levi?" says one of the judges.

"Yes," I whisper.

"We'll begin with a few scales."

They ask for D minor, G major, E minor, B flat major. With each execution, I relax. I'm playing under the expected tempo, and I stumble once in the last scale, but otherwise every note comes out pure and in tune. They invite me to continue with my solo.

This is the moment I've been waiting for. I think back to what Aradi Imael told me about playing with my whole self. Taking a deep breath, I let all my worries and all the pain of this winter flood through me. I embrace them. Then I tuck my violin back under my jaw, lift my bow, and begin.

I am a soul unmoored from my body, floating far above this city buried in snow and sorrow. The violin sings of its own accord. The first crescendo swells with my love for Caleb. My strings murmur with whispers of death at the Ikhad. A tricky passage brings to mind the mysteries of the Hagramet text, and with three dark chords, I sound the depths of my alliance with Azariah. Finally, the raw desperation pours through, for Sarah, for Leah, for Caleb. Aching sadness, crippling fear, and smothered hope mingle in the music. I play the Shevem as I never have before.

When I finish, the calluses on my fingertips are hard, the skin white. I feel exhausted, but also purged. The room is absolutely silent. I can tell I've done well, more than well. I muddle through the sight-reading excerpts, hardly aware of what I'm playing. After the last snippet of music, it's all over.

"My thanks, Levi," one of the judges says. "Decisions will be mailed in a few weeks."

Nodding awkwardly, I reach for my music. The three women bow their heads, intent on their notes. The only sound is the scratching of their pencils. I walk from the room. Triumphant euphoria surges in my veins, settling to a quieter confidence as I calm down. I can do anything now.

THE SHEVEM STILL swirling through my head, I return to the Street of Winter Gusts and Caleb's bedside. His face is waxy, the skin under his eyes a bruised blue. He tosses under the covers, his breath whistling in his nose.

I sit on the edge of the bed and stroke his face. When he opens his eyes, I begin to sign. I tell him about the Hagramet text and the harmful magic and Azariah's and my plans. My hands fly in complete silence, speeding to the cure.

I'll heal you, I sign. *Soon. I promise.*

He twists under the blankets, pushing his face toward a cooler patch of pillowcase. I brush the sticky hair from his brow and kiss him on the forehead.

Then I walk through the drizzle to Old Spinners' Street.

The pavement is slick and dark with moisture, and the low gray clouds seem to press down on the apartment buildings. Gadi Yakov's worn face is tender when she invites me in. The children are all gathered in Leah's bedroom and start like rabbits when I enter.

"Marah!" Yael and Ilan chorus, swarming me with outstretched arms. Ari claps his hands on Leah's bed. Touched by their affection, I let Yael and Ilan tug me to their sister. She's sitting up, sipping an infusion of bee balm meant to ease her cough. Strands of her now lank hair lie plastered to her temples, and her black eyes have sunk deeper into their sockets. The exhaustion is carved into the hollows of her face.

"I'll send them out, if you want," she says, so softly I have to strain to hear her.

"No, I don't mind," I say, clasping her hands.

"Oh, good. It's lonely without them."

Her hands feel like heated stones in mine. "You're feverish again."

"It's nothing," she says, pulling away, but her cheeks are very flushed.

Ilan distracts me by climbing onto my back. "Do you know any stories, Marah?" he asks.

"She knows lots," Leah says. "Come here. Let Marah breathe."

"Leah tells us stories, but she never gets to the end," Yael informs me.

"I make them up," Leah says when I glance at her. "When

I don't know what happens next, I start a new one. I'm good at beginnings." Her laughter is feathery.

"Leah, you should be resting," I say, prying Ilan's fingers from around my neck. He latches onto my arm instead. I draw Yael to me too, comforted by these warm, innocent bodies against mine.

"I'm tired of resting, Marah." She gives me a significant look. "I'm not going to waste these days."

Right then, Gadi Yakov appears in the doorway and summons the children. "It's time to go outside. In this weather, you won't want your cloaks after five minutes."

"Let's find Raspberry in the park!" Yael says, rushing into the hall. Ilan screams with excitement and dashes after her.

"Do you think Raspberry's all right?" I ask when everyone's gone.

"I have to believe he made it," she says with a faraway expression. Then she asks, "How was your audition?"

"Pretty good. I'm happy about it." I grin, still electrified by my solo. It keeps playing itself over and over in my head.

"But never mind that," I hurry on in an undertone. "Azariah and I have found the cure to the dark eyes in the Hagramet text. The cure, Leah! And Tsipporah's taking us to buy ingredients tonight. You're going to get well, I promise, and everything will be all right."

"Everything's all right when you're here," Leah says. "Sometimes when I'm alone, I feel so angry. When you're here, it's easier to bear."

"You don't believe me," I say. "Why don't you believe me? We're going to make the cure!"

She closes her eyes. "You will. Yes. I—I hope you'll cure Caleb."

"I'll cure you too."

Leah slumps against her pillow. "Marah, it would help if you'd just—"

"I want you to get well, but you act like it's hopeless!" I jump up and storm to the door, but the iciness of the knob on my palm brings me to my senses. I look back. Leah's staring at me, her cracked lips parted.

My heart splinters. I stagger back to the bed. "I'm sorry. I'm sorry, I'm sorry."

She looks at me, tears shimmering in her fathomless eyes. "I don't want to die," she says.

You won't die, I want to say, but instead I say, "I know. Just hang on, all right? Hang on a little longer." I breathe deeply. "I want to hear one of your stories."

Leah half sobs, half laughs. "You're the one who knows real stories."

"I want to hear a story no one's ever read, that has no end."

"Oh, Marah," she says.

18

AT NIGHTFALL, I PLUNGE INTO THE MOIST DARKNESS OF the city, my cloak drawn around my shoulders, my lantern held aloft. Dim lights flicker in windows here and there. Despite the thaw, the air is chilly and fills me with a cold hopelessness. It takes a monumental effort to push on to the Ikhad.

The marketplace is eerily empty. The stalls, draped with canvas for the night, loom in the dark. Two figures hover by the corner roof post next to the book stand, lanterns bobbing between them.

"Marah?" Azariah's voice is high.

"It's me," I breathe, trembling with relief. "Tsipporah?"

She takes a step forward and squeezes my hand in greeting.

"Tsipporah, this is my friend Azariah Rashid," I say, gesturing to where he stands awkwardly apart from us.

In a detached voice I almost don't recognize, Tsipporah

says, "You didn't mention your friend was a kasir."

My heart skips a beat. "He's all right, Tsipporah."

"You give me your word?"

"Yes," I say, moving to stand beside him.

"Very well," Tsipporah says, still sounding distant. I should've told her about Azariah before. "Let's be on our way. We've far to go."

She takes off at a surprising speed. Azariah and I stride after her.

"How was your audition?" he asks.

"Excellent." It feels good to remember it, to remember how sure of myself I felt both while I was playing and afterward. An echo of that assurance washes over me now, and I cling to it.

The neighborhoods begin to change, the apartment buildings giving way to dilapidated tenements and shady boardinghouses. Tsipporah leads us through seedy streets where tramps snore by the gutters and the stench of liquor and horse dung floats in the humid air. Gas streetlights are scarce, and we meet only a handful of workers trudging home from the factories, a few women dragging children inside. I've never been in this part of town, and I feel like an outsider in my own city.

At some point, the cobblestones dissolve into mud that sucks at my shoes. I raise my lantern to get a better look at our surroundings and realize the dwellings have become little more than shacks. We've reached the outskirts of the city.

"Where are we going?" I murmur to Tsipporah.

"The forest," she says.

The forest! When I was small, Father would tell me spooky stories about the forest as he tucked me into bed at night, tales of great bears and crafty panthers, of mysterious lights that lured travelers into ravines. If he only knew where I was now.

Tsipporah hurries onward, and Azariah and I creep after her as a fine rain begins to fall. The lane narrows so much that Azariah's thick wool coat brushes my shoulder. Once, he stops and twists around, holding his lantern high and peering into the darkness behind us.

"What is it?" I ask.

"I thought I heard someone," he says, but there's nobody there. We continue after Tsipporah.

The rain intensifies, and our feet squelch at every step. My mind wanders from the untranslatable Hagramet words to worries about the cost of contraband ingredients, but every few minutes I catch myself mentally playing the Shevem— bowings, fingerings, and all.

After a while, we leave the slum and enter a wide open space. A wall of darkness rises ahead. I breathe in the scent of evergreens and wet earth as the rain descends in curtains through pines and leafless aspen trees. Tsipporah shuffles ahead into the dark, and we follow, tramping on the slippery leaves that carpet the narrow path.

Eventually, I distinguish a light ahead. Then many lights,

more than there should be in these wild woods. Blinking, I step into a clearing after Azariah and stare at the sight before me. Wooden poles sunk deep into the ground support taut cloth roofs. Spruce branches scrape the sides of sodden tents, as well as more outlandish structures improvised from boards and scrap metal. People move briskly through the glade, weaving around each other in a practiced dance. And I hear music. Fiddles, keening over the thrum of hushed conversations, and drums, pounding somewhere unseen. It's practically a village. I can't believe it exists in what I thought was a desolate forest.

"What *is* this?" says Azariah in awe.

"The forest market," says Tsipporah.

"The black market," he says.

"Ha," says Tsipporah. "This isn't all of it."

I throw her a startled look. "This is where the Hagramet grammar came from."

Tsipporah grins. "Very good, Marah."

"But don't the police find you?" Azariah says.

"Of course not," Tsipporah scoffs. "We're too clever. I've been coming here since I was a girl and have never once been caught. Now move along. Night won't last forever."

We advance toward the fire crackling under a proper roof at the center of the clearing, but two men block our way. One is small and thin and looks like a Laishidi immigrant, from the jungle country south of Xana. His coarse, straight black hair gleams in the firelight. The other man is burlier, swarthy. His piercing gaze rests on me and Azariah.

"Who are they, Tsipporah?" he says.

"They're with me," she says. "You can trust them."

The Laishidi doesn't even twitch. "The boy's a kasir, if I'm not mistaken."

Azariah goes rigid beside me.

"Tsipporah's word is good enough," the burly man says with finality. His companion slides grudgingly aside, his eyes still fixed on Azariah. Tsipporah shoves us forward and winks at the men as I wonder at her influence.

While Azariah and I warm ourselves by the fire, Tsipporah flits from one acquaintance to another. Before I've even rubbed the numbness from my fingers, she returns and asks to see our ingredients list.

Azariah extracts a sheet of notebook paper from deep inside his coat. "We need a certain amount of each item, and the more the better, because we want to make as large a batch of the cure as we can . . ."

I stop listening to Azariah's nervous instructions. According to the Hagramet text, a spoonful is a sufficient dose. Much depends on the nature of the unknown ingredients, though. And on the prices. I look away when Azariah pulls out his coin purse, afraid to be associated with such wealth in a place like this.

We agree to split up so we can return to the city as soon as possible. Azariah slips Tsipporah a handful of coins, and she sets off to buy the known ingredients, leaving us to investigate the untranslated ones. I follow Azariah out into the rain, feeling uneasy without Tsipporah. The barely restrained hostility in the sea of faces around us almost makes me take Azariah's hand.

"Tsipporah said she has a friend in there who can read Hagramet," he says, pointing to a large tent.

As we approach, I hear the sound of a violin. The music is showy, studded with flourishes, and even through the soaked cloth, the fiddler's skill is dazzling.

It takes much batting to find an entrance in the endless folds of sopping material. At last, Azariah lifts a dripping sheet of fabric, and I duck inside. The musician breaks off in the middle of a chord. Confronted by seven dirty, unfriendly faces, I fail to produce an audible greeting.

"City kids," someone mutters in disgust.

The fiddler steps toward us, stooping under the tent cloth, his instrument and bow clutched in one fist. An oil lamp illuminates a leathery face with knobby cheekbones and a lustrous mustache.

"Who invited you in here?" he growls.

Feeling Azariah's presence behind me, I whisper, "Adam."

"What's that?"

"Toviah Adam," I manage to say more clearly. "You were playing his 'Winter Caprice.'"

The fiddler's eyes widen, his menacing expression fading.

"Well, well," he says, amused. "What have we here? A little musician?" His companions continue to scowl at me and Azariah, their distrust palpable.

"I play violin," I say.

"Is that so?" the man says, a hard gleam in his eye. He shoves his fiddle at me, as if telling me to prove it.

I hesitate, intimidated by his aggressive manner and the suspicious stares of everyone else in the tent. Then I take the instrument. The scarred violin is a rich red-brown, its scroll carved into a lion's head. Though the Shevem is still coursing through me, my thoughts drift to "Where Wind Blows Not," that concert piece our medsha loved so much for its words of longing. I lift the stranger's bow and draw it across his fiddle's strings.

As I play the melody, I hear a voice begin to sing along. At first, it's only the fiddler himself, but then the others join in until I'm accompanying the whole tent. They recognized the tune, and they all know the words to the folk song.

When I stop playing, their antipathy has melted away. Two wizened old ladies are smiling at me.

"You know your traditional Ashari music," the fiddler says with approval as he takes back his violin. "Who are you anyway?"

"We're friends of Tsipporah's," I say.

"Ah!" he says with new respect. "Why didn't you say so right away? Call me Yochanan. At your service."

Azariah looks expectantly my way, so I scrape up my courage. "We have some words of Hagramet we need translated, sir. We heard someone here can read it . . ."

"That would be me," he says.

"Oh!" I say, startled. "Well, could you . . . ?"

"Can you pay?" Yochanan asks. "Sorry, but I can't be handing out favors, even for Tsipporah."

Azariah opens his purse, and I catch a glimpse of what it contains. In addition to plenty of one- and two-stone coins, he has silver falcons and gold crescents, larger denomination coins I've rarely seen.

Yochanan reaches out a callused hand for the falcon Azariah is proffering. For one heart-stopping moment, he doesn't withdraw his hand, as though the payment is insufficient. I don't have the nerve to bargain. But then he closes his fist.

"That's a fat purse, boy," he says, his voice cooler. Azariah draws himself up, his expression haughty. I realize these are the first words anyone in the tent has addressed to him.

"Show me these Hagramet words," Yochanan says.

Azariah hands him a damp page with the three undecipherable ingredients copied onto it. Yochanan holds the paper close to his nose, his mustache twitching as he mutters to himself.

"Strange words," he says.

"What are they?" I ask.

Yochanan gives me a long look. It is not unfriendly, but he clearly wonders what we're up to. "First, ground cardamom. A foreign spice. Expensive, but available in the city. Might be cheaper here though. Next, black eggs—"

"What?" Azariah interjects.

"Black eggs. Aged till the yolks turn to ash and the whites to amber. Delicacy from Narr, though they made them here too, in the days of Hagram. Potent stuff." Yochanan dips his head toward one of his companions. "Divsha sells them."

"And the last word?" I ask.

"Ah, yes . . . Hope you're rich, because this is the tea."

There's a solemn silence as Yochanan waits for our reaction. But I'm confused. "That's not the word for tea."

"Not the tea you drink every day. The heavenly tea," Yochanan says. "The tales from Hagram all tell of it. But the kingdom collapsed, folks forgot where they came from, and only a few remember the stories."

"So . . . can we buy it?" I ask.

"Yes, but better watch out. Costs a fortune, and it's dead illegal."

"My thanks," Azariah says impatiently. "Can we buy black eggs now?"

"Of course. Divsha!" Yochanan nods to a silver-haired woman. "Got any on you?"

Divsha arches her back as she stands. Despite her hair, she looks young. She can't be Ashari, not with her beaky nose and wide-set eyes. Is she from Narr? I didn't think there were any Narri in Ashara. In school, they always said Narr was the most uncivilized land in the world. Judging by his expression, Azariah's heard the same thing.

Divsha thrusts one hand into her huge, shapeless coat. "How many?"

"Two," I say.

She produces what look to me like two ordinary chicken

eggs. Beginning to grasp how things work around here, Azariah unties his purse again. Divsha names her price, and he hands the coins over without discussion. We mumble our thanks and make to leave.

"Wait!" Yochanan raises the oil lamp higher. "A last word of advice, for free. There's heavenly tea in the next clearing. Find the sand-spawned woman named Basira."

I wince at his vulgarity. To my horror, Azariah spins around and glares at Yochanan.

"The next clearing?" I say, trying to shield Azariah from view.

"Did you think all of Ashara's illegal merchandise would fit in one clearing?" Yochanan smiles. "You'll find Basira in the orange tent, but be careful. She's a strange one. Won't sell to just anyone. Be sure to pay her properly."

"Right," I say, anxious to leave.

"Keep up your fiddling, now," says Yochanan. "And give Tsipporah my greetings."

"We will." I prod the tent cloth until a section billows outward. Azariah and I escape.

"Now what?" he says, his voice throbbing with fury.

"We buy some cardamom. Then we find Basira."

"I can't believe that Yochanan."

"I'm sorry he insulted you. He didn't know you were Xanite. Not that that excuses him." I glance sideways at Azariah. "But it might help if you'd . . ."

"What?" he says through clenched teeth.

"Act a bit less like a kasir," I say apologetically.

"How do you suggest I do that?"

"Keep your head down. And try not to sound so superior all the time."

I hear him suck in air and brace myself for a retort, but he says, "You're right."

Purchasing cardamom proves easy, but I'm starting to feel tired, hungry, and homesick. I don't like being so far away from Caleb. I feel as though I've traveled to another star and left my feverish brother behind.

Azariah grabs my hand as we skirt another tent. The heavy cloth beats in the wind, and it feels like we're brushing past the heaving side of some enormous beast. The lights of the next clearing twinkle through the trees.

It's slow work forcing our way through the tangle of underbrush. Twigs snatch at our clothes and scratch our wet faces. It seems like a miracle when we break through into the second clearing. The bonfire draws us like moths.

While Azariah examines his mud-spattered clothing in the firelight, I peer out into the shadows. Behind us, there's a tiny orange tent set off a little from the others. I nudge Azariah, and we walk toward it.

"Hello?" I call, hoping my voice carries through the drenched cloth.

"Come in," someone replies.

The tent is dark inside, lit only by a tiny oil lamp and now by our lanterns, which we set on the ground. An ancient woman sits at a round wicker table, her hands folded on the embroidered tablecloth. A silver and turquoise ring gleams on her finger.

"I am Basira," the woman says. "Come closer."

The unexpected richness of her voice pulls me deeper into the tent, and I shuffle forward. The lamplight catches in the golden threads of the tablecloth, transforming them into mesmerizing wires of flame.

"Who are you?" asks Basira. Her eyes are light like Tsipporah's, only less green, more like the color of water. I find it difficult to look away from them.

"I'm Marah," I say.

"I'm Azariah." He forges bravely ahead. "We'd like to buy some heavenly tea."

"First I will see what you have to give to me," Basira says. I hold my breath, remembering Yochanan's words. *Be sure to pay her properly.*

She tilts her head as if in invitation, and I notice a couple of stools half-hidden by the folds of the tablecloth. Azariah and I drag them out and sit down.

Basira fixes her attention on Azariah. "You are Xanite, aren't you?"

"Yes," he says, startled.

She addresses him in Xanite, and he replies in the same language, looking self-conscious.

Basira smiles, satisfied. "I will give you the heavenly tea you ask for if you tell me a story."

"A story?" Azariah says, perplexed.

"A Xanite story," Basira adds, gazing serenely at him.

He looks helplessly at me, and I feel a spurt of alarm.

"If it's a tale you want," Azariah says, "Marah knows lots, don't you?"

"Not Xanite ones," I whisper.

"Oh." His forehead creases. "But Sarah says you're good at storytelling . . ."

I shake my head. While I'm reluctant to entrust him with this crucial task, it's clear Basira wants it to be him.

Azariah closes his eyes, and I wait in trepidation. At last he speaks. "I think . . . Maybe . . ." He faces Basira. "I know the Xanite creation myth, the story of the beginning of time written on the temple scroll . . ."

Basira nods.

"It's in Xanite, though," Azariah says shakily, glancing at me.

"You may tell it in Ashari," Basira says.

"All right." Azariah pauses. "Before the river of time began to flow, the waters of the world lay trapped inside a great boulder, larger than the heavens themselves." He closes his eyes. "The boulder rested below the sands of the earth."

Basira's face is glowing with something other than the lamplight.

"These sands wrapped the barren earth in their countless grains. And in the waters inside the boulder under the sand slumbered a spirit, the greatest of the spirits, who is Kohal."

I shiver. I should've had more faith in him.

"There came a time when Kohal awoke and smote the boulder. The waters erupted out of the sands, and a river called Time, huge and invisible, began to flow through the heavens. Outside the waters, other spirits multiplied until they were without number. These spirits are eternal and are with us still, because they are outside Time.

"The river's current gave rise to mortal life. Plants grew thick in its waters: seaweed and flowering vines and trees bearing fruit. The fishes and the great whales swam in its depths, and the eagle and the thrush flew alongside them. All the animals of the desert and the forest and the mountains dwelt on the river's sandy bottom, and humankind walked among them."

I could listen to him for a while yet, but I sense the story is already drawing to a close.

"All mortal life flourishes still in the river of Time," Azariah says solemnly, "but none can ever scrabble onto its banks."

I let out a sigh. There is a brief silence. Basira's eyes are shut, and her expression is faraway, as though she is seeing another land.

Then she takes a breath. "My thanks. The heavenly tea you require is yours."

Without asking how much we want, she hands him a small leather bag tied with a red cord.

"But your price," Azariah says.

"You have shown reverence for where you came from and trust in each other," Basira says. "There are too few people who honor their ancestors or befriend those different from themselves. This tea is yours."

Almost speechless with disbelief, we thank her and duck out of the tent into the night. As new rain patters on my head, I feel as though I'm waking from a dream.

19

IT FEELS MUCH COLDER BACK IN THE FIRST CLEARING, AND
I'm shivering. We find Tsipporah in the swollen crowd
around the fire. She has the cub's foot, the oxalis tubers, and
the perilla oil in a bag tied to her belt, and Azariah and I
have the black eggs, the cardamom, and the heavenly tea.
The three of us plunge back into the dark forest, Azariah and
I trudging behind Tsipporah. The creak of the glistening
black trees and the incessant whisper of the freezing rain are
soothing, or maybe it's just that I'm exhausted.

For a while, nobody speaks. Then Azariah says in an
undertone, "That was bizarre, in the tent with Basira."

"Yes. Your story was good though." I hesitate. "You're
pretty devout, aren't you? I've noticed the Maitaf on your
desk . . ."

He doesn't answer right away. "I like being observant," he
says at last. "In the Maitafi fane, and in the Xanite temple."

"Do you say the prayer to greet the dawn?" It's the only
habit of strictly practicing Maitafi I know of.

"Usually only in the wintertime, when the sun rises late," he says sheepishly.

We emerge from the woods and pass through the slum into the city. Soon the buildings are familiar. Before we reach the Ikhad, Tsipporah stops at a small street that leads to the river.

"This is where we part," she says. "You know your way home from here, and it's time I went home too. Here." She unties the bag containing the rest of the ingredients from her belt. Azariah takes it from her.

"My thanks, Tsipporah," I say, though the words feel inadequate.

"Yes, my thanks," Azariah echoes.

"I wouldn't have done anything less for you, Marah," Tsipporah says. "Go home safely, both of you."

Then she heads toward the river, the tip of her shawl fluttering behind her.

I stifle a yawn. "You should come to my apartment," I tell Azariah. "It's the middle of the night, and we're soaked."

"All right," he says, his expression intensely grateful.

We start trudging toward Horiel, but we haven't gone far when a voice shatters the rain's gentle murmur.

"Azariah! Marah!"

I spin around. Behind us, a figure steps from an alley.

"Channah?" Azariah and I say in confused unison.

She raises her lantern, and her black coat glitters with rain. There's something unsettling in her expression.

"I've been sent to take you to the Assembly," she says,

taking a step toward us. "With the ingredients for the cure."

I gape at her.

"How do you know about the ingredients?" Azariah demands.

"I've been following you," she says. Her face is drawn, her eyes flickering with uncertainty.

"Following us?" Azariah glances anxiously at me, and I remember he thought he heard someone behind us in the slum, on the way to the forest. An age ago.

This makes no sense. What does Channah have to do with the Assembly?

Memories come floating back to me, all her probing questions in the auto, the way she knew about the foreign dignitaries attending the Second Councilor's funeral . . .

"You're a kasir," I say.

"What?" Azariah exclaims.

Swiftly, Channah arranges her hands at chest level and utters a word. Icy shock seizes my muscles, and my legs fuse to the street.

Azariah looks wide-eyed from me to Channah as I struggle against the spell. "You are a—"

He breaks off, turning back to me and dropping his lantern. It clangs on the cobblestones as the flame goes out. He twists his fingers, shouts an incantation, but nothing happens.

"You're a spy!" he shouts at Channah. "The Assembly sent you to keep an eye on us, didn't they?"

Channah doesn't deny it. "Please calm down. I don't want to hurt you," she says, a note of desperation in her voice. "The auto's right up—"

"What've you been doing in our household?" Azariah insists.

Channah swears under her breath. She curls her fingers into another sign and speaks. Black smoke billows into my mind, snuffing out the world around me.

I WAKE UP on the ground, my eyelids leaden. Rolling onto my side, I wince at my stiff back and sore legs. The air around me is cold and musty. I open my eyes and gingerly raise my head. My lantern burns on the concrete floor, illuminating crates stacked against stone walls.

"Marah?"

Azariah is sitting against a large wooden box, so weary he can hardly hold up his head. I feel as spent as he looks.

"Azariah, what—?" I press my palm to my pounding forehead. "Where are we? What happened? Did Channah . . . ?"

"We're in my house," he says, sounding embarrassed. "In a storage room in the basement. I . . . I tried to fight her, but she's a much stronger magician. She brought us in an auto, a government model, and then she smuggled us down here and locked us in. The whole time it was like I was drugged. I helped her *carry* you."

Pressing my hands to my sides, I realize the pockets of my cloak are flat. "The ingredients!"

"She took them all," Azariah says.

I feel like crying, but I'm too exhausted. Then a new wave of panic crashes over me. Mother. She must be beside herself.

"Azariah, I'm so tired."

"I know," he says. "Sleep."

"But we have to—"

"Sleep," he insists, his voice already muffled. "We can't do anything until we rest."

So I stretch out on the floor again, and Azariah extinguishes the lantern.

I expect to sink into slumber at once, but I don't. In the dark, the storage room could be infinitely large or as close as a tomb. My breath keeps holding itself, and I have to release it with a pained gasp. I imagine Azariah's river of time rushing through the blackness, and in it I see faces: the Seventh Councilor, Channah, Melchior, Tsipporah, Basira, then Azariah, Sarah, Leah, Caleb, and Mother. My heart aches, but I don't want it to stop. Better to hurt than to be numb, better to feel than to forget . . .

The next thing I know, I'm staring up into Azariah's pinched face. His brown eyes reflect the lantern light. The floor is unforgiving under my aching back.

I sit up and rub my eyes. "Is it day?"

"How can we tell?" Azariah says. "I feel better though. Are you rested?"

"Rested enough," I say. "Did Channah say anything else to you when she brought us down here?"

"Nothing useful," he says. "She asked me where the

Hagramet book was. I wouldn't tell her, but she said it didn't matter, she knew it was hidden somewhere in my study. It must've been her who broke in there Tenthday night."

I struggle to straighten out my swirling thoughts. "She was eavesdropping on us all along, wasn't she? She must've reported us to the Assembly. But why are they pursuing us so secretively? I felt something was wrong when we thought about telling someone what we'd found, remember? This just proves the Assembly has something to hide."

"But what?" Azariah says. "They want a cure to the dark eyes, everybody does. This should be cause for celebration."

I stand up and walk in a circle around him. "Unless they have some ulterior motive . . . Don't look at me like that. I have no idea what it could be. But it *is* strange that the cause of the dark eyes should be explained in a book the Assembly has banned."

He frowns. "They didn't specifically ban that book, they banned Hagramet books."

"It amounts to the same."

"But Marah, the Assembly instituted the ban a hundred and sixty years ago. It can't have anything to do with the dark eyes."

"Well, when do you think the neutralizing spells were lost?" I ask. "Surely at least a hundred and sixty years ago, since no one remembers them today. What if they were lost *because* Hagramet books were banned?"

He opens his mouth to retort and abruptly closes it, looking uncertain. "Maybe there is some connection," he says at last, "but that doesn't explain what the Assembly is doing *now*."

I purse my lips. "At least you agree they appear to want very tight control over the cure? I wonder if they even want people to have one . . ."

"Of course they must!" Azariah almost chokes on his words.

"Well, we can't just keep talking. We have to get out of here and retrieve the Hagramet books and take back the ingredients."

Azariah swallows. "Assuming we accomplish all that, where do we go?"

"Home," I say, picturing Mother at the kitchen table, her face haggard. "I mean, my apartment."

"Are you sure? Channah knows where you live."

"I don't know what else to do. And I need to see Mother." I glance at the door.

Azariah follows my gaze. "It's locked. And not just with a key."

"You're a magician."

"Didn't I tell you how strong Channah was? I tried while you were unconscious."

I twist the doorknob, but the lock won't budge. I rattle it back and forth a few times and then start pounding.

"No one ever comes down here," Azariah says.

I look around at the bare walls, the dusty crates, the cracked ceiling. "We could try knocking up there."

"I think she thought of that. There are a lot of spells around here."

"How do you know?"

"I can feel them," he says. "The spells draw the ambient magic into currents. It's a tug, like a breeze."

"Then won't other people in the house feel them too?" I say.

"Not unless they come close enough."

I rest my forehead against the door. When it quivers, I jump back, almost losing my balance.

"It moved," I say.

"I didn't hear—"

The door shakes again, and this time we both hear a thud outside.

"It's her," Azariah says. "Get back."

The bolt slides over with a deafening click, and someone peers in, shining a lamp into the storage room.

"God of the Maitaf," says Melchior. His eyebrows arch as he looks from me to Azariah. Our clothes, dried stiff, are plastered with mud and strewn with twigs and dead leaves.

"Go back," Melchior says over his shoulder. He blocks the doorway, straining against whoever's behind him. "Uncork another bottle of mead. I'll be right there. Go!" He elbows someone we can't see and steps into the storeroom, closing the door. "What the hell is this?"

"How did you open that door?" Azariah asks.

"I broke the lock spell."

"You did?" Azariah says with undisguised shock.

Melchior glares at him. "I let people underestimate me. What are you doing down here?" He acts like we've encroached upon his territory. Apparently somebody does come down here.

"Channah shut us in," Azariah says. "You have to help us get out."

"Channah?" Melchior stares at us both. "What's going on? What happened to your clothes?"

Azariah's jaw clenches. "The forest happened. Melchior, we've found a way to cure Sarah, but Channah stole what we need."

"*What?*" Melchior seems unable to form words as disbelief, hope, and anger mingle in his expression.

"Channah's a kasir," Azariah says. "All the spells on this room are hers. I think the Assembly placed her here to spy on Mother and Father."

"We really have to leave," I put in.

"Look," Melchior says with an impatient gesture, "why don't we ask Mother or Father for help? They could—"

"No!" Azariah says. "If we draw them in, it'll bring the whole government crashing down on us, on Channah's side."

Melchior's face hardens. "Fine. But if I help you now, I want all this explained to me. Especially what you said about curing Sarah."

"All right," Azariah says.

"I know how you can leave without being seen," his brother begins, but I cut him off.

"We can't leave until we get what Channah took from us. Where is everyone in the house?"

"Father's at work," Melchior says. "Mother's with Sarah."

"Sarah." Azariah's voice almost breaks. "How is she?"

"Her fever's gone, but the illness is in her chest now. She can't sleep for coughing."

"What about Channah?" I ask.

Melchior frowns. "My friends and I passed through the servants' hall coming down. I'm sure I heard her moving around in her room."

"So she's still here," I say with relief. "Melchior, what if you tell Channah Sarah's asking for her, to get her out of her room?"

"As if Channah cares about Sarah," Azariah says spitefully.

"She has to pretend to, at least," I counter.

The seconds trickle by until Azariah says, "Let's try it. We have nothing to lose."

20

MELCHIOR CRACKS OPEN THE DOOR, PEERING INTO THE gloom. When he beckons us, Azariah and I slither into the corridor and press ourselves against the wall. A rumble of laughter reaches us from somewhere nearby.

"It reeks of Xanite saltweed," Azariah mutters. "Have you been smoking down here?"

Melchior ignores him, concentrating on casting a new spell on the storeroom lock. Then he leads us through a black passageway to a staircase that rises in the shadows. I follow Azariah so closely my nose almost touches his muddied coat. Halfway up the steps, we hear a muffled crash from somewhere in the basement. Melchior curses.

"If I don't get back there soon, they'll destroy the place or come marching upstairs and spoil everything for you. Shimon's half drunk."

"You've got to be joking," says Azariah.

"What do you expect? There's no school." Melchior stops near the top of the stairs. "Wait here."

I hear a prolonged squeak, and then a shaft of light chases away the darkness. Melchior slips out of the stairwell, leaving us in blackness again. His footsteps move away and then return. When he peeks in and nods, Azariah and I pass into a narrow hallway I've never seen before. There are four closed doors ahead, two on either side. Melchior opens the nearest one on the left and waves Azariah and me inside. Before he shuts us in, I glimpse the silhouettes of brooms and the gleaming edge of a bucket. The closet smells of soap.

I hold my breath, listening to the tap of Melchior's shoes. He knocks on the door diagonally across from the broom closet.

"Channah? It's Melchior."

She answers the door, and I can just follow their exchange. Melchior passes on Sarah's request, and Channah demurs. But when Melchior pleads with her, she abruptly consents. The next instant, her door closes with a crack.

Both sets of footsteps start off toward the other end of the house, but a moment later Melchior's heavier ones turn back and pass us by, headed for the staircase to the basement. Then all is quiet in the servants' hallway.

"He's gone to control his friends," Azariah whispers. "Let's hurry."

We step out of the broom closet and cross the hall to Channah's room. Azariah reaches his hand out tentatively.

"Her door's unprotected," he murmurs.

"She couldn't have cast a spell in front of Melchior," I point out.

We enter her room. It's not very big; Azariah's study is more spacious. Just across the threshold, I almost bump into the foot of the bed. The other furniture is plain: a desk and chair against the far wall, a dresser in one corner, a bookcase in the other. The closet door hangs ajar.

Azariah's Hagramet text and my grammar, along with our notebooks and lists, are fanned out on the rumpled bedspread. I gather them up as Azariah seizes the lumpy bag lying on the desk. He plunges his hand into it and holds up the black eggs for me to see. I rush over and peer into the bag while he touches each of the other items: the packet of dried cub's foot, the loose tubers, the flask of perilla oil, and the jar of cardamom.

Azariah and I glance up at each other.

"The heavenly tea's missing," I say.

He runs his hand down the front of his coat. "It was in my breast pocket, by itself."

The surface of the desk is empty now. I turn toward the bookcase, but except for three or four small volumes, it's bare. Azariah checks the desk drawers, to no avail. I begin to wonder, a sick feeling intensifying in my stomach, if the tea is on Channah's person.

"Take these," I say, pushing the books in my arms on Azariah. "Take the ingredients too and go. I'll meet you at the road when I've found the tea."

"What? I'm not leaving you here."

"Go," I insist, starting on the top drawer of the dresser. I don't feel the slightest qualm digging through Channah's stockings. "And find some food if you can, I'm starving. Go, Azariah! Better for her to catch one of us than both of us!"

He leaves, finally, though his face is distorted with clashing impulses. When he's gone, I rifle through Channah's shirts. Nothing. The dresser has three more drawers. This is taking too long.

I try to imagine what Channah would've done with the pouch of heavenly tea. Would she really have hidden it in her dresser while leaving everything else in plain sight on her desk?

Then I notice the closet door again. I pull it open so violently a puff of air rushes past my face. Her winter coat is hanging right in front of me. I slide my hand into one of the pockets, and my fingers brush leather. I grab the little bag, my knees weakening at the sight of the bright red cord securing it.

Stuffing the heavenly tea into my cloak, I flee Channah's room without checking whether the coast is clear. No one's around, though. I tiptoe down the hall, praying I'll recognize where I am in the Rashid mansion once I'm out of the servants' quarters. I turn down a carpeted corridor, stopping at a doorway that opens on my left. Peeking in, I realize it's the living room. I can get to the front entrance from here.

I start to creep across the living room, heading for the opposite doorway and feeling terribly exposed in the wide spaces between the furniture. I'm halfway across when Channah walks into the room from the other side. I freeze, my muscles taut with terror. Channah recovers first and is upon me at once, her hand squeezing the flesh of my upper arm so tightly I let out a gasp.

"How did you get out?" she says, a tremor in her voice. "Where's Azariah?"

I clamp my lips together.

Her eyes widen. "The ingredients." She starts to drag me toward the servants' quarters, but I dig my heels into the carpet.

"Please," I cry, "I just want someone, anyone, to make the cure! Otherwise my brother is going to die!"

Channah's grip loosens. Her resolve seems to waver, and I notice the dark circles under her eyes and the sheen of perspiration on her forehead.

"Why are you doing this?" I whisper.

"The Assembly wants to make the cure," she says mechanically. She swallows, avoiding my gaze.

"But we were going to. Why are you hindering us?"

"Because I have no choice," she says bleakly. "It's too late—I can't—" Her expression fills with anguish. She looks at me, and I get a strange feeling. For weeks, I believed she was a halan, until I learned the truth last night. But right now, she doesn't seem like a kasir. I feel like we are both halani again, like before.

"Marah, just leave. I won't follow you."

"What?" I'm sure I've misheard.

"Go. Hide someplace the Assembly won't find you. Now, Marah!"

I step free of her grasp, dazed by my victory. What happened? Is it a trap?

Channah's jaw tightens, accentuating the skeletal look of her face. "Leave, for God's sake!"

I sprint past her, out of the living room, and down the hall to the front door. The cold hits me as I stumble out of the mansion. And there's Azariah, hunched against the wind and swirling snow, hiding behind the gatepost at the end of the driveway. When I reach him, I fling my arms around him.

"Marah!" he cries, half flummoxed, half relieved. "Do you have the tea?"

"Yes!" I pull away. "God of the Maitaf, I was so scared."

"Me too," he says, his cheeks pink.

I'm still shaking. "Azariah, she let us go."

"What?"

"Channah . . . She let me escape. She told me to hide."

Azariah looks nonplussed. "That doesn't make any sense. Why would she let us go?"

"I don't know. It was like she changed her mind."

He shakes his head. "I don't trust her. We'd better leave."

"Did you have time to find any food?" I ask.

He passes me a bag of dried sweet potatoes. I take a handful and bite into a chewy strip.

We pass through the open gates onto the birch-lined road and trudge toward the city. The snow falls thickly, obliterating hoofprints and tire tracks, muffling and purifying the world. It rises above our ankles, slowing our brisk pace. The air is a soft, sleepy gray, tinged pink by an invisible sunset.

Once in the city proper, I lead the way to my apartment.

When we go by Leah's street, walking in exhausted silence, my throat tightens. It feels like an eternity since I last saw her, yet it was only yesterday.

At last we reach the landing outside my apartment. The floorboards creak under us, and I hear footsteps.

Mother looks out into the hall, her face stiff and ashen. I lurch toward her, and she draws me into the kitchen, squeezing my hands, practically cracking the bones.

"Marah Levi," she says in a strangled voice. "Where have you been?" Her words pulse with relief and fury.

"I meant to come home," I say, swallowing hard. I try to apologize but start to cry instead.

Mother pulls me to her, and I rest my forehead on her shoulder. I make an effort to hold in my tears, but I only feel myself unraveling further.

Somehow Azariah is still standing forlornly on the landing. I'm dimly aware of Mother inviting him in and telling him where he can wash up, and then she and I are floating down the hall. We enter her bedroom and sink onto the edge of the bed.

"Marah," she murmurs. "Marah." She tries to lift my chin, but I just sob into her chest.

She strokes my hair for a few minutes as we huddle together in the chilly room. Her wardrobe looms in the shadows. I used to crawl inside as a child and press my cheeks against her dresses, breathing in the scent of cedar. I remember feeling so safe. I want to feel that way again.

"There, Marah," Mother says. "We'll talk about it in the

morning. You and your friend must be hungry, and you're covered in mud."

She coaxes me to my feet. In the bathroom, I run some water in the tub. As usual, the hot water comes only in fits and starts, but I wash most of the grime off myself. After changing into clean clothes, I join Azariah at the table, too tired to feel embarrassed about the tearstains on my cheeks. He's washed his face and hands, but we don't have any men's clothes to lend him. Mother says she'll borrow something from the neighbors in the morning. We fight to stay awake as she feeds us bread and soup.

After our hasty meal, I show Azariah to my bedroom. In the lamplight, I can see Caleb cocooned in blankets.

"You'll have to sleep on the floor, but there's a mattress," I tell Azariah. "I'm going to sleep in Mother's room."

He nods, lowering the sack of ingredients. I jump at the sound of clinking glass, but Caleb doesn't stir. We bid each other good night, and then I follow Mother to her bedroom.

I WAKE IN the night, disturbed by the touch of small hands on my arm. Blinking sleep away, I push the blankets off and start to sit up. Caleb hovers over me, his whole body trembling. I swing my legs out of Mother's bed and wrap my arms around him.

Caleb starts to cough. On the other side of the bed, Mother snores softly. Anxious not to disturb her, I hurry my brother out of her room. Keeping one arm around his shoulders, I feel my way down the hall.

In our bedroom, Azariah is awake, a dark shadow hunched on the mattress.

"Marah?" he says. "Your brother woke up and . . ."

"Can you light the lamp?" I ask.

I hear him fumbling for it in the dark. He mutters a word, and the flame appears. Caleb wrests himself from my embrace.

You have to go away, he signs.

I ignore this. *You need to get back in bed.*

No. His hair sticks to his forehead, and his black eyes are wide. *You have to leave the apartment or something bad will happen.*

A chill reaches deep into my bones. *Can we wait until morning?* I sign.

No, Caleb signs frantically. *You have to leave now.*

Azariah is standing rigidly near the radiator, staring at us.

"Caleb says we have to go," I whisper. "Now."

Azariah's shoulders sag. "How can he know that?"

"The intuition." I tuck my brother in again, then kick the mattress under the bed to hide any signs of someone else having slept here.

My thanks, I sign to Caleb, whose dark eyes are still fixed on me. *Tell Mother . . .* My heart is breaking. *Tell her not to worry.*

Our departure is a blur, but time slows out in the night, where the freezing darkness eats away at hope. We trudge in silent misery through the rising carpet of snow.

After ages and ages of staggering forward and stumbling

against each other, we stop. We're somewhere in the north-eastern part of Ashara.

"That house there, does it look abandoned?" Azariah whispers.

I nod. A ragged piece of paper nailed to the door flaps in the icy breeze. We go inside, grateful for the relief from the biting wind. The house is silent except for our breathing. Azariah runs his hand over the staircase banister.

"Dust," he says. "Let's go up."

The first room we find upstairs is empty but for a heap of quilts. The eerie desolation of the house makes my skin crawl, but Azariah just rips into the dark hill of blankets. Without another word, we both collapse onto the floor, wrapping ourselves in things we can't even see.

21

IN THE MORNING, THE ROOM IS AWASH IN SUNLIGHT. I RUB my eyes and sit up. Azariah is already awake, kneeling over the Hagramet text and the translation notebook, packets of ingredients laid out all around him.

I shake off the faded quilts and, taking care not to step on anything, move toward the window. The snow has muted the tracks we made last night. I strain to read the sign on the corner townhouse.

"We're on the Street of the Weavery," I say. "Gishal District."

Azariah nods. "We're going to have to go out. I took a look around the house while you were still sleeping. There's almost nothing useful here besides a few more blankets, and as far as I can tell, the gas is shut off. And we have nothing to eat, of course."

"We need more ingredients too," I say. "How are we going to buy everything we need?"

Azariah produces his coin purse from inside his coat. "I still have money."

I brighten. "I thought Channah had taken everything."

"No, she was quite a scrupulous thief," he says bitterly.

I consider what day of the week it is. After these tumultuous last nights, it takes me a moment to figure out it's Thirdday.

"The Ikhad's open today," I say. "We're lucky. We can find the rest of the ingredients, and some food."

"We need a stove," Azariah says. "Not just to cook, but to make the cure. So that means fuel, and some lanterns would be handy too . . . It's going to be awkward trying to carry all this back here without attracting attention."

I rub my cold hands together. "Maybe if we had someone to help us . . ."

Azariah ponders this for a second. "Melchior."

I don't answer right away.

"Marah, he's the only one. Our parents will ask too many questions, and mine are in enough trouble already."

"You're right," I say. "But how are we going to get in touch with him?"

"I wonder if he might go looking for me at your apartment," Azariah muses.

"That's it!" I pick my cloak up off the floor and throw it on.

"Where are you going?"

"The Maitafi Graveyard."

"What?"

"My mother works there. She can send a message to Melchior for us."

"I'll come with you," Azariah says, rising.

"No. Go to the Ikhad. Buy the rest of the ingredients, if you can, and anything else you can easily bring back. Food."

He nods. "Be careful, Marah."

"You too."

THE MAITAFI GRAVEYARD lies at the edge of Gishal District, near the city limits. When I reach its wrought-iron gates, I follow a tamped-down path to a low building just inside the cemetery walls. To my right is a desert of blindingly white snow, concealing hundreds of graves. I can distinguish a few scattered trees, and in the distance, a clump of dark-clad men. Grave diggers.

Inside, the administrative building is like a cave. I press myself against the stone wall, blinking as my eyes adjust. Then I hear her voice.

"—Fourthday, yes. Which fane?"

Several men converse in low voices, huddled together at the counter along the far wall. I glimpse Mother between their heads. She's bent over a black book, writing.

At last, she says, "It's taken care of. I'm sorry I can't spare the litter bearers until—"

"The fane has its own," one of the men interrupts. "But we have no mourning cloth left, and the congregation has no funds . . . We're trying to buy medicine, help a member who was fired by the kasiri . . ."

"Wait here a moment," Mother says. "Another fane left me a new bolt of cloth."

She disappears through a doorway and returns with a length of blue linen, which she spreads out on the countertop. "Will this be enough?"

"It's too much," one of the men says. "He was five years old . . ."

His voice breaks, and Mother stiffens. "Please take it all," she says, folding the cloth.

The men exit in silence, throwing me curious glances as they pass. When the door closes, Mother covers her face with her hands.

"Mother!" I rush to the counter.

She turns, gripping the edge of the countertop. "Marah."

"Mother, I—"

"Two policemen came to the apartment before daybreak," she says, opening a hinged gate in the counter. She draws me into the back room, where a bolt of blue linen lies partly unrolled on a table, a pair of heavy scissors nearby.

"What happened?" I ask.

"They searched the place for you and Azariah. When they questioned me, I told them I hadn't seen you since Firstday. They left in a fury."

Abruptly, she embraces me. The words I mean to say are stuck in my throat.

"That's not all," she says, her voice muffled. "After sunrise, someone else came. Melchior Rashid. He was looking for his brother."

I pull away. "What did you tell him?" I ask urgently.

"I didn't know what to say. He said he'd return in the evening."

"When he does, tell him where we are." I give her the address of the abandoned house. "But you mustn't come. Tell Melchior to."

"Why mustn't I come?" Mother says, clutching my shoulders. "Tell me what's going on, Marah!"

Mustering the steadiest voice I can, I say, "There is a cure for the dark eyes."

"The books you and Azariah have been studying?" Mother asks. "The rare herbs Tsipporah went with you to buy?"

I nod.

"I don't understand. Why have you kept this cure a secret, when all of Ashara needs it? Where do the police come in?"

I tell her everything, leaving out only what would just alarm her further, like the dinner with the Seventh Councilor and Channah catching me in the Rashids' living room. Mother looks shocked enough as it is.

"Do you believe me?" I ask when I reach the end.

"After this morning, how can I not believe you?" Mother says. "But I don't understand the Assembly's intentions in all this."

"Neither do we," I say. "That's why we're going to hide until we've made the cure. How . . . how is Caleb?"

"The same. The downstairs neighbor is watching him today." She strokes my cheek. "How can I let you go?"

I squeeze her hand. "We have to do this."

Mother hunches her shoulders against some invisible tempest. "I'm making a mistake, Marah. Keep me from making this mistake. If your father were here, he would not let me let you go."

There's a sharp pain lodged in my heart. "You're not making a mistake. I'm doing this for Caleb."

She gazes at the shimmering blue cloth pooled on the weather-beaten tabletop. I wonder if she's looking into the past, remembering the last time Caleb was gravely ill. Or how empty the apartment felt after Father died.

There's a noise outside, and we glance up. The grave diggers pass by the window, their shovels swinging, too dirt-caked to glint in the sun.

"I have to go now," I say. "Soon I'll bring Caleb the cure."

"I'll wait for you," Mother says. "At home. I'll arrange for the grave diggers and the litter bearers to take care of everything here while I'm gone. . . ."

"My thanks. And send Melchior. Please."

She holds my gaze for a moment before saying, "I will."

AZARIAH RETURNS TO the abandoned house shortly after I do, bearing a sack of provisions and ingredients. To eat, he's bought a loaf of bread, a huge wedge of cheese, some hard sausage, and an abundance of dried fruit. For the cure, there are more herbs and spices.

"I didn't get the yellownut oil," he says. "The vendor at the Ikhad was out. I can try a shop tomorrow."

"Or maybe Melchior can get it for us," I say. I tell him about seeing Mother at the Maitafi Graveyard.

After indulging in a filling lunch, we spend the afternoon reading and rereading the translated instructions, practically committing them to memory. I study which ingredients are separated, the order in which they are combined, and the different temperatures at which the potion must be kept for various intervals of time.

Azariah focuses on the spells he must cast, practicing the incantations separately from the hand shapes. After about an hour, he switches to trying to recreate the neutralizing spell again. Out of the corner of my eye, I see him bending his fingers into intricate arrangements. A sharp scent permeates the bedroom as he casts an initial spell. Then he mumbles an incantation over and over, modulating through different sounds.

"I've got to be close," he bursts out at one point. "I think the hand shapes are right because *something's* moving. The magic is like sludge though."

We take a break to compose a list of additional items we need from the outside world. As dusk falls, we pace the bedroom to ward off the numbing cold. I wish I had my violin with me. I haven't touched an instrument in almost two days, and after all those weeks of intense practicing, it feels like a part of me is missing.

The thump downstairs comes after nightfall. Crouched in the corner, wrapped in a blanket, I almost choke on one of the last sweet potato strips.

"It's him," I say, coughing.

Azariah goes down to investigate. The creak of the steps announces his return with someone else. Then the bedroom door swings open, and Melchior sets a flickering lantern on the floor.

"*This* is where you're living?" he says.

"We could use some help," Azariah says, following him in.

"You'd better tell me what you're up to," says Melchior, his face dark with worry. When we remain mute, he tosses a damp newspaper onto the floor.

"What's that?" says Azariah.

"Take a look."

I crawl out of my blanket and seize the paper. My eyes are drawn to the black numerals on the front page.

DEATH COUNT: 398

Feeling dizzy, I turn the page.

CITIZENS!
ANYONE WITH INFORMATION CONCERNING THE
WHEREABOUTS OF THE KNOWN SUBVERSIVES
MARAH CHAVAH LEVI
AND
AZARIAH JALAL RASHID
SHOULD IMMEDIATELY CONTACT A
GOVERNMENT OFFICIAL.
THOSE WITHHOLDING INFORMATION OR AIDING

THE INDIVIDUALS NAMED ABOVE SHALL BE
ARRESTED AND IMPRISONED.

I gasp, and Azariah leaps to my side, stooping to read the notice. The wavering light makes the shadows play wildly on his face, striping the horror there.

"The police came to our house last night," Melchior says. "They wanted you and Marah, and they wouldn't say why."

"What did Channah do?" I ask.

"Channah's disappeared," Melchior says. "She was gone by the time the police arrived."

"She went to the Assembly," says Azariah.

"Are you sure?" I say. "She let us escape with the ingredients for the cure. Isn't that aiding us?"

"Well, clearly she's a practiced liar," Azariah snarls.

"But why would she go back to the Assembly after—?"

Melchior clears his throat pointedly. "This cure. What is it? And why is the Assembly after you? Surely it can't be because you've found a cure."

"We haven't made it yet," I say. "It looks like the Assembly wants to silence us and take absolute control over the cure, but we don't know why."

Melchior looks between me and his brother, still unsatisfied. Sighing, Azariah invites him to sit and offers him a handful of dried apples, which he refuses. Then Azariah tells him the story from the beginning.

When he's done, Melchior is silent for a long time. Eventually, he says, "It's a lot to take in."

Azariah hands him our list. "Do you think you could bring us these things? The stove is especially important."

Melchior's hand closes around the page ripped from the notebook. "I'll bring you what you need."

"My thanks," Azariah says.

"Then I could stay and help you," Melchior begins, but Azariah shakes his head.

"Please, I'd rather you stayed with Mother and Father and Sarah. The government mustn't become suspicious of you too."

"I'm good at being unremarkable," Melchior says with a bitter smile. "But Azariah, that's another thing. Mother and Father are at the breaking point. First you go and disappear on them, then the next thing they know, the government wants your hide."

Azariah's face is pale and stretched. "Tell them I'm all right. But nothing else."

After Melchior leaves, something new occurs to me. "He could be arrested for helping us."

"He'll be all right," Azariah says with conviction. "Melchior can take care of himself."

DURING THE NIGHT, another snowfall blankets the city. Melchior returns late in the morning, a sack flung over his shoulder and a big jug under his arm. The frozen breath of winter howls into the house after him.

In our bedroom workshop, he first takes out new provisions: dates, jars of vegetable soup, wizened apples, bread, cured meat, and a bag of hard candy. There are also two mismatched tea glasses and a small tea tin.

"That's water," Melchior says, pointing at the jug. "The ingredients you need are in the bag. And I brought you a stove, a thermometer, and matches." His brow furrows as he sits down on the floor. "There was an article in this morning's paper assuring everyone the Assembly's still making good progress on the cure."

"I think they're lying," I say. "If they're pursuing us and trying to keep our discovery quiet, I seriously doubt they're developing a cure themselves."

"Do you mean they never even tried to find a cure?" asks Melchior.

Azariah makes a sound of dissent.

"Of course they must've tried," I say. "Before they learned we'd found one."

Melchior rubs his chin with his knuckles, still skeptical. "The only possibility . . . Maybe they're afraid there won't be enough of the cure, and they want to heal the people they like first."

I shudder as the Rashid brothers share a look filled with dread. I imagine they're thinking their family isn't among the Assembly's favorites.

"For that matter," Melchior adds, "how much of the cure will there be in this first batch?"

"We're not sure," Azariah says.

"A dose is only a spoonful," I say. "I'd guess we'll have enough to heal dozens, but not hundreds."

"You won't even be healing dozens holed up in here," Melchior says.

I look down. I don't like to think that he's right.

"Our first objective is to save Sarah and Caleb," Azariah says in a fragile voice.

"Caleb?" says Melchior.

"My brother," I say.

Melchior looks at me again, his lips parting silently. Then he says, "I've been thinking about what you said yesterday. Isn't it true the cure won't be enough if those neutralizing spells aren't revived? The harmful magic will keep building up."

"Let's worry about one thing at a time," I say.

Melchior concedes with a tilt of his head.

"Have the police come back to our house?" Azariah asks.

"No," says his brother. "I'll keep an eye out though. And I'll watch for you too. You *will* be coming home, won't you?"

"With the cure," Azariah says fervently. "Maybe even tomorrow, if all goes well."

Melchior rises. "I'll come back tomorrow morning. Then we can go home together."

"I doubt we'll finish making the cure before tomorrow afternoon," I say.

"I'll come early anyway. Just to check on you." Melchior retreats into the corridor and adds, "Good luck."

No sooner has he left than I reach for my notebook and Azariah starts fiddling with the little laboratory stove. In spite of everything, excitement sparks in my chest. The cure's going to be real.

We begin by pouring some water into the cooking pot Melchior brought us. While this heats on the stove, I compulsively check the original Hagramet text, mouthing the ancient words and searching for the slightest translation error.

A quarter of an hour later, Azariah says, "It's bubbling. Can I begin the first spells?"

I hesitate. The spells are the aspect of this whole endeavor that troubles me the most. Part of it is an instinctive distrust of magic. The other part is the fear that the spells Azariah learned aren't identical to the ones cast over a thousand years ago. But he's trusted me as a translator, so I owe it to him to trust him as a magician. Besides, at this point we don't have the luxury of avoiding risky gambles.

"Go ahead," I say. "I'll start chopping the oxalis roots."

We don't talk much as we work except to confer on particular points of the instructions or to allot ourselves tasks. The water comes repeatedly to a boil. First, we dissolve a generous measure of beet sugar into it. Later, we toss in minced oxalis tubers and sprinkle dried cub's foot into the pot. Azariah combines all the dry spices, including the ground cardamom, and performs some more of his layering spells over them, while I soak half the heavenly tea leaves in the perilla oil and the other half in the yellownut oil. We add all these mixtures to the potion at the appropriate times and allow it to simmer.

In some ways, preparing the cure feels like practicing for my audition. The fierce concentration is the same. So is the methodical nature of the work. Unlike when I was learning my Shevem solo, though, Azariah and I only have one chance to get through the whole recipe, and we can't afford to make a single mistake.

While the herbal brew bubbles gently, we peel the black eggs. I prick my thumb on a jagged fragment of shell and lick away the blood. Azariah cleans the knife Melchior supplied and slices the eggs, grimacing. "Yochanan called these a delicacy?"

What were once the egg whites do in fact look like dark amber, except more gelatinous, and the yolks are an unappetizing gray. Their sulfurous odor mingles with the acrid smells left in the wake of Azariah's spells. Despite our misgivings, we dutifully drop the slices into the pot at the right moment.

The next two hours involve depositing bundles of herbs into the cure and fishing them out again when they've steeped long enough. It all feels false, more like a science experiment than real medicine.

Near the end of the day, we reach the point where the mixture must cool and thicken overnight. We switch off the stove and set the pot under the window.

"I'm starving," says Azariah. "Where are those dates?"

We fall upon the food Melchior brought us. Our stomachs filled, there's little to do but go to bed. The sooner we do, the faster morning will come.

"Good night, Azariah," I say.

"Good night, Marah."

Swaddled in cast-off blankets, I curl up against the relentless cold. Strains of the Shevem echo in my ears. Maybe somewhere far away the Qirakh judges are making a decision about me. With the high of my audition long gone, it's all too easy to fret about every flaw in my performance. I definitely messed up that last scale, and I've since realized all the mistakes I made in the sight-reading.

I have to get into that school. If I do, I'm sure everything will be all right. School is something normal, something stable to look forward to after this frightful time is over.

If only the night weren't so long.

22

"MARAH, COME LOOK!"

I fling off my blankets, gasping at the chilly air. The dawn light has just touched the rooftops across the street, and the windowpanes glitter with frost. Azariah is prodding the cure. He holds up a wooden spoon, and the golden syrup hangs down in ropes, flowing back into the pot.

"It's thickened perfectly!" I say.

"Here, have an apple," Azariah says jubilantly, ripping open the sack of provisions.

"We're not done yet," I say, but I can't stop smiling.

In fact, there is still much to do. Though most of the ingredients have already been added, today's instructions prove trickier, with more precise temperatures and steeping times and more spells. More than once, we halt the entire process for as long as we safely can to consult the original Hagramet and discuss my interpretation again. By the time the cure has completed its final stretch of simmering, it's past noon. I've licked seven successive pieces of hard candy down to nothing out of sheer nervousness. But now, as we switch off the stove, searing joy wells up in my heart, almost as painful as sadness.

"We can bring it to Caleb and Sarah today," I say, scarcely able to believe it. "It just has to cool a bit."

"Shouldn't take long in this freezing house," Azariah says, grinning.

Only over a hurried lunch do we realize Melchior never came.

"Do you think something happened to him?" I ask, feeling shaky inside.

"He can take care of himself," Azariah says again, though he sounds less sure this time.

"Maybe he thought he'd be followed," I say.

"Then he was right to stay away."

The cure is still warm, so I make a pot of tea while we wait. As I gulp down my drink, a thought I've been pushing away nudges up against my mind again.

"Azariah . . . don't you think our homes are being watched?"

"What are you saying?" he says, an edge to his voice. "It's dangerous to deliver the cure, so we should wait?"

I press the hot tea glass to my cheek. "I was thinking last night. I know a way of getting to my apartment without going through our building door. But your house is isolated, and that road is so exposed . . ." His expression makes me falter.

"I don't care," he says. "I'm going. Melchior said he'd watch for me, remember?"

We finish our tea in silence. Then we gaze into the pot under the window. The cure is golden brown and slightly viscous. It's translucent enough for us to see the unsavory sediment of blackened tea leaves, crumbled black eggs, and other herbs crusting the bottom of the pot.

"It looks revolting," Azariah says. "What if we've done something wrong?"

"Have some faith," I say, sick with anxiety myself. "We were very, very careful."

I take the flask that once held the perilla oil and he the one for the yellownut oil, and we each scoop up a small amount of the cure. I make sure to take enough for Caleb and Leah.

"Come straight back," I tell Azariah as he tucks away Sarah's dose. "After this, we have to decide how to get the cure to the rest of Ashara."

We part ways in the deep snow outside, the wind choking off our voices. As I flounder around the block, the brittle layer of ice on the new snow cracks under my feet. A cart rolls past, followed by a few mournful pedestrians.

Guarding the flickering hope in my heart, I walk toward Horiel District. A swish of black catches my eye. I look up and duck my head again. A spectacled woman stalks past, her haughty gaze sweeping the street, her black coat rippling around her boots. Is she an ordinary kasir or a police officer in plainclothes hunting for us? I clutch the flask deep in my cloak and hold my breath until she's gone.

Finally, I near the Street of Winter Gusts, and though I'm burning to see Caleb, I make a cautious approach. With the hood of my cloak obscuring my face, I walk past our street and turn onto the next one. There are no kasiri in sight, no one who looks especially watchful, but my heart thumps nonetheless. I wait until the street is deserted and enter the apartment building directly behind mine.

In the entryway, I find the door to the basement and descend the dark stair. In Horiel, the apartment buildings' lower levels are all connected through a series of mostly unlocked doors. Caleb and I used to play down here among the boilers and the coal, exploring mysterious rooms and getting lost in the maze.

The basement is pitch black, of course, and I didn't think to bring a lantern. Feeling my way along the wall with one hand, I shuffle forward, skirting a pail, a few tools, a discarded chair. The obstacles seem endless, and I want to scream with impatience. In my blindness, I find myself reliving with terrifying clarity the futile race toward Father's steelworks. My legs twitch at the memory.

When I reach the wall opposite the stair, I sweep my hand across it till I hit a doorknob. The door swings open. I trip over the threshold into the basement of our apartment build-ing. This is more familiar territory, and I swiftly find my way up to the entrance hall. From here, I pound up the staircase, wiping my blackened hands on my pants as I climb.

When I reach the fourth floor, I burst into our apart-ment, excitement and terror mounting in my chest. From our bedroom comes the sound of quiet singing. I nudge the door open.

"Marah!" Mother leaps from the edge of the bed as though she's seen a ghost.

"I have the cure," I say, my heart twanging.

Caleb stirs and opens his eyes. I'm in time. This nightmare is about to end. I'm so thankful I could weep. Instead I draw the slender flask out of my pocket. In the bottle, the cure glows like honey.

"Bring him something to drink," I tell Mother.

While she's in the kitchen, I sit on the edge of the bed and cradle Caleb's face in my hand. I can see the blue veins in his eyelids and temples. Mother reappears with a glass of lukewarm tea. My hands shaking, I uncork the flask and tip a mouthful of the cure into the glass, trying to forget I'm about to feed my brother a concoction invented by a long-dead civilization.

Mother swirls the tea and raises Caleb's head, bringing the glass to his mouth. We watch in anxious silence as he drinks. After swallowing the last gulp of tea, he sinks back onto his pillow, his lips shining. His eyelids flutter shut. He looks just as he did before.

"Give it time," Mother says, reading my thoughts.

It feels good to be sitting with her, at Caleb's bedside, the three of us together. Thinking Caleb has fallen asleep, I brush the hair from his forehead. He rouses at my touch, opening his eyes, and I gasp.

The darkness is beginning to fade from his irises. His

eyes are still darker than normal, but they're unmistakably brown, a rich brown like the color of cloves.

"Mother," I say in a hushed voice, though she's already seen. "It's working."

Caleb gazes questioningly at us, bewildered by our excitement.

Your eyes are brown again, I sign, tingling with joy.

I linger a few more minutes before rising from the bed. It's almost impossible to leave, but I must go to Leah now. Holding the corked flask in my fist, I edge toward the hallway.

"When will you be back?" Mother says, her haunted eyes following me.

"Soon," I say. She knows as well as I do the battle isn't won, but what can I tell her when Azariah and I don't know what we're going to do next?

I leave the same way I came, through the basements, and emerge in the sunlight on the next street over. The coast looks clear, so I walk to the end of the block and peek around the corner. A tall kasir woman is striding down the avenue in my direction, and this time there's no doubt: a silver badge flashes on her coat.

I recoil and press myself against the bricks just underneath the street sign. If there are police in Horiel, they're looking for me.

I dart into the nearest apartment building. A young boy is in the foyer, fetching the mail.

"Who are you?" he says, his eyebrows dipping into a suspicious frown.

"I'm—meeting a friend." I take long breaths over my galloping heartbeat.

The boy scowls, but he retreats up the stairs. I wait in the unfamiliar entryway for as long as I can bear. Then I start counting. Only when I reach two hundred do I dare crack open the building door.

Instead of returning to the avenue where I saw the kasir, I take a roundabout path through un-shoveled alleys to the Avrams' apartment. Gadi Yakov answers the door. At the sight of me, she goes very still. The hope and triumph I felt at home have disappeared, replaced by a feeling of deadness, like a thick fog.

"Come in, Marah," she says at last, her voice brittle. "Are you in trouble? You're welcome here if—"

"No," I say, confused. "I came for Leah . . . I came to . . ."

I make a sudden movement toward the corridor, but Gadi Yakov holds me back.

"Marah," she says, her gaze filled with pain and pity, "Leah's gone."

I draw an excruciating breath. No. It can't be true. I would have known. Like with Father. I would have sensed it.

"When?" I breathe.

Gadi Yakov closes her eyes briefly. "She died five nights ago."

It's difficult to count back when we've been on the move so much, but I know that was the night Azariah and I went to the forest. The night Channah captured us.

"I want to see," I say numbly.

"See what?" Gadi Yakov says, alarmed.

I brush past her, rushing to the end of the hall before she can stop me. The bedroom is empty.

"Marah." Gadi Yakov is in the corridor behind me.

"I have to go," I say in a voice not my own.

"If you're in any danger, we'll protect you," Gadi Yakov says, sounding broken. "You're Leah's best friend. You're like another daughter to me."

"I can't stay," I say, clutching the flask inside my cloak. Leah floods my mind, memories, fragments of conversations. Leah laughing, holding Ari, tuning her violin. The images crowd inside me, and yet I still feel a vast emptiness.

I sway in the drafty stairwell, deaf to Gadi Yakov's parting words. Maybe I'll come back tomorrow and Leah will be here. Part of me believes it. Part of me knows it's not true, knows I won't come back, knows Leah will never be anywhere again.

In the street, a bitter gust caresses my face. For once, the cold can't penetrate deeply enough. I want to feel it in the marrow of my bones, but I don't. I feel nothing.

At the sound of crunching snow, I look up and see billowing black coats. I hold still, almost convinced I'm invisible.

"Stop," says a square-jawed kasir in a voice crisp with authority. He opens his coat to reveal the metal insignia pinned to his vest: the diamond-shaped badge of the First Councilor's Corps.

I glance up and down the street. Empty.

"She's the right age, and this is her neighborhood," says

his companion. I'm almost certain it's the tall woman I saw before. She keeps her gray-green eyes trained on me as she circles behind me. "Are you Marah Levi?"

I bolt. But the gap between the two kasiri that looked wide enough a moment ago snaps shut, and I run straight into the man's pillowy stomach. He grunts, staggering, but the woman seizes me by the upper arms, her hands like talons.

"Let me go," I shout, even though I know anyone who hears me will take one look at the kasiri and draw the curtains across their windows. "My name's not Marah Levi."

"Then why did you run?" the woman demands.

My mind scrambles for the right words. I can't afford another error.

"I was scared!" I bleat. Who wouldn't flee when accosted by two official-looking kasiri in the street? "I'm just on my way home."

"What's your name?" asks the man, brushing off his coat.

"Leah Avram," I say. The wind rushes through my ears, and I feel light, too light.

"She could easily be lying," says the woman.

"Look, Avimelech, we can't detain every fourteen-year-old girl we—"

"We're five blocks from her apartment, Barak." The woman's grip on my arms tightens, and I suck in my breath.

"Fine," says Barak. His gaze drills into me. "We'll accompany you home so you can show us your papers. Go on, lead the—"

"Marah!"

God of the Maitaf. The kasiri start. Channah is standing at the mouth of the nearest alley.

"It *is* her," Avimelech says, clutching me to her.

"What are you doing here, Yishai?" says Barak. For a second, I don't know who he's talking to, but then I realize Hadar probably isn't Channah's real surname.

Sarah's tutor descends upon us, her black coat flapping. "Let her go!"

What is she doing? My captors gape at her, but Avimelech recovers first.

"So, our rogue spy resurfaces at last?" I can hear her contemptuous smile as I fight to break free of her. "Don't tell me you've been lurking in Horiel ever since you let the children escape the Rashids' house."

"You cannot do this," Channah says, her face blazing. "To save the kasiri and let the halani die . . . It's unforgivable."

I stop struggling. Save the kasiri? Let the halani die?

"Can this be?" says Avimelech, still holding my arms. "Yishai wants to save the sparkers?"

"Treason," mutters Barak. "They should never have assigned her to pose as a sparker. She was bound to revert."

"Oh, that's right," Avimelech says. "You were a changeling, weren't you, Channah?"

Channah's hands move like lightning. Avimelech screams, doubling over. I burst from her loosened grip and take three steps before the air itself seems to bind me, like the sticky threads of a spider's web. I don't know which of them cast the spell, but I can't run. When Barak lunges for me, Channah darts in front of him, and they collide.

"The girl, Barak!" Avimelech shouts between incantations directed at Channah. The kasiri are all on their feet again, locked together by invisible forces, their hands contorted to shape the magic, their lips forming precise syllables. Dull flashes of light flit between them.

Barak stumbles toward me again, but Channah shouts a word, twisting her fingers, and he strains against invisible fetters. The women's hands move like fighting birds. Channah chokes out another spell, and both her adversaries cry out.

"Listen to me, Marah!" Channah shouts. "The Assembly wants the cure for the kasiri. They will never give it to the halani. If you're captured, the sparkers will die. Now run!"

She looks me straight in the eye and aims a spell at me. My unseen shackles burst even as I pull against them, and I fall headlong onto the street.

"Traitor!" Avimelech screams as I drag myself up. Her face is radiant with hatred, all of it focused on Channah as she sets her fingers into an intricate sign.

Channah's hands are between spells, and she gathers them to her chest, as if to shield herself. Then Avimelech utters a word, and silver leaps from her palms. Channah shudders and collapses. A silent scream burns up through my throat.

"God of the Maitaf!" cries Barak. "You didn't have to kill her!"

I hear the horror in his voice, but then I'm running, darting down the narrowest alleys in Horiel, seeking the places the kasiri won't go. The wind freezes my cheeks, but I can feel the sweat under my arms. Channah betrayed everyone, and now she's dead. Ripples of shock sweep across my skin. I keep running.

IT TAKES HOURS to return to our hideout. I dare not venture onto any thoroughfare, choosing only the darkest passages. When I reach the abandoned house, Azariah isn't there. It's long past dusk, and the cold engulfs my bones. Inside I feel an icy nothingness.

I stumble across the bedroom, groping for a violin case that isn't there. I need to play my grief, I need to play to find it. I need the music to teach me how to feel again. I can imagine ripping anguished chords from the strings, the violin screaming while I cannot. But I have no instrument here.

So instead I light a lantern, wrap myself in a quilt, and huddle under the window. I tell myself I'll never see Leah again, but I can't muster any response. I tell myself I saw Avimelech kill Channah before my eyes, but I feel only raw emptiness.

I don't know how long I've been watching the flame quiver in the lantern when I hear the door scrape downstairs. Moments later, Azariah walks gingerly into the bedroom. His eyes are blank and chilling, his coat dusted with snow.

"Marah," he says tonelessly.

I start to rise, the quilt slithering from my shoulders, but I don't have the strength to stand. Azariah sinks to the floor beside me, and I cling to him, or maybe he clings to me, just to have something to hold on to. My tears fall soundlessly as I tremble against Azariah. At last I let him go, wiping my face on my sleeve.

"What is it?" he asks hoarsely. "Not Caleb?"

"No. I gave him the cure. It works, Azariah, his eyes are brown again . . ." My voice quavers. I can't bear my happiness and grief at once. I feel like I'm going to split open.

"It's Leah," I say. "I was too late." Through my tears, everything glitters. I wipe my eyes again and see the look on his face. "What's wrong?"

He takes a ragged breath. "Sarah is dead."

The pain is like a dagger driven under my breastbone. For some reason, it stops up my tears. Azariah scoots away from me on the floor. He brushes the back of his hand across his eyes. I stand up and edge toward the hallway.

"No, don't go," he says, looking straight at me, his eyes glistening. I return to his side. I can't imagine Sarah gone. This is all wrong. I want to be with my brother, and Azariah should be with his family.

When he has mastered himself, he says, "It was Melchior who told me. I never even made it to the house. He was coming to the city to tell me about Sarah, and we met on the road. He said when he got home yesterday, Sarah's fever had spiked, and she started fighting to breathe and . . ."

He lets out a shuddering breath and then says in a muffled voice, "She died last night. I can't believe it came to this. If we'd been one day ahead . . . Marah, she was eight years old."

We sit in the semidarkness, contemplating the unfathomable depths of the world's injustice and wondering if we will ever be able to forgive ourselves.

23

"THERE'S SOMETHING I HAVE TO TELL YOU," I SAY IN THE morning between sips of tea, breaking our night-long silence.

Azariah, sitting under the window with his knees drawn up, looks expressionlessly at me.

"Channah's been killed." Haltingly, I describe what happened.

"They sent Avimelech after you?" he says. "She's high up, being groomed for the Assembly . . ." He snaps out of his torpor. "Are you sure Channah said the Assembly intends for the halani to die?"

Hearing him say it so bluntly, the shock reverberates in me again. "I'm sure."

"*Keeping* the cure from the halani? But it's so—"

"It's true," I say. "When Channah told me, Avimelech called her a traitor."

Azariah says nothing.

"Don't you see?" I say, gripping my glass. "Channah never went back to the Assembly. She changed sides."

"If she hadn't been working for them in the first place, we would've finished the cure in time for Sarah," he says, trembling with rage. "What even made her switch? She just ended up dead."

Avimelech's changeling remark burns bright in my memory. "Azariah . . . she was born a halan. I think when I told her Caleb was dying, when I asked her why she was doing this, she remembered. Maybe she had a brother once, or maybe she thought of her birth parents—"

"I don't want to hear it," Azariah says.

I wait until he looks calmer before saying, "I think we should concentrate on two things: getting the cure to people who need it and revealing the truth about the cause of the dark eyes to everyone. Kasiri won't adopt the neutralizing spells until they understand why they're necessary."

He rests the back of his head against the wall and stares at the ceiling. "How are we going to do those things?"

"Well, we could take the cure to the Maitafi Graveyard."

Azariah looks at me. "You're saying we should give the cure to your mother to distribute?"

"Yes." I pray she'll be there today. "We'd have to be careful. But she's bound to know people who need the cure, and she'd be discreet."

"Fine," he says. "What about revealing the truth?"

"That's harder." I set down my empty tea glass and rub my numb fingers, trying to think.

"Maybe if our families helped us, and each person told more people . . ."

I shake my head. "It'd still be too slow. We need something that will reach a lot of people right away."

"We could preach it in the fanes," Azariah says sarcastically. "Or print it in the newspaper."

I sit up straight. "That's it!"

"What?" He draws back in surprise. "Marah, people don't believe half of what's written in the paper."

"If we print something denouncing the Assembly, I'm sure everyone will want to believe it at this point."

Azariah pulverizes a crust of bread between his fingers. "Then let's do it tonight."

AFTER NIBBLING ON some bread and cheese, we leave for the Maitafi Graveyard. I clutch the pot containing the cure to my chest. A thin stream of halani on their way to work trickles through the streets of Gishal District.

At the graveyard, we approach the stone building. A diaphanous rope of smoke unravels above the chimney. Inside, a small crowd is gathered in the main room, mostly women in fringed shawls, with a few bearded men mixed in. A man with long hair tied back in a ponytail has his arm around the shoulders of a girl Melchior's age, who is holding a viola. The mourners take no notice of our arrival.

As Azariah and I step forward, I realize everyone is huddled around a table that wasn't there the last time I came. On it lies a slender body draped in blue cloth. I stop in my tracks.

Azariah steers me by the elbow, first toward the counter where Mother is and then into the back room. Here I get another shock. Caleb is sitting on a stool wrapped in a quilt, watching a teakettle on the wood-burning stove in the corner of the room.

I rush to his side, setting the cure on the floor. The quilt slides to the ground as Caleb flings his arms around me. When he pulls back, the gauntness of his face frightens me. But his eyes. They're soft and brown, no longer like black marble. We don't sign. There are no signs. The joy rising in my chest feels like pain.

"He's still weak," Mother says. "But he's just strong enough to walk, and he wanted so much to leave the apartment . . ."

Caleb holds my hand while Mother makes tea. Crouched in front of him, I struggle to wrap the quilt around his shoulders again with my free hand. Azariah intervenes, pulling it into place and gathering the corners in Caleb's lap.

A sound swells from the front room, the deep-voiced viola singing a solemn line. Azariah and I both turn toward the doorway. The instrument sounds uncannily human, and the melody is stark and austere, like music that might have risen out of the depths of the earth. It stirs something in me. The musician breaks off, and I hear men and women chanting in unison, imitating the preceding line of music. Then the violist plays a new line.

"It's the sung prayer," Azariah says. "From the service for the dead."

I give him an odd look.

"I've heard it lots of times," he says. "Normally it's conducted in the fane, with the whole congregation there . . ."

"They're holding the funeral here because the roof of their fane collapsed under the snow," Mother says, handing Azariah a glass of tea. She nudges the pot on the ground with her shoe. "What's this?"

I stand up. "It's the cure," I whisper.

She gives me a startled glance. "Did you go to the Avrams yesterday after . . . ?"

"Mother," I say, forcing the words out though it feels like coughing up nails, "Leah died."

My eyes are painfully dry. Mother stares at me a moment and then wraps her arms around me. For a second, I feel like there might be something to hold on to, but the sensation is fleeting.

I turn to Caleb again. *Talk to me*, I sign. *Are you really well? Are you tired?*

He shakes his head, suppressing a cough. *I'm really well. I miss you.*

His gaze slides to Azariah, who's standing slightly apart. When he notices Caleb watching him, his eyes soften, but his lips remain tight. I know he's thinking of Sarah.

Out in the front room, hinges squeal, and shovel blades scrape the floor.

"It's time to send the procession to the grave," Mother says, moving toward the doorway. Azariah goes after her, and I follow him. Caleb starts to rise from his stool.

"No," says Mother. *Stay by the stove.*

In the main room, she instructs the grave diggers in an undertone. Already, the bearers of the dead are arranging the blue-shrouded bundle on a litter. I look away. By the window, the young violist stands with her instrument held in the crook of her elbow.

"I apologize for the delay," Mother says, approaching a middle-aged man standing at the foot of the litter. "The head grave digger will lead you to the grave now."

"My thanks," the man says. "We have not quite finished the service."

"Oh, I'm sorry," says Mother, stepping back in embarrassment.

The man nods to a woman standing nearby.

"The crossing of the last threshold," she announces, her voice papery.

Finding her place in her Maitaf, she begins to read a stanza. This must be the threshold passage, the last prayer Maitafi recite for the dead. Like the prayer to greet the dawn, the threshold passage is one of the Maitafi prayers so well known that every Ashari has heard of it.

The woman falters. She repeats a line, reads another. Then her voice catches and grinds to a halt.

One of her companions draws near. "Here, Devorah, let me—"

But Azariah takes up the new stanza, uttering the words deliberately, his voice very low. He speaks from memory, not even glancing at the woman's Maitaf. His monotone strengthens into a fervent recitation. All the while, his eyes are fixed on the litter.

When he reaches the end of the prayer, he turns and stalks into the back room. The head grave digger opens the door for the litter bearers. The procession files out into the cold.

I hasten to the back room. Azariah is standing in a square of sunlight.

"Drink your tea before it cools," Mother says behind me.

"We need to go," I say, turning around. "We brought you the cure because we hoped you could distribute it. We thought you would know who to give it to."

Mother hurries to the stove and presses a hot glass of tea into my hands anyway. "The woman who read the threshold passage has a son with the dark eyes."

"Please give some to her," I say. "And to anyone else. A spoonful is enough."

"I will," she says.

Azariah starts buttoning his coat. I kneel in front of Caleb again, wishing I could stay. It's unfair to have only these short snatches of time with him. *Be well*, I sign.

He smiles and nods at the tea glass wedged between his knees. *Oversteeped. Mother forgot it was white tea.*

I laugh and then stop before I cry.

Mother accompanies us to the door. As we step out into the dazzling snow, she says, "You can't stay in hiding forever."

It's true, but I don't know what to say. So I just wave, trying to reassure her, and Azariah and I leave the graveyard.

The sun seems too bright, making me skittish. Even so, nothing can quell the joy of seeing Caleb well—not Azariah's silence, not the thought of that blue-clad body being laid into the earth forever.

I glance sideways at Azariah. He's biting his lip so hard I expect to see blood. Impulsively, I say, "I'm sorry."

"For what?"

"I'm sorry you had to . . . You shouldn't have come. I didn't mean for—"

"Just drop it, Marah," he says brusquely. A few gritty steps later, he apologizes.

"I didn't know Caleb would be there," I say. "It must've been—"

"I was glad to see him too," Azariah says. "I couldn't bear it if . . ."

A fierce ache overpowers everything else swirling madly in my chest, and I swallow hard. For a second, the pain and compassion I feel for Azariah are so crippling I wish the burden were mine instead. But I know I would never be able to let Caleb go so he could have Sarah back.

24

IN THE EVENING, WHILE SLURPING LUKEWARM VEGETABLE soup with Azariah, I consider what to print in the newspaper. My gaze strays to the crumpled *Journal* tucked behind the stove. We haven't looked at our wanted notice since Melchior brought it. It occurs to me now that whatever we print tonight will not only be our way of making the truth known but our response to the government's public charge of subversion.

I rip a sheet out of one of the notebooks, reach for a pencil, and scribble *Citizens!* across the top of the page. Azariah watches me as I ponder what to write. The message must be clear, succinct, and above all, true.

The dark eyes is caused by harmful magic.
It can be cured with an herbal potion
prepared with spells.
We have brewed the cure and know it is effective.
The Assembly wishes to keep the cure a secret

in order to give it to the kasiri
but deny it to the halani.

Join us in stopping this evil.

Marah Levi
Azariah Rashid

I sign our names with a grim flourish and hand Azariah my scrawled draft. "How's this?"

He reads it. "Next we should tell them the Assembly's poisoning their water."

"It's not believable?"

"No, it's fine. The councilors will be hard-pressed to contain the uproar after this." He hesitates. "Are you sure about printing our names?"

"Yes," I say at once. "We might as well stand up to the Assembly."

Azariah's jaw tenses. "You're right. We'll show we're not afraid to accuse them."

I am afraid, I almost say, but I push that thought away.

LATE AT NIGHT, we set out for the newspaper office. We found the address in the paper Melchior left us: Seven Mirala Street. Azariah remembers passing Mirala Street on some Firem excursion, so he leads the way with a lantern.

I slip my hands into my pockets to warm my fingers and feel the cold glass of a flask there. It holds Leah's dose of the cure. I realize I forgot to pour it back into the pot before we gave it to Mother.

Eventually we emerge from a small street into an imposing square. The cobbles give way to huge flagstones. Across from us, a massive brick façade rises above two arches wide enough for autos to pass through. The First Councilor's official residence.

I recoil into the shadows. "You didn't say we were going to Yehodu Square!"

"Mirala Street's right off it," Azariah says, peeking around the butcher's shop on the corner. "The newspaper office is pretty close to the Magnificent Apartments."

I survey the square again. Thankfully, all the windows of the Magnificent Apartments are dark. It's chilling to think the man who lives there wouldn't mind if I were dead.

"Let's go," says Azariah.

We advance along the edge of the square until he indicates a dark chasm between two storefronts. We turn onto Mirala Street. Halfway down the block, there's a lit doorway. We approach the lamp like a pair of moths and find a plain door with a brass plaque in its center.

THE JOURNAL
7 Mirala Street

Azariah glides up to the dark window. I catch my breath. For all we know, five kasiri are standing guard behind the door.

"It's all right," he says. "There's only one man. He's sleeping, and he's not a kasir."

"Are you sure?"

"He certainly doesn't look like one."

Before I can protest, he opens the door. The hinges are mercifully well-oiled, and we slip inside. Azariah fiddles with the knob, whispering an incantation over his bent hands.

The room is cramped due to all the newsprint stacked along the baseboard. The First Councilor gazes out from his portrait on the wall, his still face betraying nothing. In the middle of the room, a grizzled man snores in a chair, a flat cap over his eyes, his patched coat brushing the floor. An oil lamp burns on the table.

Azariah gestures at another doorway, and I follow him into the next room. Huge machines loom before us like monsters. We advance together between two rows of equipment and find thousands of copies of tomorrow's newspaper piled at the back of the room.

"They're done for the night," I say. "Only the guard is here."

Azariah bends to read the headlines. "'Gavriel Daniel Chosen Next Firem Assistant Headmaster.' Oh, look, it says he's First Councilor Yiftach David's nephew. I'm sure he got the job completely on his own merits—"

"Azariah, it's past midnight," I say, agitated. "The distributors sell newspapers early. They could be here by six to collect—"

"Which gives us five, maybe six hours to print an insert

and slide it into as many of these as we can," he says, nudging a stack of newspapers with his foot.

"But how?" I say.

Azariah turns back to the machines, his lantern swinging. I approach the closest one, trying to guess how it works, but I can't make anything of its awkward design.

"I think you'd better wake the guard," I say at last. "With any luck, he actually works here and knows what to do. Try to persuade him to help us. I'll keep looking around."

Azariah leaves the lantern with me and threads his way back through the rows of machinery. I return to investigate the back of the room more closely. Behind all the stacks of newspapers, there is a counter against the wall. I raise the lantern. Ghostly light bobs over dozens of compartments filled with metal letters and labeled with spidery handwriting. This must be the type, but nothing suggests how to assemble a proper message so it can be printed.

A muffled exclamation reaches my ears from the front room, making me jump. I hear Azariah hastening to reassure the guard and then introducing himself. This elicits another cry of surprise; the night watchman recognizes Azariah's name.

Shuddering, I perch on the typesetter's stool and reach into a compartment. The metal pieces are cool on my sweaty hands and streak my skin with ink. I can hear Azariah speaking earnestly again, but in Xanite.

A minute or two later, he emerges from the eerie forest of machinery with the night watchman shuffling behind.

"It's all right, Marah," he says. "This is Faraj. He's Xanite too. Faraj, Marah."

"Hello," I say, attempting to smile at the guard.

Faraj's gaze is wary under the brim of his cap. Gray stubble spreads across his hollow cheeks.

"He can work the machines and everything," Azariah says.

I reach into my cloak for the folded piece of notebook paper. Turning to the guard, I ask hesitantly, "Will you print our notice?"

"Be glad to," he says. "Only, what do you expect me to do afterward?"

"Afterward?" I say blankly.

"When my superiors find out I helped you," Faraj says matter-of-factly.

Azariah and I share worried looks. We can't protect Faraj. If he helps us, he might have to flee too. At the very least, he'll lose his job. How can we ask that of him?

"If we make it look like we forced you . . ." Azariah begins.

"We could tie you up," I say to Faraj, embarrassed to be suggesting such a thing.

"Tying up wouldn't be enough," Azariah says. Not quite meeting Faraj's eyes, he adds, "I could cast binding spells."

"If it's all right with you," I say quickly to the night watchman.

Faraj reflects for a moment. At last he says, "You can use spells, so long as you tell me what they do."

"My thanks," I say with relief, smoothing out the piece of paper with our text and offering it to Faraj.

He limps to the nearest machine and sits down at it. "This is a linotype machine."

In front of him is something like a typewriter keyboard. He peruses my scribbles and begins to type. To his left, little blocks of metal engraved with letters begin to form lines of text.

"Matrices," he explains.

A line of matrices gets carried away into the machine. Then a bar of metal falls into a tray with a clatter.

"Slug," Faraj says.

When they're ready, he collects all the slugs and takes them to a worktable. There he arranges them in a metal tray the size of a newspaper page.

"Wait here while I make the stereotype," he says, hobbling away with the tray.

A few minutes later, a loud sound shatters the quiet. I stifle a shriek.

"God of the Maitaf, Marah," Azariah says, though his voice is frayed with fear.

A machine groans to life nearby. I follow Azariah into a third room, where Faraj is standing next to another mysterious machine. Newsprint from a roll on top passes under a round cylinder with our text on it and appears at the bottom, perfectly readable.

"Rotary press," Faraj says. "Prints three thousand copies an hour."

I stare at the night watchman, then at Azariah. We both smile.

25

SOMEONE ROUSES ME, WHISPERING ABOUT DISTRIBUTORS. I stir, wincing at my muscles' protest. Azariah's head rests on my shoulder, and we're both wedged in the corner of the printing room. Faraj stands nearby, and I realize it was his voice that woke me.

I shrug. "Azariah."

He raises his head, squints at me, and stands up. "What time—?"

"I think the distributors are coming." I seize Azariah's proffered hand and struggle to my feet.

The worst part of the night came after Faraj printed several thousand copies of our notice. Fifty thousand papers had already been trussed for the distributors. We didn't have time to print enough notices or to insert a new page into every newspaper. We did all we could, but it was slow work.

To fight off drowsiness, Faraj sang in Xanite. His voice was unexpectedly warm, and the tunes sweet, but they were more lulling than energizing. Azariah hummed along when he knew a melody, and together they taught me a little nursery rhyme and laughed at my pronunciation. When Azariah told the night watchman I was a violinist headed for Ashara's Xanite music school, he grunted in admiration. I was too sleepy to explain I hadn't been admitted yet.

Faraj told us to rest, finally, but now it feels like I've slept only a few minutes.

I hear voices through the door that opens onto the alley. Faraj lifts a bundle of newspapers, and Azariah and I follow suit, staggering after him. The alley is still dark. I can just make out a crowd of boys and older men, with a few women scattered here and there.

"Where's Yechezkel?" Faraj calls. "And Afdal? Naomi? If you usually sell out, come forward."

"Is there a special edition?" someone asks.

"Just sell them." Faraj thrusts his bundle into a girl's arms. Somebody relieves me of my burden, and I stumble inside to fetch more.

Time blurs. In, newspapers; out, distributors. Shuttling back and forth, again and again. No newspapers left. I find Azariah in the front room.

"Let's go," I say blearily.

"Where's Faraj?" he says.

The night watchman shuffles through the doorway. He fishes a ring of ancient keys from his trousers pocket, lets them drop to the floorboards with a clatter, and looks at us.

"Faraj, my thanks," I say. "We owe you a great deal."

"Yes, my thanks," Azariah says. "I'm sorry we have to—I mean, if there's anything—"

Faraj holds up one callused hand. "I've done my part. Now bind me."

He sits down in the chair he was sleeping in when we arrived. Azariah steps forward nervously. "The first spell will paralyze your arms and legs," he tells Faraj. "Is that all right?"

The guard nods.

Azariah positions his hands. When he pronounces the incantation, orange light pulses at his fingertips. Faraj is utterly motionless, and if the spell was cast well, he won't move until the kasir newspaper staff arrives in a few hours.

"Can you move your limbs?" Azariah asks.

"No," says Faraj.

"Now I'm going to do a muting spell," Azariah says. "To show you couldn't call for help. You won't be able to speak until someone uncasts it."

The night watchman nods. Azariah performs his spell. Afterward, the only sound in the newspaper office is our breath.

BACK AT OUR hideout, I sleep all day and wake up at sunset. In my quilted cocoon, I feel warm and exultant. We pulled off our mission to the newspaper office without coming to any harm. Feeling Azariah's gaze on me, I roll onto my side. He's sitting under the window, the Hagramet text in his lap.

"What do you think's happened?" I ask.

He shrugs. "I have no idea."

We hear a knock downstairs.

"It's got to be Melchior," he says in a strangled voice, bounding out before I can untangle myself from the blankets.

The stairs creak, and I hear Melchior and Azariah arguing in Xanite. When the brothers appear, Melchior throws me an appealing look and says, "My parents want Azariah to come home now. You too."

"Me?" I say, scrambling to my feet.

"We can't," Azariah says.

"You must," Melchior says. "They've seen the newspaper. Everyone has. The time for hiding is over. Mother and Father are ready to take on the Assembly." Melchior's iron gaze flickers for a moment. "Word of the cure has spread like wildfire. People believe it's out there already."

According to him, people are mobbing the District Halls in both kasir and halan districts, demanding the cure. Mothers come carrying their sick children bundled up in blankets. The waiting rooms are overflowing with people who refuse to budge, while latecomers camp in the streets outside.

Picturing the desperate throngs storming the District Halls, I go cold. Will there be another slaughter like the steelworkers' massacre because of us?

"Fine," says Azariah. "I'll come home."

Melchior lets out his breath. "Father has the auto two blocks away."

Azariah gapes at him, then swears in Xanite. "What if I'd refused?"

"I wasn't leaving until you agreed," Melchior says.

After packing up our belongings, we leave the bare room for the last time and trudge downstairs. Melchior leads us to his father and the automobile I've only ever seen Channah drive. Thinking of her, a star of confusion and pain flashes in my heart.

By the light of the headlamps, Banar Rashid looks haggard as he nods to me. Azariah accepts his restrained embrace before we all get into the auto.

At the Rashids' house, Gadi Faysal welcomes us, her face as smooth as glass. Her hair is twisted into a knot and adorned with a copper ornament. The realization that the copper is for Sarah makes my stomach lurch. Gadi Faysal kisses Azariah's forehead and then takes my hand in hers.

"It's good to see you, Marah."

She shows me to the guest bedroom. I wash first, in deliciously warm water. Afterward, I put on the skirt and blouse Gadi Faysal has found for me. They fit even less well than that velvet dress, but they're better than my own filthy clothes.

The spare bedroom is no less sumptuous than the rest of Azariah's house. The four-poster bed has three pillows and heavy curtains that can be drawn closed. There's also a desk and a bookshelf displaying bronze figurines from Xana, Laishidi masks, and a curious flute made of a gourd with three pipes sticking out of it. I study it for a few minutes, wondering what it sounds like and whether I dare touch it. Deciding I'd better not, I flop onto the bed and promptly doze off.

Only a moment later, it seems, someone knocks on the door. "Marah? It's me."

"Coming!" I slide off the bed and rush to the door, tucking my hair behind my ears.

Azariah flushes when I burst into the corridor. His hair is damp, his skin scrubbed clean.

"I told Mother and Father everything while you were resting," he says as we walk to the dining room. "They were stunned, but they believed me."

I feel a rush of relief. The grown-ups will handle everything now.

Melchior, his face brooding and sad, is already in the dining room. The Rashid parents sit at either end of the table, which looks too long without Sarah. Only Melchior can swallow more than a few mouthfuls of the meal.

When the dishes have been cleared, Banar Rashid faces Azariah and me.

"The Assembly has been dealt a serious blow," he begins. "Now that you've exposed the councilors' abhorrent design . . ."

"Ashara will not stand for it," Gadi Faysal says. "They've gone too far."

"There are pressing matters to which we must attend," Banar Rashid continues. "The government must initiate mass production of the cure, along with a fair and efficient system for distributing it. Study of the neutralizing spells must commence immediately with a view toward their reinstatement in the very near future."

"How are we going to make those things happen?" I ask impatiently.

"We go to the Assembly Hall tomorrow," Gadi Faysal says, setting her fist on the tablecloth.

"But tomorrow's Eighthday," Azariah says. "The Assembly doesn't meet on the weekend."

"They'll be there," Banar Rashid says grimly. "They were this afternoon. This is a crisis. We'll force a public hearing."

"Who's we?" I say.

Azariah's parents look gravely at each other.

"We are willing to spearhead these efforts," Gadi Faysal says, "but we do not expect to be alone tomorrow. The notice you and Azariah published has provoked outrage among kasiri and halani alike. The Assembly's power appears to be broken."

After our council, everyone retires. Azariah and Melchior accompany me down the corridor to the guest bedroom. I step inside, expecting them to leave, but Melchior leans in the doorway.

"I think Mother and Father are being too optimistic," he says.

I raise my eyebrows. Optimistic isn't quite how I'd describe his grief-stricken parents.

"They believe the Assembly's lost its grip on power," Melchior clarifies. "I'm not so sure."

"What are you trying to say?" Azariah asks him.

"Just that we should be careful."

I look between the brothers. "Careful how?"

"Maybe I should stay out of it," Melchior says. "I'm the Rashid the Assembly has taken the least notice of. It might be better for everyone if it stayed that way."

Azariah looks struck. "That's a good idea. Marah and I will go to the Assembly tomorrow with Mother and—"

"We will?" I say, alarmed.

"*I* want to," he says. "But if Melchior's right that this isn't over, he should stay away until we're certain the Assembly's going to distribute the cure to everyone."

"In case you need me," Melchior says.

"That's the plan?" I say, underwhelmed.

Melchior shrugs. "It'll have to do." He straightens from the door frame. "Now let's get some sleep."

Azariah bids me goodnight and follows his brother out. I pad over to the window. The curtains are drawn, and the moonlight reflected off the snow outside bathes me in a silvery glow. I'm alone in the unfamiliar guestroom, far from my family.

Someone has set out a nightgown for me. I change into it and slide into bed, but I can't sleep. I miss having Azariah near. The stiff coverlet and the heavy canopy of the four-poster bed feel oppressive. With the bronze statuettes and the gourd flute gleaming on the shelf, I feel like I'm staying in a museum. Forcing my eyes shut, I remind myself how close we are to saving Ashara and try to hang on.

AZARIAH AND I emerge at the same time for breakfast and find Melchior and his parents in the dining room. Gadi

Faysal offers us bread, honey, and pickled melon. Azariah joins Melchior at the far end of the table. Every so often they exchange a few inaudible words. I drink a glass of piping-hot tea, wishing it would burn away my anxiety and restlessness.

When the door knocker clatters in the entrance hall, Banar Rashid leaps up to answer. Gadi Faysal remains in her chair, stiff as marble. Azariah and I share a panicked look, then he nudges his brother. The next instant, Melchior is gone, through the kitchen.

Banar Rashid returns a moment later, flanked by two kasir police officers. A third follows close behind, his diamond-shaped insignia glaring.

"Chanoch Asa, First Councilor's Corps," he says, tapping his badge.

"I know what you are," snaps Gadi Faysal.

"Your charm has withered since we were in school, Nasim," Asa says, smiling. Then he looks at the rest of us. "I didn't anticipate such luck. Your son Azariah seems to have reappeared. And this must be the famous Marah Levi."

I force myself to meet his gaze even though my hands are shaking in my lap.

"You've all been summoned to the Assembly Hall," Asa continues. "The automobiles are waiting. Jalal, Nasim, may I request the pleasure of your company? The children can ride in the other auto."

I look to Azariah's parents, hoping for some hint they'd expected this, but there's only a horrified silence. Finally, Banar Rashid and Gadi Faysal follow Asa out of the room.

Azariah and I hasten after them, with the two silent officers bringing up the rear.

Outside, the autos' polished black armor reflects the distant sun. I feel a curious lack of terror as Azariah and I climb into one of the vehicles. At least we're together.

The autos roll into the city and down the wide boulevard that cuts across the northwestern districts of Ashara. As we near the city center, the streets fill with people, all walking in the direction of the Assembly Hall and engaged in fierce discussion. Halani and kasiri brush shoulders as the street grows clogged, and some of them even speak to each other.

Our driver has to slow the automobile to a walking pace as the people on foot overtake the street. When he sounds the horn, the halani shrink away, but the kasiri stare hard at the two autos easing past them.

Wild hope lifts my spirits as I gaze out at the throngs. If all these people are descending upon the Assembly Hall for answers, the crowd will be even thicker there. The Assembly can't harm us in front of so many witnesses, especially if kasiri and halani are united.

A few minutes later, the auto comes to a complete halt and then lurches forward again. Azariah and I peer through the windshield in time to see a uniformed officer of the First Councilor's Corps waving us through a police blockade. On either side of us, Ashari are packed together so tightly they form a solid wall outside the auto windows. People are shaking their fists and shouting to be let past, but the officers' hands are poised to cast spells. The threat of deadly magic keeps the mob at bay even as our auto glides through.

Beyond the line of police, the street is deserted. I realize with a sick feeling how isolated we are now.

We drive into the plaza and pull up in front of the Assembly Hall. One of our escorts leaps out of the auto and yanks open the back door. "Out."

I move clumsily after Azariah. His parents are standing together, hands clasped, on the steps of the hall. Banar Rashid's expression is apprehensive, Gadi Faysal's defiant.

Asa oozes up the steps, motioning for us to come. Struggling to swallow, I trudge toward the massive oak doors. Once I pass through them, I don't know if I'll return.

26

WE ENTER A SOARING ATRIUM. THE GREEN MARBLE floor is so polished it looks icy. Government employees in black suits swish past us wearing harried expressions, stopping now and then to exchange a few clipped words. The army of clerks stationed behind a long counter are in an uproar, crashing into each other as they run back and forth waving memoranda. Asa leads us through the chaos, keeping a close eye on us and his subordinates hemming us in.

For a time, everybody is too wrapped up in their personal sliver of the crisis to notice our presence. Officials sail by, arguing about the necessity of locking down the District Halls and the rumors that several cases of recovery from the dark eyes have been confirmed. A few steps farther, I catch sight of Seventh Councilor Ketsiah Betsalel.

"I'm telling you to recall all police officers assigned to the far suburbs and the rural outposts," she shouts at somebody. "Those are your orders! Where do you think they're more needed: here or in some godforsaken hamlet?"

Finally, a gaunt, elderly kasir spots the Rashids and me being ushered across the atrium. "Jalal? God of the Maitaf, is it your son Azariah?"

Banar Rashid starts to say something, but Asa cuts him off. "They are not to be spoken to."

The old man stares in alarm. "What do you know, Jalal? Should we—?"

A woman grabs him by the arm and tries to jerk him away. "What are you doing? Stay away from Rashid, he's in disgrace."

Heads begin to turn. While some kasiri trip over each other trying to give us a wide berth, others slow in their mad dashes through the Assembly Hall. Asa tenses.

"Guards!" he shouts, loudly enough to punch through the hubbub. Around the atrium, the officers in charge of the hall's security leave their posts and advance toward us. The effect on the government kasiri is immediate; they almost all return to going about their business. Only a brave few try to keep up as Asa hurries us toward a wide staircase ahead.

"Was the notice true?"

"What are we to believe?"

"Why have you been arrested?"

"It's them, it's the children!"

Banar Rashid turns abruptly to face the atrium. "Azariah and Marah printed the truth!"

Asa swears and silences Banar Rashid with a spell as his deputies whirl around, bellowing incantations that force even the most persistent kasiri to scatter. Then the officers hustle us up the steps to a door, where Asa casts a spell. Pasting on a horrible grin, he holds the door open for the Rashids and me. With the other two officers pressing us from behind, there's nowhere to go but in.

No sooner have we entered the room than the door slams shut. In front of us, on a dais, two men and a woman are seated at a stone desk. On either side of us are long benches, empty except for a boy about Melchior's age holding a portable writing desk on his lap.

From the portraits I've seen and the distant views I've had of him in public, I recognize the man seated in the middle of the desk as Yiftach David, First Councilor of the Assembly. He's a small, gray-haired man, not particularly imposing, but his eyes are deep-set and utterly unreadable. A gold watch chain loops across his vest.

The man on Yiftach David's right is taller and heavier set. Like Asa, he wears the diamond insignia of the First Councilor's Corps. His sturdy face gives the impression of indomitable will. The woman on David's left has a sapphire pendant at her throat. Her face, coldly beautiful, shines with detached intelligence. All three are immaculately dressed in black.

Yiftach David rises very slowly. His face is pale and pinched, his eyes dusky. Could he be ill himself? I can't quite discern whether his eyes are black or just naturally dark.

"My dear Rashids," he says. "Gadin Levi." Then he gestures to his colleagues. "This is Ehud Tsuriel, the captain of my personal Corps, and Kalanit Hoshea, one of my advisors."

Gadi Faysal steps forward. "Do you mean to silence us, David?"

Acting as if he hasn't heard her, David looks past us to Asa. "Leave us."

Asa turns to Banar Rashid and mutters a counterspell. Then he and his men withdraw.

"David, this is absurd," says Banar Rashid, his voice back. "Just what do you intend to do? No one will support the Assembly in this depravity."

"Is that what you call it, Rashid?" the First Councilor says, sounding disappointed. Then his tone grows colder. "Come here, Gadin Levi. And you, young man."

Azariah stiffens, but I obey, and he follows me. Gadi Faysal makes a noise in her throat as David fixes his gaze on us. I can scarcely breathe.

"Where is the cure?" he asks.

Silence. Even the scribe, hunched over the few lines scratched on his paper, holds his breath.

"Where is the cure?" David repeats, his white knuckles grinding into the stone tabletop.

"It's gone," I say in a brittle voice.

"A likely story," snaps his advisor Hoshea.

"It's true," Azariah says. "It's all gone."

My hand strays to my cloak pocket where the glass bottle lies hidden. Panicking, I clasp my hands behind my back.

David doesn't seem to notice. "Who are your accomplices?" he asks.

"There was no one but us," I lie, my whole body trembling. I pray Mother has given away the rest of the cure by now.

"No matter," says the First Councilor. "We will find them."

His attention returns to Azariah's parents, but his advisor isn't done with us. "Do you know how many laws you've broken?" she demands. "Breaking into the newspaper office, attacking the night watchman, printing that notice, which, by the way, was bald sedition—"

"But we told the truth!" I say.

David looks at me and laughs. There's a manic, almost feverish, gleam in his eyes.

"Enough!" Banar Rashid strides forward and pulls me and Azariah behind him. "Your renegade minority will never succeed in this mad plot. Healing the kasiri and leaving the halani to die? The public will demand the cure and make no distinction between kasir and halan."

Now David's advisor laughs. "Who do you think will be called renegades when this is over, Rashid?" She nods toward the police captain, who is still sitting there as though made of stone, his face empty of emotion. "The Corps has surrounded the Assembly Hall. We will paint you as subversives who sought to incite the citizenry to overthrow the government. There is no known cure for the dark eyes yet. Your allegations are lies, a ruse designed to topple the Assembly, all the crueler for having raised false hopes."

"Peace, Hoshea!" the First Councilor says, raising one hand. "It may not come to that."

"It's too late anyway," protests Banar Rashid. "The people are convinced."

"The people are easily swayed," David says. "In one direction as in another. Do you believe we would have any difficulty discrediting a nobody halan girl and a Xanite family with known radical leanings? Soon the Assembly will quietly begin making the cure and healing those stricken with the dark eyes. That is, those kasiri . . ."

The emphasis on the word *kasiri* is delicate but unmistakable. Banar Rashid walks up to the dais, Gadi Faysal at his side.

"You cannot do this," he tells David.

Azariah rushes to join his parents, and I follow him. As I squeeze past Azariah's shoulder, the First Councilor turns. From this close, I can see his eyes *are* black, the pupils gone. My heart skips a beat.

"But we *can*," David says, his face glowing with excitement. "All in anticipation of the day when Ashara boasts a pure citizenry of ka—"

"We're all of us Ashari!" I shout, hot rage rushing up through me. "This isn't just your city. And the plague is because of *you*, because of kasir magic!"

"Marah's right," Banar Rashid says. "The fault is ours. The halani are innocent victims. How can you abandon them to suffer the consequences of our mistakes?" His voice is passionate, almost pleading.

David peers down at him, his eyes like onyx. "You misunderstand. We are not taking advantage of a chance occurrence. On the contrary."

My arms prickle with foreboding. The Rashids' silence seems to encourage David.

"This plague," he says, slightly breathless, "has been almost two hundred years in the making. It was designed precisely to purify Ashara, to build a city of kasiri where magical bloodlines would never be diluted or die out."

God of the Maitaf. This can't be real.

The Assembly created the dark eyes.

27

THE WIND HOWLS ACROSS TWO CENTURIES, RUSHING past my ears. David's face is rapt, and deathly pale.

How is it possible? Two hundred years in the making? Somehow they must have convinced kasiri to stop casting the neutralizing spells, so that the harmful magic began to accumulate . . .

The police captain makes a sudden movement as if to rise, and I realize with a jolt of terror that because of the knowledge we now possess, we might never leave this chamber alive.

"I don't believe you!" I blurt out. The captain goes still. "If you created the dark eyes, you'd have the cure."

"We did," David says, looking not at me but at the still speechless Rashids. "The Assembly guarded the book containing the cure very carefully and outlawed the study or possession of Hagramet texts so knowledge of the language would be lost. However, all four copies of the Hagramet book were believed burned in the fire that destroyed the

Assembly Hall seventy years ago. It now seems they were not *all* burned."

I look at Azariah in astonishment, but he's staring at the First Councilor, his expression a mixture of disbelief and revulsion.

"You—you knew all along," he splutters, "but you pretended not to—you acted like you were doing all you could, closing the schools—"

"The danger of contagion proved an excellent pretext for that," David says with delight. "Shutting down the schools allowed us to reassure the public we were taking the illness seriously while simultaneously hampering the spread of subversive ideas among students."

I remember standing in the schoolyard with my friends on that day that now seems so long ago, arguing about underground meetings and the intuition as our power. I want to tell David he was right to fear Ashara's students.

"But Yiftach, why?" Banar Rashid struggles for words, looking ill. "Why are you bent on . . . on *purifying* Ashara?"

The First Councilor draws himself up, his face blazing. "When the cold times came, it was the magicians who ensured the survival of the northlanders, was it not? Without our kind, the remnants of Erezai would have perished, and the city-states would not exist. At its founding, Ashara was half kasir and half halan. Yet over time, the kasir population began to decline while the halan population slowly rose."

"What of it?" Gadi Faysal says icily. "These are historical facts—"

"So you agree they are true!" David leans forward, staring intensely at Azariah's parents. "But they are not mere statistics. You are foreign-born. Your family does not remember how the number of children born with magic dwindled over the decades or how intermarriage, before it was outlawed, diluted kasir blood. A hundred years after the cold times began, the Assembly decided to act. It had to.

"As Xanite immigrants, you may not feel our history as keenly as we do. But as kasiri, surely you can understand what a catastrophe, what a *tragedy* it would have been for Ashara's magicians to disappear while the common sparkers, who would not even be here today were it not for us, endured."

Contempt flares inside me. Of course. Fate threatened to wrong his poor, precious kasiri while we ungrateful halani had all the luck.

"But why didn't the Assembly call off the plan when the cure was lost?" says Banar Rashid. "Surely the councilors must have realized how reckless it would be to continue!"

Reckless? How about evil? But David, triumphant, takes the question to mean he has persuaded Banar Rashid of the rightness of the Assembly's original intent, if not the wisdom of how they proceeded.

"We had already dedicated too many years to our purpose," he explains, his forehead gleaming. "We could not give up." He speaks as though he were one of those councilors, though the fire happened before he was born. "The Assembly remained confident that when the illness emerged, the city's best scientists and magicians would be able to rediscover the cure."

"But they failed," says Gadi Faysal. She gestures at me and Azariah. "Two children did better, so you went after them." She darts forward, like a falcon swooping down on David. "Because of you, my daughter is dead."

David flinches. "As a kasir, she should not have died. I sincerely regret—"

"How *dare* you?" Gadi Faysal's voice is so terrible it should be deadly. "Her life meant nothing to you. And she didn't deserve to live because she was a kasir. She deserved to live because she was a human being. She was just a child!"

Yiftach David says nothing.

"You'll never succeed anyway," says Gadi Faysal. "Not all kasiri's children are born magicians."

"Such children will be . . . dealt with," David says.

Does he mean killed? The ordinary kasiri will never let it happen. There'll be a revolution. Or will there be? *The Corps has surrounded the Assembly Hall* . . . David's ready. The kasiri will be living in the city he envisions before they understand what's happening. And then, in a generation or two, they'll forget there ever were sparkers. We'll become nothing but a story.

Banar Rashid's face is rigid with horror, but all he says is, "David, this scheme is impossible. Today, the halani represent two-thirds of Ashara's populace. Take them away, and you guarantee the collapse of the city."

"I assure you, we have detailed transition plans in place,"

David says. "It is true the sparker population has continued to grow most unfortunately since the Assembly first conceived of unleashing the dark eyes. But this merely proves how prescient those councilors were! They foresaw the need to protect us from becoming an ever-shrinking minority overwhelmed by the ungifted masses. Don't you see? Ashara *must* become a city of kasiri!"

Gadi Faysal makes a sound of disgust. "You feared extinction, so you turned around and condemned the halani to extinction instead? That is truly vile."

"We will never stand with you in this," her husband adds.

All of David's eagerness evaporates. His eyes flash like polished jet.

"I gave you more credit than you deserved," he says, his voice hard. "Now I see how it is. I should have known your radicalism would blind you. Magicians who put sparkers before—"

A tremor shudders through his body, and his legs buckle. His advisor leaps up to catch him, and he collapses into his chair. My heart thuds.

"You've as good as killed yourself," Gadi Faysal tells him, still livid. "Now are you satisfied?"

"I may die before we prepare the cure again," the First Councilor says, his black eyes glassy with fever. "It is a sacrifice for a better future, as your daughter was."

"Sarah was not a sacrifice!" I burst out as Azariah gives a wordless cry of rage beside me.

David doesn't even glance at me. "Enough," he rasps. "I must address the city. It's time."

I watch in despair as he grips the edge of the stone desk and, with great effort, rises again. In a moment, he will stand on the steps of the Assembly Hall and tell all of Ashara that our cure is a lie while, imprisoned in this chamber, we await our death. The truth will die with us, and the halani will never be healed. Caleb will die, and then Mother, all my friends, Tsipporah and Aradi Imael . . . until the dark eyes has destroyed all the halani.

"Wait!" I cry. This can't be the end. There must be some way I can stop David in his tracks and make him change his mind. Somehow I have to make him see.

In a moment of clarity, I decide what I must do.

28

I THRUST MY HAND INTO MY POCKET AND TAKE OUT THE flask.

"Marah, what are you doing?" Azariah says.

I walk up to the dais and hold the bottle out to Yiftach David.

"This is the cure," I say. "All that's left."

David seems to have turned to stone. I hold my breath. Then he reaches across the desk with trembling fingers and takes the flask. I don't let his hand touch mine. Summoning his last reserves of strength, he walks around the desk to stand before me.

He fumbles with the cork and tosses it aside. Then, his dark eyes burning with hatred, he throws his head back and downs the cure.

There's a shocked silence. David flings the glass bottle to the floor, where it shatters. He scorches me with his gaze, furious with me because he now owes a halan girl his life, furious with himself because he couldn't resist the offer of the cure. Without warning, he strikes me across the face. I stagger back, a flower of pain unfurling on my cheek. Stunned, I touch cold fingertips to my face.

"What are you doing?" Azariah shouts at the First Councilor, flying up to the dais, his fists clenched.

"Get back here!" Banar Rashid tells his son.

Azariah seizes my hand.

David stares at me, his lips still shining. He takes a step toward me, and I shrink from him.

"Leave her alone!" The scribe, the boy, shoves the portable desk off his lap and jumps up from the bench. His inkwell smashes on the floor, the ink spattering everywhere. "Father, she saved your life!"

Father? Shaking, I turn toward the scribe. He's gazing at me with his clear, light eyes as though he's never truly seen a halan in his life.

David turns swiftly and speaks an incantation, his hands fluttering. There's a flash of light. The boy pitches forward, but not before I see the resemblance to David in his jawline, his forehead . . .

I scream. The boy is on the ground, facedown, dark ink seeping everywhere like blood. Azariah takes a step toward him.

"Leave him!" David cries. His son groans and rolls onto his side, curling up like a little child.

I look at the broken glass on the floor and then up at David. It's all over now. He hasn't changed his mind. I thought my act of mercy would force him to see me as a person and to reconsider wiping out the halani. If anything, I've only fueled his hatred of us. My heart hardens, and I curse myself for giving him the cure.

There are shouts behind us, and half a dozen kasir officials explode into the room.

"Fire!"

"The city's on fire!"

"Then put it out!" David yells.

"The hall is burning!"

The kasiri, chests heaving, are clustered near the entrance. David hesitates for a moment, then steps down from the dais. At the door, flanked by his subordinates, he turns back, seeking out his son. For the first time, a trace of remorse crosses his face.

"Tsuriel," he orders the police captain, "bring Adriel and come."

The captain pulls David's son to his feet and slips his arm around him. The boy can hardly stand, but he twists his head around and locks eyes with me again. The underlings hasten out, followed by the captain with David's son Adriel, and finally David himself. He looks over his shoulder at his advisor, who has stepped down from the dais and is fingering her sapphire pendant.

"Guard the prisoners, Hoshea," he tells her.

"As you wish," she replies.

David rushes out. The next moment, Hoshea is shouting rapid-fire incantations, magic budding on her fingertips. I cringe, but she aims her spells at Banar Rashid and Gadi

Faysal. When the sparks subside, Azariah's parents stand frozen like statues. They don't even seem able to blink. Beside me, Azariah braces himself for his own round of paralyzing spells, but David's advisor glances down at the two of us with disdain and turns away.

"I don't know why Yiftach didn't just kill you," she says. "I knew you would never—"

A strident incantation bursts out next to my ear. My mouth falls open as Hoshea crumples to the ink-spattered floor. I turn to see Azariah with his hands held out stiffly in front of him. "Did you—?"

"I didn't kill her," he says. He lets out his breath and hurries to free his parents.

"Where did you learn that spell?" Banar Rashid asks, waving toward the unconscious advisor as soon as he can move again. "And the counterspells for binding? You're only in Final!"

"I've done some reading on the side," Azariah says.

His parents' awe is soon eclipsed by the direness of our situation. As Gadi Faysal examines the locked door, her face sharp with concentration, I imagine flames licking toward where we're trapped in the heart of the Assembly Hall.

"There are coded spells on this door," she announces. "Only a handful of authorized officials will know the codes, and it's almost impossible to break them."

Banar Rashid joins her and casts some spells himself, his brow furrowed.

Then Azariah says, "Hoshea must know the codes."

His parents exchange glances, and Gadi Faysal, looking nauseated, kneels beside David's inert advisor.

"Wake her, Azariah. I'm ready." She rises on one knee, her fingers rigid in an elaborate sign.

Azariah looks fearfully at her, then crouches and shakes Hoshea's shoulder. With a moan, she opens her eyes. At the sight of us, she recoils and struggles to sit up. Her gaze fastens onto Gadi Faysal's hands, and she freezes.

"Do as I say, or you're dead," says Azariah's mother. The whole thing would seem absurd if Azariah didn't look like he was about to be sick. Though I can't sense it, I imagine the tension Hoshea must feel in the air, the magic brewing like a storm, and suddenly Gadi Faysal doesn't look so ridiculous.

"Stand up and go to the door," she orders. She keeps the spell trained on Hoshea's chest as they get to their feet. The two women move together toward the exit.

"Unseal the door."

Banar Rashid, Azariah, and I hover around Hoshea and Gadi Faysal, anxious to pass through the doorway but afraid of drawing too near.

Veins stand out in Hoshea's neck. She seems transfixed by Gadi Faysal's bent fingers. Then she utters a set of words, her hands dancing. Banar Rashid lunges for the doorknob, and—we're free.

Instantly, Gadi Faysal rearranges her hands and speaks. Hoshea collapses again, but this time, Banar Rashid catches her and drags her out onto the landing. I tumble out after him with Azariah. The atrium is swarming with kasiri, three times as many as before, and the hall rings with cries.

"Get out of the building!" shouts Gadi Faysal, waving me and Azariah away. "Wait for us outside. We'll meet you as soon as we've dealt with her."

As she and her husband ease Hoshea onto a marble bench, I seize Azariah's hand and run. We pass through the crowd unnoticed, like ghosts, and burst out onto the steps of the Assembly Hall.

Smoke and snow.

29

BILLOWING BLACK CLOUDS BLOT OUT THE SKY. IS THAT ash on the ice? I can't stop shaking. But we're out.

Azariah and I dash down the steps into the panicked horde filling the square. The police blockade must have broken. Some people brandish torches, caught up in the frenzy, eager to destroy now that pandemonium reigns, but already others are fighting the small fires burning here and there in the plaza. Halani come running with sloshing buckets of water, and ordinary kasiri rip off their gloves and cast spells to smother the flames.

The roiling sea of people almost rips my hand from Azariah's. We press forward until we break free of the human eddies and find ourselves in a part of the square that is almost empty. It only takes a moment to see why.

To our right, along the eastern wing of the Assembly Hall, broken windows vomit flames. As we watch, a dozen government clerks spill out of a side door and stagger toward the blaze, averting their faces from the heat. Waves of blue light flare from their outstretched hands as cinders settle on their suits.

For a moment, Azariah and I just stand there, breathless.

Then he turns to me and shouts over the roar of the fire and the crowd. "Why did you do it?"

"What?" I stare at him, uncomprehending.

"Why did you give David the cure?"

I shudder as I remember the First Councilor plucking the flask from my fingers. "Azariah, this isn't the time!"

"It was the last dose, Marah!" His expression is betrayed.

"I don't know!" I cry. "I—I thought if I saved his life when he was ready to kill me and my people he—he wouldn't be able to go through with it, he'd have a change of heart . . ." It made sense at the time, but now it sounds crazy.

Azariah gapes at me. "Marah, David is irredeemable."

"I know it was for nothing!" I say, angrier at myself than at him. I wish I'd never saved David.

Two clerks stumble away from the fire and lurch across the cobblestones toward us, one coughing as he bats at his smoldering jacket cuff.

"It was boys with firebombs! Kasir boys!" the other official bellows at his companion. "They looked like Firem Secondary students. I saw them throw bombs through the windows. They'll pay for this!"

The heat of the flames is intensifying, and Azariah and I plunge back into the crush to escape the scorching air. Everyone's shouting for order, for the cure, for the councilors' heads, for news. Amid the chaos, a wagoner struggles to calm his terrified horse. Then by some miracle, we spot a familiar figure pushing his way toward the hall's front entrance.

"Melchior!" Azariah screams over the din.

Melchior turns in confusion, then reaches out a sturdy hand to his brother.

"I was about to go in for you!" he says, his voice thick with relief. Clustered around him are a handful of boys with sweaty, dirt-smudged faces. Their wild eyes burn with a tremendous anger. Shock scuttles across my skin.

"Was it you?" I croak. "The firebombs?"

Melchior nods.

Azariah's jaw drops. "Are you insane?"

"They'll contain it," his brother says roughly. "Where are Mother and Father?"

"They're dealing with Hoshea."

"Who?" says Melchior, but before he can reply, another of his Firem friends appears at his side.

"Word is David's left the hall," he says.

"Let's find him," one of the other boys says.

"No—wait—" Melchior reaches out a hand, but his classmates are already marching off. "Forget it." He pulls Azariah and me toward the edge of the choked square. The cobblestones are littered with jagged pieces of glass. Looking up, I realize some of the apartment windows that face the square have been smashed.

"After Asa took you away, I drove into the city and rounded up my friends," Melchior is explaining. "When we saw the Corps had blocked off the Assembly Hall, I feared the worst. I thought I might be able to get past the guards and find you in the hall if we created some chaos. My friends were happy to help. Shemuel's brother has the dark eyes. But things got a bit out of hand—"

"Melchior, there's more," I break in.

He swears. "Why is there always more!"

I have no answer. We look across the plaza. From somewhere behind the Assembly Hall, a new plume of smoke rises into the glittering blue sky.

"We need to find Mother and Father," Azariah says. "They said they'd meet us."

"Let's go that way." Melchior nods toward the western wing of the hall, which is not on fire.

This side of the square is more crowded, probably because it appears safer than the smoky eastern side. As I squeeze through the packed bodies, treading on a soiled scarf and tripping over some kasir's lost hat, I wonder how we'll ever find Banar Rashid and Gadi Faysal in this mess.

"Up there!" Melchior shouts, pointing to a tall, narrow scaffold clinging to the façade of the western wing. He elbows his way to the foot of the structure, Azariah and I sticking close behind. The three of us clamber up a ladder to the first plywood platform.

"One more," Azariah gasps. "Need to be higher."

I reach the next level first and kick aside a paint-speckled drop cloth so the boys won't get their feet tangled in it. Then I make the mistake of looking down. The square is much farther below us than I expected, and the scaffold shifts and creaks under our weight.

Swallowing, I drop to my knees and crawl to the edge of the platform, scanning the sea of heads for Azariah's parents. There must be thousands of people down there. I hope to God Mother and Caleb are safe at home. But could Shaul and his brother and the other students from the pharmacy be here? Might Gadi Yakov's grief have moved her to protest? Would Aradi Imael march? During rehearsal, she always kept her politics to herself. What did she think when my name was printed in the newspaper like a criminal's, two days after my Qirakh audition?

"God of the Maitaf," Azariah says beside me. I follow his gaze and catch sight of what we couldn't see when we were down in the square ourselves. Along the northern edge of the plaza, opposite the Assembly Hall, ranks of kasiri in black uniforms are colliding with each other in sprays of colored light.

"It's the First Councilor's Corps," Melchior says.

"But they're fighting each other," I say. As we watch, it becomes obvious that the Assembly's elite force is divided against itself. Even as the officers clash, the crowd in the square is growing, swelling like a storm cloud. The throngs are attacking the Corps too, and their greater numbers threaten to engulf the police.

Melchior shoves his brother. "Look for Mother and Father!"

Azariah tears his gaze from the north edge of the square

and glances down, but the violence is quickly spreading toward us and the hall.

A column of Corps officers plows its way into the center of the square. The crowd throws itself upon them like a pack of wolves, civilian kasiri's spells flashing while halani wield bricks and metal rods.

The mob targets one officer with particular viciousness, separating him from the rest of the column, driving him this way. Suddenly, I glimpse his face. It's Tsuriel, the captain of the First Councilor's Corps. His left temple and the side of his neck are wet with blood.

I jerk back on the scaffold, my mouth filling with saliva. Azariah's face is drawn. Melchior keeps searching the crowd for his parents, swearing steadily in a mix of Ashari and Xanite. I grind my palms into the plywood, feeling paralyzed. I can't think of what we should be doing. Controlling the fires? Keeping people safe? Stopping the councilors?

I hear Azariah gasp. Before I know what's happening, he's tugging me to the far side of the platform. From here we have a clear view of the clogged southwest corner of the square and the Assembly Hall's western portico.

Yiftach David is standing on the portico steps, alone, trapped between the protesters on the porch and the crowd on the cobblestones pressing in around him. A man in a ragged coat throws a rock at the First Councilor's head and misses. David spins around, hands crooked. A bolt of silver light, and the rock thrower falls. There's another body already slumped at the foot of the steps.

"Ouch, you're hurting me," Azariah says, wresting his fingers from my desperate grip.

"It's hopeless," Melchior says. "He's outnumbered fifty to one, a hundred to one . . ."

There are kasiri shooting spells at David, but he wards them off, swaying on the porch steps. Then the mob surges forward, undaunted by the First Councilor's barrage of spells. Not flinching at the sparks, the halani fall upon David with their broken boards and bricks. He disappears from view.

Suddenly, a burst of light flares up from the portico, concealing everyone on the steps in a sheath of gold. The next instant, it's gone. People spring back to reveal an inert David.

I look to the brothers. Melchior's face could be carved of stone. Azariah's eyes are huge, his mouth hanging open.

"What is it?" I ask.

"I've—I've never seen it," Azariah stammers, "only read, but—that gold light—I think he killed himself."

Relief floods my veins. I sag on the scaffolding. Some part of my mind tells me I should shudder with horror, but all I feel is the tension bleeding from my body.

A sound comes from below, a chanting that spreads through the crowd until the whole square rings with the words.

"David is dead!"

I creep to the edge of the platform again. Despite the clear chorus rising from the plaza, not everyone is chanting. Firefighters battle the blaze in the eastern wing while bucket brigades struggle to douse the small street fires. In the middle of the square, units of the First Councilor's Corps are still skirmishing with each other and the masses.

"What are they doing?" I say. "Their commander is dead!"

"There are still five councilors left," Melchior says grimly.

We watch helplessly from the scaffold as the fighting continues below. I lose all sense of time, stuck in a nightmare of drifting smoke, flickering spells, and dull chanting.

Then a voice loud enough to split open the sky booms through the square. "Citizens!"

Azariah claps his hands over his ears, and I seize his coat to keep him from toppling off the scaffold.

"People of Ashara, this is Yehudit Chesed."

I know that name. Yehudit Chesed is a member of the Assembly, but I can't remember which one until Melchior says, "It's the Fifth Councilor."

We look wildly around the square for her, but her voice is so amplified by magic it's impossible to tell where it's coming from.

"Yiftach David is dead, and the Assembly will not stand against the people any longer. I beg you, lay down your weapons and cease casting spells so that no more blood may be shed and no more lives lost."

Yehudit Chesed's voice drowns out every other sound. A hush falls over the square.

"Where is she?" I ask. "Is this real?"

"I swear to you that the cure for the dark eyes will be given to all, halani and kasiri."

"There!" Melchior points at two figures on the front steps

of the Assembly Hall. One is a woman with glossy brown hair and flawless posture. I squint at the young man next to her. When I recognize him, I catch my breath. Standing beside Yehudit Chesed, his shirt stained down the front with ink, is Adriel David, the First Councilor's son.

30

HALF AN HOUR LATER, AZARIAH, MELCHIOR, AND I tramp through the city toward Horiel District. We gave up on finding Gadi Faysal and Banar Rashid and can only hope they'll eventually think to look for their sons at my apartment. The boulevards are as packed as the Ikhad on Tenthday. Apocalyptic scenarios and wild rumors circulate among neighbors and strangers.

"What news?" they call out to us. Have we come from the Assembly Hall? Can the cure be obtained closer to the river? Have the councilors made a statement yet?

"David is dead," I keep saying. "The Assembly has fallen."

People grab my sleeves, imploring me to tell them more, but I shake them off, walking forward in a stupor.

On the Street of Winter Gusts, a growing flock of Horiel residents is gathering in front of my apartment building. With the Rashid brothers on my heels, I push through the crowd, determined to reach the door. I didn't expect it to be wide open and funneling people into our entryway. As I cross the threshold, someone shouts, "It's the Levi girl!"

"Kasiri!" someone else cries.

Gadi Yared, our meddlesome neighbor, pounces on me, gripping my wrist. "Have you brought us the cure?"

I struggle to tear away from her, and then I see them, at the foot of the stairs. Mother, struck dumb in midsentence trying to fend off the inquiries of half a dozen neighbors. And Caleb.

"Marah!" Mother breathes. She takes a step forward, but Caleb dashes across the entryway and throws himself at me. I catch him in my arms. The foyer erupts. It's as if all of Horiel District is stuffed into this tiny space, clamoring for answers from me.

"Leave her alone!" Mother shouts as she fights her way to me. "Do you have any idea what she's gone through?"

The journey up four flights of stairs is nightmarish. On each landing, more tenants spill out of their apartments and join the train following us to our door. Here, Mother turns to face the onlookers.

"Leave us in peace!" she snaps. "My daughter and her friends need rest."

Then she sweeps us into the apartment and slams the door in their faces. There is a muffled outcry from the landing.

Still clinging to my arm, Caleb leads me to the table. Mother busies herself at the stove, setting water to boil and heating a pot of something savory.

"Please sit down," she tells Azariah and Melchior, who are still standing awkwardly by the door.

"We can't eat your lunch," Azariah says. "You weren't expecting us."

Mother shakes her head. "There's more than enough food. After yesterday's burial, the fane gave me six jars of soup."

So she went to the cemetery yesterday. "The cure," I say. "Have you . . . ?"

"I gave it all away," she says. "To Maitafi congregations and to people in Horiel."

She ladles up bowls of soup for everyone and begins frying bread with Caleb's spice mixture. "Marah, after the notice appeared in the newspaper yesterday, a mob passed through our street, headed for the District Hall. This morning I left for the graveyard, but the streets around the Assembly Hall were so crowded I turned back. Where have you been?"

Haltingly, I explain what took place after we printed the notice in the newspaper. Azariah and Melchior help me tell the story while we eat. They wait for me to sign what I can to Caleb. He and Mother listen without reaction, as though they've exhausted their ability to be shocked.

I'm stumbling over David's death and Yehudit Chesed's announcement when an engine rumbles in the street. Before I can blink, Melchior is halfway to the window. Azariah and I leap after him. In front of our building, Banar Rashid and Gadi Faysal are getting out of an auto, their black coats streaked with ash.

A few minutes later, they're embracing their sons in my family's kitchen. After I've made the necessary introductions, Banar Rashid takes a deep breath. "The eastern wing of the Assembly Hall is still burning, and there is rioting in the streets from the hall to Yehodu Square, but there is no doubt the plot to eliminate the halani has failed."

No one replies.

Mother finally offers them tea, but the Rashids are weary and eager to go home. Melchior disappears into the stairwell. Azariah and I clasp hands on the now empty landing, and then he too is gone.

After they leave, I go to my room. Caleb follows me. I sink onto the blue-and-white quilt on the bed, my steadiness beginning to crumble.

I'm glad you're home, Caleb signs, sitting next to me. His eyes are so serious, and the gentlest brown.

I wrap my arms around him. I'm so weary, so relieved, so happy that I'm alive and that he is and that the Assembly will never hurt my family now . . .

I pull away. *Do you know Leah is dead?*

Biting his lip, he nods. He leans against me, his silky hair pressed against the wool of my sweater. *She's still here*, he signs.

I shut my eyes, hold him close, and rest my forehead on his crown.

We stay like that until Mother knocks softly on our door.

"I understand if you don't want to talk, Marah, but it's your friends. From school."

Waiting for me in the kitchen are Miriam, Devorah, and Shaul. Before I can greet them, Shaul envelops me in a crushing hug. He reeks of something I can't identify.

"Shaul, what—?"

"You brought down the Assembly!" he says in a choked voice. For a second, I think he's crying, but the idea is ridiculous. This is Shaul.

He releases me, his face radiating a kind of savage joy. "You're a hero, Marah!"

All at once I recognize the scents clinging to him: gasoline and smoke. The understanding of what this means hits me hard in the stomach. Overwhelmed with pride and sadness in equal measure, I almost burst into tears.

"We came as soon as we heard you were home," Devorah says. "Since the newspaper yesterday, everybody in Horiel's been dying to see you."

I don't know how to respond.

"The things you've done!" Miriam exclaims. "And who's Azariah Rashid?"

"Oh," I say, even more at a loss. I glance nervously at Shaul, certain he would not react well to hearing Azariah's a kasir. "He's . . . Well, it's a long story."

"I ran into my brother's friend Yoel by the Assembly Hall," Shaul says eagerly, saving me from having to explain. "There's going to be a big meeting at the pharmacy tomorrow to decide what we're going to do. Yoel told me to invite friends." Shaul grins. "Do you three want to come?"

Devorah, Miriam, and I look uncertainly at one another, and I feel a new wave of exhaustion overtaking me.

"Don't worry, you can decide later. Everything's going to change now," Shaul says with elated optimism. "The sparkers are unstoppable now. The kasiri won't rule us again."

31

I SLEEP AND SLEEP. I WAKE FIRST IN DARKNESS, THEN IN pale light, rising at last late in the morning. Mother has gone out and returned already, having gleaned all the news she could. The District Halls, half of which have had their windows broken, are dark and empty, she says, yet there's a mysterious order in the city. Possibly because most of Ashara is afraid to go to work.

The Rashids' auto arrives unexpectedly in the afternoon. I rush out of the apartment building into the cold sunlight. The mere sight of Azariah lifts my spirits.

"My parents want to talk to you," he says. "And I wanted to see you."

"Me too," I say. Up and down the street, doors are opening and neighbors are piling onto their doorsteps. I pretend not to see them.

Melchior brought the auto, and his reckless driving out of the city triggers memories of Channah. I can picture her behind the wheel, a kasir and a spy, right beside me. A kasir and a spy, dead at my feet. I inch closer to Azariah, who is muttering what sounds like another attempt at the neutralizing incantation to himself. His nearness is comforting.

As we roll up to the Rashids' mansion, I start to see the autos. First one, perched lopsidedly on the edge of the driveway. Then two more, then four, then a whole fleet of black automobiles parked between the house and the outbuilding, not to mention two carriages.

"What on earth . . . ?" I begin.

"Mother and Father have a lot of people over," Azariah says apologetically. "They came of their own accord. I should've warned you. We don't have to have anything to do with them, though."

Melchior snorts as he cuts the engine. "If you want to avoid them, you'd better go through the kitchen."

So Azariah and I enter the Rashid mansion the way Channah took me the first time I set foot here. The warm kitchen smells of mulled wine, but the cook is absent.

"Have you heard anything?" I ask Azariah as we steal down the hallway. "With half the government gathered in your house?"

He makes a face. "It's not half the government. They're mostly my parents' friends. They're all in the living room, so if we just—"

A stout kasir rounds the corner and plows into Azariah. He sputters an apology and then exclaims, "If it isn't the boy! And you must be Gadin Levi. You *are* a halan!"

I stiffen.

"Everyone's been waiting to meet you," the stranger says, giddy. He seizes Azariah by the arm and, ignoring his protests, tows him toward the living room. I trail after them, glowering at the back of the kasir's head.

The living room is overflowing with kasiri: women in sober dresses, their hair pulled back into sleek buns; graying men in suits clasping goblets of mulled wine; even a smattering of what look like university students. If it weren't for everyone's solemn expression, it would appear the Rashids were hosting a party.

"Azariah and Marah are here!" the kasir clutching Azariah announces to the room. The response isn't what he hoped. The closest guests turn to regard us, and a number of them nod politely to Azariah in recognition. Then they resume conversing in urgent tones.

It dawns on me that, unlike the information-starved halani in Horiel, these people don't need us. They have Banar Rashid and Gadi Faysal to tell them about our exploits and Yiftach David's revelations. They know better than two Final students who the important political players will be in the aftermath of yesterday's events. I don't know whether to feel relieved or slighted.

While the portly kasir makes vain attempts to interest nearby visitors in quizzing Azariah, I drift through the living room, listening and watching.

"—lack of democratic structures is at the root of all this. The Assembly is a self-perpetuating institution, and what we must secure for ourselves above all is the right to vote on who governs—"

"—don't trust her at all, why do you think I'm out here at Jalal and Nasim's and not in the city? There must be a total purge, in my opinion—"

"—realize David's plan would have brought about the economic ruin of Ashara, which just proves he was a lunatic who surrounded himself with lunatics. I have always said—"

As the Rashids' guests strive to outdo one another in condemning the councilors, I silently ask them where they were when Azariah's father was reprimanded by the Assembly. And as they trade ideas for reforming the government, I become increasingly aware of the fact that there are nothing but kasiri here. If these are the people who will rebuild the city, who have already taken it upon themselves as their natural responsibility, where do the halani come in? I should've asked Shaul to bring me to the pharmacy today.

Slinking past another cluster of kasiri, I notice a familiar figure hovering in the corner. It's Lavan, the Seventh Councilor's secretary. Whenever one of the Rashids' guests passes by, he smiles hopefully, and when the visitor inevitably refuses to acknowledge him, he slumps and takes a consolatory sip of wine. What is he doing in the home of the very people he was helping his employer investigate for disloyalty just a few weeks ago? Did he figure out which way the wind was blowing and abandon Ketsiah Betsalel?

Someone taps me on the shoulder, and I whirl around.

"I'm sorry, I didn't mean—oh, it *is* you. The name Levi . . . You're the little deaf boy's sister."

It's the kasir from the Horiel District Hall, the one who delivered Caleb's summons and visited our Final class. I'm too startled for words.

"You don't remember me, of course," the mild-mannered kasir says.

"I do," I stammer. "I didn't know you were acquainted with the Rashids."

"I'm not, really," he says ruefully. "I heard there was to be an informal meeting of reformists here, and I finally mustered the courage to try to join their circle."

I recall how this man offered to take Caleb to the District Hall and tried to answer Shaul's questions, and it strikes me that he isn't a bad person. But like so many kasiri, he was too cowardly to question the Assembly openly. He's almost pitiful, but I still resent him.

"The Rashids are very brave people," he's saying, "as are you, Gadin Levi. I wish—"

"Excuse me," Gadi Faysal says, materializing beside us. "If I might borrow Marah . . ." Her tone is chilly, and she looks pointedly across the room to where Banar Rashid is extricating Azariah from a clump of guests.

"Of course," says the District Hall kasir, backing away from Gadi Faysal. "Forgive me."

Azariah's parents whisk us away to a parlor at the back

of the house where Melchior is already seated in a silk-upholstered divan. Next to him, a few logs crackle in the marble fireplace.

Banar Rashid joins Melchior, and Azariah and I sit down opposite them on an identical divan. Gadi Faysal draws an armchair closer to the fire and attends to the tea service on the low table before us.

"My thanks for coming, Marah," says Banar Rashid when the steaming glasses have been passed around. "Nasim and I want to share with you what has transpired and come to light in the last day. I apologize for the crowded house, but it was something of a spontaneous reunion . . ."

"Go on, Father," Azariah says.

"Well, the fires have all been put out," Banar Rashid says. "The blaze in the hall's eastern wing saved us, of course, but even so, it's lucky there were so many people around to contain it. No one knows who set—"

Melchior clears his throat. "It was me and my friends. At least at first."

His parents stare at him.

"Well, it was quite the diversion," says Gadi Faysal, clutching her tea glass in both hands.

"Indeed," her husband says, stroking his beard. "In any case, Yehudit Chesed, the Fifth Councilor, is in charge now."

"Still?" I say in disbelief.

Banar Rashid looks taken aback. "It's only been a day, Marah."

I shift on the divan, my stomach twisting. *I don't trust*

her at all, one of the guests said. Surely he meant Yehudit Chesed?

"I understand if you're wary of her," Azariah's father says, "but she's made it clear she wishes to leave the government as soon as possible, and there are many of us who would prevent her or anyone else from seizing power. She declared she had long had qualms about the scheme to destroy the halani, and then yesterday . . ." He hesitates. "Yehudit Chesed's change of heart was thanks to you, Marah."

"Me?" I say.

Banar Rashid and Gadi Faysal share a significant look.

"Adriel David witnessed you giving his father the cure," Banar Rashid says. "It was an extraordinary act. He was so affected he sought out the other councilors to tell them what you had done. Only Yehudit Chesed was moved by his account of your actions. The shock of hearing that a halan girl had offered the cure to David finally convinced her to abandon the Assembly's plot."

Azariah throws me a stunned look. My heartbeat is very loud in my ears. So healing David counted for something after all.

"I understand," I say at last. I still don't like that she's in charge, but I remind myself that Channah changed her mind and decide I can wait to judge Chesed for myself.

"What about the rest of the councilors?" asks Azariah.

"The Third, Fourth, and Sixth Councilors have disappeared," his mother says. "They may have fled to other city-states. Ketsiah Betsalel remains, and after she acknowledged the plot was wrong, Yehudit Chesed placed her under protection." The tightness of Gadi Faysal's jaw suggests she doesn't think Betsalel deserves it.

"How about Hoshea?" Azariah says. "And Tsuriel, the captain of the Corps? We saw—"

"Tsuriel was bludgeoned to death," Gadi Faysal says abruptly.

"Nasim," Banar Rashid protests as I cover my mouth.

His wife ignores him. "Hoshea made the same choice as Yiftach David."

So much death. Banar Rashid sighs and closes his eyes, as though plagued by a headache. Azariah mutters something under his breath. I gulp down a sip of tea.

"Yehudit Chesed has revealed many details of the Assembly's plot," Banar Rashid finally continues. "It seems the Assembly phased out the neutralizing spells two centuries ago by claiming that magical advances had rendered them superfluous. Within two generations, few even remembered their existence.

"Meanwhile, candidates for the Assembly were closely observed until it was certain they could be included in the conspiracy. Additionally, in each generation, two or three kasiri who had proven their trustworthiness and loyalty to the Assembly were selected to preserve knowledge of Hagramet."

"Hoshea was David's lead Hagramet scholar," Gadi Faysal breaks in.

I murmur in surprise. There's so much to take in.

Banar Rashid's gaze is sympathetic, as though he understands. "I only have one more thing to tell you," he says. "It seems the District Hall firings were connected to the dark eyes. The halls were destined to become centers for distributing the cure to kasiri, so the Assembly decided it could no longer risk employing halani in them." His expression grows pained. "They were also preparing for a day when there would be no halani to do administrative work."

I can't believe it. *This* is why Mother was fired?

"That's disgusting," Azariah says, recovering first. "But surely halani will be in the government now? Actually governing, I mean?"

"There are already halani involved in forming the provisional government," Melchior says.

"Good," I say, for a moment acutely conscious of what divides me from the Rashids. It's not enough to have liberal-minded kasiri on our side. We need our own voice.

"Now, Nasim and I were asked to approach you two about something," Banar Rashid says delicately. "The dark eyes epidemic is not over. The Fifth Councilor has gathered the best pharmacists in Ashara in preparation for producing the cure in large quantities, but they need the instructions from you."

"We could get the translation to them by tonight, if you would deliver it," I tell Banar Rashid.

"Of course," he says. "My thanks. I'm sure they would want me to express their gratitude as well."

"Ashara owes you a great debt," adds Gadi Faysal.

The idea both frightens me and fills me with pride. There's

a shadow of a smile on Azariah's face that must reflect my own. For the briefest instant, though, his mask slips, and I glimpse the pain etched in his face. Our grief is still raw under our happiness. And suddenly it feels like this revolution has come at the price of Leah's and Sarah's lives.

I set down my tea glass and stand up. "My thanks, Banar Rashid, Gadi Faysal. I'd like to go home now." Before they can offer me a ride, I add, "I can walk." I know the way now, since Azariah and I walked to the city after escaping the storage room.

"Don't be silly," Banar Rashid says, getting up. "I'll drive—"

"Father, we'll walk together," Azariah says.

"And how will you get home?" Gadi Faysal asks.

"I'll walk back."

"It'll take you hours," she says.

Neither of us says a word. When his parents realize we won't back down, they let us go.

Outside, the western sky is just turning rosy as cold blue encroaches in the east. We skirt the battalion of automobiles and set out on the road to the city.

"We did it," I say.

"We did," he says. "There's still so much work to do, though."

"I know," I say. But a powerful swell of hope rises in my chest.

A sense of tranquility settles over us as Azariah and I

tramp through the quiet, snowy world. A lone automobile glides past us on the road. Azariah murmurs to himself every so often, but I don't ask what he's saying. Above us, the first stars are winking in a dome of blue silk. From time to time, we lift our faces to their cold majesty.

IN THE CITY, we find the streets wonderfully alive. Children play in the grimy snow, carters lead horses to their stables, women call to each other from their doorsteps. At an ordinary intersection, Azariah stops, his gloved hands clasped in front of him. The white plume of his breath dissolves into the shadows.

"Marah, I think—" He retreats toward the gutter, tears off his gloves, and twists his bare hands, speaking softly.

"Azariah, what—?" At my feet, a scrap of newspaper flames briefly and crumbles into a pile of black flakes. I wrinkle my nose at a whiff of bitter magic.

"A simple combustion spell," he says, his eyes burning with concentration. "Now . . ." He reshapes his hands and utters a string of deliberate syllables. The bitter smell fades at once, replaced by a faintly sweet scent, like hay.

"You did it," I breathe. "The neutralizing spell."

Azariah nods, his eyes wide. "I didn't know what the harmful magic felt like before, but now that I've changed it, it feels right."

"How did you figure it out?"

"I was experimenting with the sounds again just now,

like when we were in the hideout. The hand shapes have always been a little tricky, but I was pretty sure I'd worked them out from your translation. When I hit on the right syllables, I could tell."

"You have to teach everyone else," I say.

"I will," he says, glowing.

Impulsively, I hug him.

32

THE WEEKS SLIP BY. EVERY DAY, THE FIFTH COUNCILOR presides over a public forum at the District Hall by the Ikhad, but I have yet to attend one. I've heard that in addition to plans for drafting a new Ashari charter and creating an elected legislature of both kasiri and halani, there's been a lot of circling back to Azariah's and my story. I can't bring myself to go.

Firem has resumed classes, but Horiel hasn't reopened yet, so I have little to do. Sometimes I read, but I always end up abandoning my book. Sometimes I help Mother with the record keeping at the Maitafi Graveyard. I play Leah's violin—my violin—losing myself deep in my soul. I wait for a letter from Qirakh.

One afternoon, I find a brown envelope addressed to me in our mailbox. My heart leaps. I flip the letter over and read *Qirakh Secondary School* on the back flap.

Terrified, I unseal the envelope and unfold the letter

inside. My gaze alights on the congratulatory first sentence. I've been accepted.

My spirits soar. I read the letter, expecting to realize I've made some mistake, but it's true. I can't wait to tell Aradi Imael.

In the afternoon, I cross the city to meet Azariah at the end of the school day. The streets are the liveliest they've been all winter, as if the fall of the Assembly has lightened everyone's mood. I walk past women bringing loaves of fresh bread home from the baker's and children building snow forts in the alleys.

When I reach Firem, I spot Azariah standing with a group of boys near the school's front steps. Their hands are hidden in the pockets of their black wool coats, and they're speaking seriously amongst themselves. When Azariah notices me, he says something to his friends and drifts out of the ring. The other boys watch him approach me.

"Hello, Marah," he says quietly.

"Your friends are staring," I say.

He gives me a crooked smile. "Well, you're rather famous."

I flush. "Azariah, I got into Qirakh."

His eyes light up. "Well done! I was sure you would."

We start back up the street, walking quickly as though we might outrun the coming evening.

"We were talking about the neutralizing spells back there," Azariah says. "Our teachers won't touch the subject yet, so everyone's been asking me. But Chesed has a committee poring over the Hagramet text now. She's already requiring officials to learn the spells."

"All thanks to you," I say. "You figured it out."

He laughs. "You reconstructed the spell."

I smile at the cobblestones.

"Chesed's more focused on the cure than on hammering out a new charter at the moment," Azariah goes on. "She's deployed what's left of the government to churning out huge batches of it. There's an army of magicians producing black eggs by the dozen in laboratories. And we're importing heavenly tea by the crate. Importing it! When it was so prized here in the days of Hagram . . ."

Azariah trails off helplessly. We slow to a halt along a wrought-iron park fence.

"They'll never meet Basira," I say. "Their black eggs didn't come from Divsha's pockets."

"And they didn't need Yochanan's translation services," he says.

"Faraj," I say. "I hope he's well."

"Tsipporah." Azariah goes pale. "Where would we be if not for her?"

"And Channah," I say, wrapping my mittened hand around one of the fence's spear points.

Azariah's eyes harden. "She as good as killed Sarah."

"Without her, I'd be dead, Azariah."

"I know. And Sarah is dead." He drags his scarf from around his throat and twists it in his hands.

"If she hadn't told me the truth, the Assembly would be watching the halani die."

"Marah."

"And she paid with her life."

"Marah!" he shouts.

I lean against the fence, looking into the park where the snow gilds the tree branches. A few moments pass in silence.

"Marah, I'm sorry," Azariah says behind me just as I turn to say the same.

"It's all right," I say, peeling away from the iron fence. "Where are we going?"

"The Ikhad," he says, as though we've always known. "To give our thanks to Tsipporah."

"Yes." Azariah offers me his hand. I take it.

SNOWFLAKES FLOAT IN the blue evening air outside our kitchen window. At the table, by the warm glow of the gas lamp, Caleb leafs through a book. Mother is due home from the Maitafi Graveyard soon. I laid my acceptance letter from Qirakh at her place.

I pick over a measure of dried split peas and rinse them. Then I inspect the spices in the pantry. Caleb raps on the kitchen table, and I turn, expecting him to suggest some appropriate seasonings for split pea soup. Instead, he taps the page in front of him.

I want to learn this.

I cross the kitchen and gaze down at the book. It's my

Hagramet grammar. What was once simply a prized possession has taken on a sacred quality in light of all that's happened. I stare at my brother. *You're serious?*

He nods. *I can learn to read a different language.*

I know, I sign. *I'll teach you. And in the spring you're going to school.*

He slumps in his chair. *They don't want me.*

They'll take you, I sign. *If I have to shout down the head-master myself.*

Caleb tries to suppress a smile and fails utterly. I laugh, my heart full.

I'll teach you the alphabet tonight if you help me make the soup, I sign.

He leaps up so eagerly he almost knocks over his chair. *Let's chop an onion,* he signs on his way to the pantry. *Is there any dried sausage left?*

Half an hour later, as the split peas simmer on the stove, Caleb and I sit side by side at the table, our heads together. I watch him copy the Hagramet alphabet onto a piece of loose-leaf. He writes painstakingly, engraving each unfamiliar letter in his memory. The hearty smell of soup fills the apartment, and I hear the creak of footsteps on the landing. Mother is home. We are all here.

GLOSSARY

Aevlia: a temperate country southeast of the north lands

Aradi: the title for a teacher

Ashara: the city-state of the north lands where Marah lives

Atsan: a city-state of the north lands

Banar: the title for an adult man

Erezai: a kingdom founded in the north lands by migrants from Xana four hundred years after the collapse of Hagram and five hundred years before Marah's time; split into the city-states

fane: a Maitafi house of worship

Gadi: the title for an adult woman

Gadin: the title for a young woman

Hagram: an ancient kingdom of the north lands

halan (plural: halani): in Ashara, a person without magical abilities

Ikhad: the largest market in Ashara, located in the city center

kasir (plural: kasiri): in Ashara, a person with magical abilities; a magician

Kiriz: a city-state of the north lands

Laishidi: a tropical country south of Xana

Maitaf: the sacred text of the Maitafi faith

Maitafi: an adherent of the monotheistic religion whose principles are set forth in the Maitaf

medsha: an instrumental ensemble consisting of three violins, two violas, two cellos, two end-blown flutes, a lyre, a horn, and percussion

Narr: a forested country far to the west of the north lands

north lands: the part of the world where Marah lives

Tekova: a city-state of the north lands

Xana: a desert country across the sea from the north lands

ACKNOWLEDGMENTS

MY DEEPEST THANKS TO DAN LAZAR, MY AGENT, WHO FIRST saw something in this book. Thanks also to everyone at Writers House, especially Torie Doherty-Munro.

Many thanks to all the people at Penguin. I am grateful in particular to Leila Sales, my editor, who made this book into so much more; to Ken Wright, my publisher; and to Alex Ulyett. A big thank you also to Nancy Brennan and Eileen Savage, for the wonderful jacket design.

To Natalie Heer and David Cook, who first read Marah's story. To Beth Pond and Brigid Gorry-Hines, my publishing buddies, for their comments and camaraderie. To Jill Jarnow, for her early input. To Jim Thomas, whose wisdom helped shape this book. To Andrew Cheng, for help with the names. To Dustin Anderson, for being so generous with his time and thoughts. To my brother, Nathaniel Glewwe, for serving as a guinea pig. To Chris Sheban, for the marvelously atmospheric jacket art.

Finally, to all my cello teachers and orchestra conductors, for challenging and inspiring me.

ELEANOR GLEWWE WAS BORN IN WASHINGTON, D.C., and grew up in Minnesota. She plays the cello and once braved a snowstorm to perform in a chamber music competition. At Swarthmore College, she studied linguistics, French, and Chinese and worked in the music library, shelving composers' biographies and binding scores with a needle and thread. More recently, she haunted the tunnels under the Minnesota State Capitol as a legislative advocate. Eleanor lives in Los Angeles, where she is a graduate student in linguistics. Visit her at eleanorglewwe.com.